TWISTED FATES

ALSO BY DANIELLE ROLLINS
Stolen Time

DANIELLE ROLLINS

HARPER TEEN

An Imprint of HarperCollinsPublishers

HarperTeen is an imprint of HarperCollins Publishers.

ISBN 978-0-06-267997-0

Typography by Jenna Stempel-Lobell
20 21 22 23 24   PC/LSCH   10 9 8 7 6 5 4 3 2 1
❖
First Edition

TWISTED FATES

PART
ONE

Once confined to fantasy and science fiction, time travel is now simply an engineering problem.

—Michio Kaku

PART
ONE

1

DOROTHY
MARCH 18, 1990, BOSTON

Dorothy sat in the passenger seat of a red Dodge Daytona, fingers tapping her crossed legs. Roman had driven, and now he was leaning against the driver's side door, staring out at the dark city streets beyond the windshield.

The inside of the car wasn't particularly pleasant. The air felt stale and smelled of old french fries and gasoline. They hadn't bothered turning on the heat, and a chill crept in through the windows, making the hair on Dorothy's arms stand up.

Oh, and the radio didn't work. If they wanted music, they had to play the tape currently stuck in the deck, a single of Paula Abdul's "Cold Hearted." They'd already listened to it at least fifty times over the last few days.

"*He's a coldhearted snake*," Dorothy thought, playing the song in her head. And she must've started humming because Roman shot her an irritated look.

She glanced at the clock on the dashboard as the red

numbers flicked from 1:18 to 1:19 a.m.

She looked up at the rearview mirror, studying the street reflected behind her. There'd been a Saint Patrick's Day party in an apartment building a few yards back, but most of the guests had trickled out by now. The door had stayed closed for the last twenty minutes. Now the street was empty, a slick of rain glistening on the pavement.

Her heart started beating faster. She inhaled long and slow, nose twitching at the smell of french fries.

"It's time," she said, reaching for the door.

Roman cut his eyes at her. "Fix your mustache first."

Dorothy twisted the mirror so she could see her face. The wax mustache perched above her upper lip was part of her disguise, but the damn thing wouldn't stay put.

She pressed it down, grimacing as the glue took hold. The skin above her lip itched. "Better?"

"You're too pretty to pass for a man," Roman said, studying her.

Dorothy's mouth quirked beneath the mustache, dislodging it again. It was a joke, sort of. She used to be pretty. But then she fell out of a time machine and got sucked into a tunnel through time and space. Her hair had turned white, and a spare bit of machinery had sliced up her face, leaving her with a jagged scar that stretched from her temple, over one eye and past her nose, and ended at the edge of her mouth. Pretty was no longer a word anyone would use to describe her.

Now she was . . .

Interesting.

"I could say the same thing about you," she said. *This* wasn't a joke. Roman was prettier than any man had a right to be, with his cool blue eyes and dark skin and messy black hair that had a way of looking intentional even when the wind had blown it into knots.

"Touché," Roman said. He'd grown a real mustache just for tonight, and he was wearing a pair of fake, gold-rimmed glasses to make himself seem older. He used the glasses to full effect now, letting them fall down the bridge of his nose so that he could peer over them, eyebrow cocked rather seductively.

The effect had him looking more like a movie-star version of a college professor than a cop.

Dorothy was far past being taken in by Roman's beauty. She made a gagging noise that caused his eyes to move to his reflection in the car window, brow creased in concern.

"Too much?" he asked, flicking a strand of hair off his forehead.

"You aren't going to find any admirers in an empty museum at one in the morning," said Dorothy.

"Ah, but there will be security cameras. And didn't you say something about a police composite sketch?"

"You want to look your best for a *police composite sketch*?"

"In the movie version of this heist, I'd like to be played by Clark Gable."

Despite herself, Dorothy grinned. No one could accuse her partner of false modesty.

"You have your dates mixed up," she said, throwing her

car door open. "Clark Gable died in 1960. This is 1990." She hesitated, pretending to think. "Maybe Ben Affleck?"

Roman shot her a murderous look.

They climbed out of the car and crossed the street, stopping outside a wrought iron gate. A brick building hovered just beyond the trees, barely more than a dark shadow under the dim, yellow streetlights.

The Isabella Stewart Gardner Museum, Dorothy thought, looking up. She frowned. In the photographs, it had seemed so much bigger.

A black box hung from the brick wall outside the gate. A year ago, Dorothy wouldn't have known that it was an intercom, but, now, she leaned in close, pressing down the button with her thumb.

Static, and then a man's voice. "Can I help you?"

"We're with the Boston police," Roman said. "We're here to check on a disturbance in the courtyard."

He flashed a small, gold badge at the camera that Dorothy had told him would be hanging above the fence. The security guard on the other side would see exactly what she wanted him to see: two Boston cops, dressed in stiff blue uniforms.

The buzzer emitted an angry growl that told her the security fence had been unlocked.

A familiar, tingly feeling of déjà vu worked its way through Dorothy's shoulders. She had a composite sketch of the thieves taped to her mirror back at the Fairmont. It was rough, but she was convinced that the smaller of the two thieves was her, dressed as a man. She'd read every news article that existed about this heist, and each one had said the same thing: the thieves were never caught.

Which made sense. If the thieves were time travelers, they never *could* be caught.

Silently, they moved down the sidewalk and toward the museum's entrance. Dorothy glanced at the twin stone panthers that guarded the front doors and felt a thrill of excitement. She'd seen them in photographs before, but now they were here, in front of her. She'd never get over that rush, when the things she'd seen in newspaper articles suddenly became real.

They pushed open the front door without knocking and walked inside, footsteps echoing against the marble. An older, African American security guard stood behind his desk. He was tall, with broad shoulders and a beard shot through with white. His eyes narrowed at them, suspicious.

This would be Aaron Roberts, then.

"I'm, um, I'm really not supposed to let people in here," Roberts said, blinking. "But you said you're with the police?"

Roman nodded. "You did the right thing, son. We had reports of a disturbance in your courtyard, and we need to check it out. Could you . . ."

Roman hesitated, tilting his head. "Well, now that's strange."

The security guard twitched and then glanced over his shoulder, like he was expecting someone to appear out of the shadows behind him. "I'm sorry. What's strange?"

"You look an awful lot like a man we've been searching

for." Now Roman was rubbing his chin. He jerked his head toward the guard, eyes on Dorothy. "Doesn't he look like Dean Morris?"

The name was made up. No one had mentioned it in any of the reports or books or articles, so they'd plucked it out of thin air. The security guard blinked.

"Morris?" he murmured.

"Would you mind stepping out from behind that desk and showing me some ID?" Roman said.

This was pivotal. There was a button beneath the desk that sounded the security alarm. It was the only one in the building. Once they got the guard away from that button, they were safe.

Aaron Roberts stepped out from behind his desk.

"I'm not this Dean guy," he said, pulling out his wallet. He tugged his driver's license loose and flashed it at Roman. "See?"

Roman barely glanced at it. "Sure you're not." He unclipped a pair of heavy-duty handcuffs from his belt, nodding at the wall. "To be safe, why don't you go ahead and face the wall for me, Mr. Roberts. Just until we get this all cleared up."

The security guard turned automatically. "But I didn't do anything."

"Don't worry, son. As long as you cooperate you won't be in any trouble at all." Roman clipped the handcuffs over Roberts's wrists.

Dorothy smothered a smile. It amused her to hear Roman call a man older than him "son."

"What the hell?" murmured a voice behind them.

Security guard number two, Dorothy thought. It was happening just like she'd read it would, just like she'd planned. It felt a bit like playing God.

She wanted to smile, but she bit the inside of her cheek, stopping herself. Moving her lip seemed to dislodge the mustache, and she couldn't risk blowing her cover, not when they were this close.

Nothing she'd read had mentioned the second security guard's name or anything about him, so she hadn't known what to expect until this moment. She turned—

And breathed a sigh of relief. He was barely older than they were, with long, gangly limbs and a spattering of acne on his forehead. Not a threat.

He looked at Roberts. "Aaron—?"

"There's been some kinda disturbance," Roberts muttered. Then, frowning, he added, "You didn't frisk me. Aren't you supposed to—"

"Sir, I'm going to need you to come here and stand next to your partner," Roman said, cutting off Roberts. "We'll have to call your names in before we move on."

Guard Number Two was staring at Dorothy, eyes narrowed.

"Sir?" Roman said again, approaching him.

The guard pointed. "His mustache is falling off."

Blast.

It seemed to Dorothy that Roman stiffened as her own fingers flew to her face. Sure enough, the damn mustache was askew. Her first impulse was to fix it, but it was too late. The second guard was already shaking his head, backing away. His eyes flicked to the security desk. The alarm.

She felt Roman's eyes on her, questioning, and she could hear what he was thinking as clearly as if he'd actually spoken the words out loud. *It's not supposed to happen like this.*

History was supposed to be on their side. Dorothy had spent so long preparing. Night after night falling asleep with a musty old book as a pillow. Hours spent staring at a computer screen, until the words all blurred and a dull headache beat at her skull. They weren't going to be caught. They *couldn't* be.

Dorothy moved between the guard and the alarm, reflexively. He was larger than she was, and she saw his eyes narrow as they moved over her body, sizing her up. He could push through her, he was thinking.

Well, he could *try* to.

Dorothy had learned many things during the last year she'd spent with the Black Cirkus, but perhaps the most useful was the location of the esophagus. There was a spot on the human body where the esophagus peeked out from behind the collarbone, all frail and weak, and if she happened to, say, jam her fingers into that spot, she could make a man twice her size cry for his mother.

This man was not twice Dorothy's size, but he still lurched

at her, and so she calmly stuck two fingers into that tender spot just below his neck and hooked them in and down.

He jerked backward, gasping, hands grabbing at his throat. "What the—"

Dorothy used that second of surprise to spin him around, wrenching both arms behind his back. He twisted, all red-faced and wide-eyed, trying to see her face.

He looked at her then, *really* looked at her, and she saw him take in the scar. The white hair.

"Jesus," he choked out. "You're not a—"

Before he could finish, she'd jerked his arm upward so it would hurt.

"Watch it!" the guard shouted, but he didn't fight as she slapped the cuffs over his wrists. "You're not even a cop, are you?"

"Not remotely," said Dorothy. She shoved the guard up against the wall, beside his partner. Now that they were both cuffed, they were no longer a threat. "This is a robbery. You don't know it yet, but it will go down in history as the greatest robbery ever performed."

Dorothy and Roman led the guards to the basement, hand-cuffed them to pipes, and wrapped duct tape around their hands, feet, and heads. Then they headed upstairs to the Dutch Room.

Dorothy had practically memorized the Dutch Room. She'd spent hours poring over photographs, wondering if the tile floor would cause her to trip in her oversize boots, if their voices would carry through the high, arched windows and into the courtyard below, if they'd be able to see in the near-perfect dark.

Her flashlight's beam bounced off green brocade walls and gilded gold frames holding the most famous artwork in the history of the world. Chairs and heavy wooden furniture had been pushed up against the walls, almost like someone had cleared the center of the room for a dance. Dorothy grinned a little at the thought. It was the 1990s. The kind of dancing she was thinking of hadn't been popular for a hundred years and the nonsense that had taken its place . . .

Well. It seemed more like convulsing than dancing, to her.

"We have a little over an hour," she said as Roman headed for a framed Vermeer.

"You're the boss." Roman pulled a box cutter out of his pocket and began cutting the painting from its frame.

Isabella Stewart Gardner had bought that Vermeer in 1892, for 29,000 francs, Dorothy thought, remembering her research. Now it was worth millions.

She tilted her head to the side, studying it. It was smaller than she'd expected it to be. Why was everything so much smaller in real life?

They packed up paintings by Vermeer, Rembrandt, Degas, and Manet, along with an ancient Chinese gu vase and a bronze eagle finial that had sat atop a framed Napoleonic flag (the flag stayed stubbornly attached to the wall, no matter how hard they tried to remove it).

Finally, Roman checked his watch. "It's been seventy-nine minutes."

"Fine," Dorothy said, stowing the final painting away in her bag. "Let's go."

His eyes narrowed. "And the guards?"

"The police will be here in six hours. I'm sure they'll let them out."

"You're terrible," Roman said. But he smiled in an amused sort of way that let Dorothy know he approved.

"Come on," she said, hitching her duffel farther up her shoulder as she started for the museum doors.

The *Black Crow* waited for them in a nearby park, its bullet-shaped body and finned tail hidden by tree branches, tall grass, and the night's long shadows. Roman loaded the stolen artwork into the cargo hold while Dorothy climbed into the cockpit and began their preflight check. Roman had spent the last year teaching her to fly the time machine. She couldn't handle the ship quite as well as he could yet, but she was getting better every day.

"Wing flaps," she murmured to herself, fingers flying over the control panel. And the carburetor needed to be moved into position, the throttle opened. She checked the EM gauge and saw that the dial was trained on *full*. They'd been going back in time nearly every day for weeks and, still, the store hadn't been depleted. How strange.

She sat back in her seat, eyes still on the gauge. The time machine had been Roman's doing, built using the blueprints he'd stolen from Professor Zacharias Walker, the father of time travel. But a time machine would blow apart the second it entered an anil if it didn't have any exotic matter—or EM— to stabilize the volatile winds of the tunnel. And Dorothy had provided the EM.

She felt a flush of pride as the memory rose in her mind, strange as always:

My name is Quinn Fox. . . . I have something you need.

Those were the words that had sealed her fate one year and two weeks ago. Just moments before, she'd been on board another time machine, begging a pilot with gold eyes to let her stay in New Seattle, with him, instead of returning her to her old life back in 1913.

And then a storm ripped her away and blew her through walls of time and smoke. She'd landed on the docks at Roman's feet a year before she would meet that gold-eyed pilot, Ash, and well over a hundred years after her mother, along with everyone she'd ever known, had died.

Dorothy could still feel the chill of the dock that she'd woken up on, and she could remember the fear that'd beat beneath her chest when she realized how alone she truly was. She'd really had only two choices:

She could offer Roman the one thing of value she'd had on her, the exotic matter that would allow him to travel through time. Working with Roman meant joining the Black Cirkus, a notoriously vicious local gang. It meant becoming someone ruthless herself.

But her other choice was to try and navigate the horrors of New Seattle on her own.

Dorothy hadn't been in the future for long, but even she knew that bad things happened to a girl who showed up in a strange place without family or friends or allies. In the end, it had been no choice at all.

And if she sometimes found herself thinking about the pilot with the gold eyes and wondering what might've happened if she'd only gone to him and explained who she was and when she'd come from . . .

Well. All she had to do was remind herself of the first time she and Ash had met, back in a churchyard in 1913. She could instantly recall the look of disdain he'd gotten in those eyes, the sound of his voice when he told her that, no, he wouldn't be able to help her.

It was that *no* she couldn't stop thinking about. She couldn't bear to hear it again, not after everything that had happened between them.

And so, over time, she'd gotten better at brushing the other, fonder memories aside.

She'd made her choice. There was no going back now.

2

ASH

Back in New Seattle, near twilight. The sky was a thin, watery green, the same color as the pea soup Ash used to get in his rations back in the war. He could almost feel the weight of it pressing down on him, like a warning of things to come.

He tensed, thinking, *Seven days.*

Professor Walker had once told him that you could pre-member something up to a year into the future. It was the "up to a year" part that Ash had been focusing on, recently. Because he'd first seen the prememory of his own death 358 days ago.

Which meant that, at best, he had seven days left to live. Less than that, probably.

Help me find Dorothy, and I'll go without a fight.

Chandra fidgeted as the guards patted Ash down. It would be easier to ignore the stormy sky if they were standing any-where other than the docks on the Aurora waterway, which was the seediest part of New Seattle. The city had always had a sex trade, but the earthquake had brought it out into the open, made it seem almost legitimate. Now the motels along what used to be the Aurora highway proudly advertised what they sold.

The misty rain had plastered Chandra's hair to the back of her neck and sent droplets rolling down her dark skin. She kept her eyes trained on the guards, lips pressed together to keep them from trembling. The two men looked more like hunks of granite than like people. The lines of their faces were sharp and hard, their eyes near black in the strange, green light. Rain glimmered off the assault rifles hanging from their backs.

Gnarled fingers dug into Ash's pockets and fumbled with the lining of his jacket, searching for weapons.

He let his eyes linger on their rifles for a moment before moving them back to the sky.

"Tornado sky," his mother would've called it.

He could picture her now, standing on their front porch, tapping one of his dad's Camels out of its pack. She'd stick the cigarette between her teeth, lighting it in her cupped hand as she watched the sky through slits of eyes.

"Storm'll blow in soon," she'd warn, shaking the match out.

But she wouldn't go inside. Real Nebraskans didn't run from tornadoes, not until the clouds turned black and formed a wall that touched from sky to ground. Not until the rain fell sideways, and the wind came through strong enough to blow you back a step.

Ash held that image of his mother in his head now: unafraid as she stared down the tornado sky. It wasn't bravery that kept her on the porch while the storm rolled closer. It was pure, animal stubbornness. Somewhere deep in her blood, she thought she could scare the storm away, keep it from taking what was hers. That same blood ran through his veins, for better or worse.

But Dorothy was never yours, said a voice at the back of his head. *And you don't even know if she survived.*

Ash flinched, like the voice was a gnat buzzing at his ear. One of the guards glanced at him, frowning. Ash gritted his teeth, keeping his eyes focused on the horizon, until the guard grunted and continued his search.

It was true, Dorothy hadn't been his. But she'd been lost during *his* mission. He'd agreed to take her back in time, to the year 1980, to search for Professor Zacharias Walker, his old mentor. He'd known how dangerous it would be to travel through the anil with such a meager supply of exotic matter, and he'd done it anyway. And then, when the EM began to fail, Dorothy had risked her life to change the exotic matter in the *Second Star* midflight, saving them all.

And then the ship had crashed. And Dorothy had vanished into the anil.

I don't think she died, Zora had told Ash in the days immediately following the crash. *She had the EM on her. . . . Maybe she only missed us by a few months.*

It wasn't an entirely foolish thing to hope for. The anil was volatile, with winds that rose above 100 knots, and storms constantly flickering around the cloudy tunnel walls, but the exotic matter Dorothy had been holding might've created a kind of protective bubble around her, keeping the anil's inclement weather at bay. Ash had never heard of a human being surviving the anil without a time machine, but he had to believe it was possible. He simply couldn't bear the alternative.

They'd lost contact with Dorothy only seconds before crashing back in 2077. If she'd survived, she could already be here, somewhere, in this godforsaken city. Ash just had to find her before someone else did.

"He's clean," said the guard, dropping his hands.

The other guard grunted, turning to Chandra. "And her?"

Chandra squirmed under his hungry eyes, tugging on her T-shirt. The shirt was intentionally too small, to show off her figure. This was a key part of their plan but, still, Ash's cheeks burned as he caught a glimpse of her bare skin from the corner of his eye. He'd spent most of the afternoon pretending her body ended at her neck.

"You know what Mac says about touching the merchandise." The first guard nodded, a hard jerk of his square jaw. "Let 'em past."

Merchandise. Ash had never realized how many muscles there were in his face, how hard it was to focus on each of them at the same time, willing them to stay still when all they wanted to do was grimace at the ugliness of what had just been said.

Not a girl; not a human being.

Merchandise.

He didn't think he'd ever hated anyone as much as he hated Mac at that moment. He didn't know the man personally, but he'd heard of him. Unfortunately. Everyone in New Seattle had heard of Mac Murphy, owner of the city's grimiest brothel. He was a toad of a human being, both in physical appearance, and in general effect on the world around him. Ash wished it were physically possible to squish him beneath his shoe. The world would be a better place if Mac Murphy were just green sludge on the sole of his boot.

There was a beat of silence, and then the second guard shuffled to the side, licking his lips. "Go on then, honey," he said, eyes on Chandra.

"Move," Ash murmured, voice low, nudging Chandra forward.

She stumbled, shoulders hunched up near her ears.

"Oh God," she said, walking steadier now. She tried, again, to tug her T-shirt lower, as though she could make it grow several more inches through sheer force of will.

Ash tipped his head as they walked past the horrible men with guns. He was careful not to move too quickly and to keep his shoulders relaxed, like this was all normal. Something he did every day.

The green sky lit up. Thunder rumbled in the distance.

Not an omen, Ash told himself.

Keep walking.

Mac's brothel crouched at the end of the dock like an

animal waiting to pounce on its prey. It used to be a motel, the kind of place with a flickering vacancy light, and rooms that could be rented by the hour. It'd been horrible even before the floods had made everything horrible; now, it was hell. Only the top two floors were still above the water, a thick carpet of black mold crawling up their dingy, yellow siding. There wasn't glass in the windows, but Mac had covered some of them with cardboard and old blankets to keep what little warmth there was left inside the building. The rest of the windows yawned open, reminding Ash of broken teeth.

Mac himself sat in a moth-eaten chair inside the first motel room off the dock, feet kicked up on his makeshift desk, which was just a moldy piece of wood balanced over two stacks of cinder blocks. The door was propped open with a brick, and Mac had a cigarette dangling from his mouth. He was a squat man with a barrel chest, and his face really did have a toad-like quality: eyes too far apart; big, peeling chapped lips. Ash half expected his tongue to flick out of his mouth and snap up a nearby fly.

Mac chewed on his thick bottom lip, cigarette dangling. "You got business here, son?"

His eyes lingered on Chandra's T-shirt, and Ash felt a flash of anger deep in his gut.

"Heard you paid for girls," Ash said, working hard to keep his voice steady.

Chandra shifted her eyes to the floor, shoulders bunched up around her ears. She sniffled in a small, pitiful way, and Ash felt a flush of pride. He knew she was scared, but this, at least, was pure performance. In fact, it reminded him of a television show about the Wild West that she'd been watching the week before. This was why he'd asked Chandra to help him out with this little mission. Zora was a crap actress.

Mac leaned back in his chair, considering her. After a moment he said, "She ain't much to look at."

It took every bit of willpower Ash had not to knock the cigarette from Mac's mouth right then and there.

He caught a scowl shaping Chandra's lips and elbowed her. She quickly transformed it into the beginning of a sob. Hands balled at her mouth, silent tears.

Mac let his chair drop back down to all fours. "But there's no accounting for taste around here. Some of my clients like 'em different. I could give you . . ." He paused, digging something out of his teeth with his thumbnail. Shrugging, he tried, "Fifty?"

Ash swallowed, barely hearing the price. He prepared himself to say the thing he'd come here to say. "Would you take it in trade?"

The words turned his stomach. People weren't things to be traded. Or, they shouldn't be. But here he was.

Mac's eyes narrowed, and Ash felt the muscles in his shoulders pull tight. Did he recognize him? Before the megaquake, Ash's face had been in the news here and there. He looked different now. His hair was longer and shaggier. He hadn't bothered shaving since Dorothy had disappeared, and he had a little scruff on his cheeks.

But, still, there were people around these parts who

might remember the young pilot who was brought back from the past by a mad scientist. Ash had been counting on Mac not being one of those people. He didn't look like the type to watch the news.

Mac's eyes lingered on him a moment longer. "You ain't one of my regulars?"

It sounded like a question, like Mac was trying to figure out where he recognized him from.

Ash tensed. "No, sir, I'm not," he said. "But I've been by the Rusty Nail now and then."

The Rusty Nail was a bar at the end of Aurora that Mac was known to frequent. Mac nodded, apparently satisfied with this explanation.

Ash exhaled, relieved. "I heard you got a new girl. Real pretty. Brown hair." *I heard she bit the last guy who tried to touch her,* Ash thought, but he didn't say that part out loud.

It was the biting detail that had caught his attention. He'd been at some trash bar on the outskirts of town when the guy next to him had yanked back his sleeve, showing off two swollen, moon-shaped welts in the crook of his arm.

"Teeth," he'd said, when he caught Ash looking. "Murphy's new whore has a temper on her."

Dorothy, Ash had thought. He could easily picture her biting any man who tried to touch her without her permission.

According to bite-mark guy, Mac's new whore had shown up in a seedier part of the city about a month ago, lost and alone but pretty as a picture. She wouldn't tell anyone her real name, but Mac was calling her Hope, and, *Hey, wasn't that ironic? Get it? Because she didn't have any hope left.* Followed by a hearty laugh.

Ash had supplied the bite-mark guy with drinks and bowls of peanuts until he was reasonably sure he'd gotten the whole story.

And then he'd taken him out behind the bar and beaten the living crap out of him.

Because *really*.

Now Mac's face broke into a crooked smile that showed off several rotting teeth. "Oh, we got a new girl all right, but she's worth a bit more than fifty." A pause, like he was considering something. "I suppose I could let her go for twice that—and that's me being generous, mind, what with you a new customer and all."

Ash had been expecting this. He dug around in his coat, pausing when he found the slim envelope he'd tucked inside the lining.

The envelope contained his savings. It came to about seventy-five dollars. Just five creased and greasy bills. It felt like nothing at all.

How was it that he was going to hand over this envelope and get a person in return?

Dorothy's face flashed into his head just then. He saw her as she'd been in those last few moments before she'd climbed out of his ship and disappeared into the storm. Grease-smudged face. Frizzed hair.

In the space of seconds, his disgust was snatched away and replaced with hope. *Let it be her,* he prayed. *Let it be this easy.*

He placed the envelope onto the rickety table, fingers tingling as he moved his hand away.

Mac grabbed the money and greedily counted the bills. "This all seems to be in order." He shoved the envelope down the back of his trousers and nodded at Chandra. "Come with me, doll."

"She stays here," Ash said too quickly.

Mac hesitated, eyebrows climbing his forehead. He looked suspicious for the first time since Ash walked in.

"Did I miss the part where you give orders in my club?" he asked in a careful voice.

Tread lightly, Ash thought, fear prickling up his spine. This wasn't some fragile ego he was dealing with, not like the guy at the bar. Mac's hatred was heartier than that.

Mac was a gasoline-soaked rag—a single match and he'd explode.

Ash weighed his words before saying, "I want to see the girl before I hand over the rest of the payment."

Mac shrugged, all casual. But the suspicion didn't leave his eyes. "If you like."

He walked out of the room. Whistling.

Chandra kept her head bowed until the hideous toad man was gone. Then she straightened, tossing her dark hair over one shoulder. Her eyes blazed. "When do I get to shoot him?"

Ash glanced at her. She had his gun tucked down her pant leg, held snug by her sock. It was the only place he could be sure no one would look for it. Guards weren't allowed to inspect the new girls before Mac did, after all. It was a flaw in the system that Ash was happy to exploit.

"After he brings Dorothy out," Ash said. "Then you can shoot his balls off for all I care."

Chandra favored him with a slow blink, perhaps imagining this exact scenario. She said, grinning, "Goody."

Fifteen minutes passed before Ash heard the approach of footsteps outside the motel room. The skin behind his ears prickled. He shifted his body between Chandra and the door.

"Now you're feeling protective," Chandra muttered, bristling.

Ash swallowed the sudden tightness in his throat. "Quiet."

"I'm just saying, you could've played the hero before, back when he was sexually assaulting me with his eyes."

Ash shot her a look, and Chandra mimed zipping her mouth shut.

Mac walked past the window first. The curtains were drawn, but Ash recognized his fat head through the yellowing fabric. A smaller shadow shuffled close behind him. A girl, her body slight and bent over.

Ash felt his breath catch.

Mac walked back into the room. "Behold," he said, lip curling in what he must've thought was a smile. "The prettiest whore in all of New Seattle!"

The girl appeared at the door. She was staring at her feet, dark hair covering her face.

"Well?" Mac looked from the girl to Ash expectantly. "What do you think?"

His voice lifted the girl's head, and her dark hair parted like a curtain, revealing skin pale as china, bow-shaped lips, and eyes like a doll's. She couldn't have been more than fourteen years old, Ash realized, the hope draining out of him. She wasn't Dorothy.

A bruise colored the skin around her left eye. He wondered if that had been her punishment for biting the last man who'd stood where he was standing now.

Mac said something else, but Ash couldn't have said what it was. His blood was pumping in his ears, so loud that he couldn't hear anything over it.

"Chandra," he said, trying and failing to keep the emotion from his voice. "Now."

Chandra lurched forward, faking a sudden coughing fit. She was faster than Ash had expected her to be, so fast that he wondered if she'd been practicing in her room back at the schoolhouse. Mac barely had time to frown at her and mutter something about bringing him sick girls before her hand was at her ankle, fingers curling around the gun tucked in her sock.

She stood, one eye closing as she took aim.

"Whoa." Mac raised his hands, backing away. He looked at Ash. "What's this? I thought we were dealing in good faith, here."

"Hey, toad face," Chandra said. "Why are you looking at him? I'm the one with the gun."

Ash shrugged. "Sounds like you should be dealing with her."

Mac's lips twitched, as though the very thought disgusted him. "You let a girl run your show, friend?"

"As frequently as possible," said Ash. "Now—"

"Wait a second . . . I know you." Mac's beady eyes flicked over to Chandra and narrowed. "Yeah, and you. You're part of that time travelers' group, right? The Chronology whatever?"

He was talking about the Chronology Protection Agency, a team of time travelers taken from throughout history and brought to New Seattle two years ago to work alongside the late, great Professor Zacharias Walker.

Mac smiled, and gave a slow shake of his head. "I've had people out looking for you and your friends for the last month. You're well hidden. That intentional?"

"It is," Ash said, a rough edge to his voice. "We got a little tired of people showing up on our doorstep asking us to take them back in time to see the dinosaurs."

"That so?" Mac chewed on his chapped lip, grinning slightly. "So you don't take requests? Say, for local business owners. There would be payment involved."

Local business owners. The phrase turned Ash's stomach. "We aren't going to take you back in time, if that's what you're asking."

"I could make it worth your while."

"No, thanks," Ash said.

Mac's eyes darted to the makeshift desk under the window. Ash followed his gaze to a small black Glock.

"Go for it and I shoot." Chandra slid a thumb over the gun's hammer. "Where do you keep the rest of the girls?"

Mac inched toward the desk. "If you think I'm going to—"

Chandra fired, sending a bullet straight through the pimp's thigh. He howled with pain, dropping to his knees. Blood leaked onto the floor.

"I was aiming a bit higher than your leg," Chandra said. "Should I try again?"

"She's not very good with that thing," Ash said.

Mac pushed his fist to his mouth and bit down on his knuckles. A tear oozed out of his eye and slithered down his cheek. He had his other hand pressed to the wound in his leg, blood gushing through his fingers.

"They're—they're upstairs," he gasped, cringing. "Room Three-C."

Ash glanced at Chandra, half expecting her to shoot again, but she only tucked the gun in the back of her jeans, scowling at Mac as she darted out of the room. The young dark-haired girl hesitated for a moment and then followed her.

Ash tipped his chin to the pimp bleeding on the floor. "Pleasure doing business."

Mac's moans followed him out into the hall; his ears were still ringing with them when he reached the stairs.

Room 3C looked flooded from the outside. Water sloshed around the bottom of the door, and the wooden frame was rotted clean through. Ash lowered a hand to the doorknob and leaned against the wood with his shoulder, hoping the door would just collapse beneath him. But it held.

"Damn," he muttered, relaxing. The curtain to the side of the door flicked as one of the girls looked out.

"Let me," the small, dark-haired girl said. Her voice was deeper than Ash expected, making her seem much older than he'd originally guessed.

The girl slipped past him and knocked softly. "Mira," she said. "It's me. Open up."

There was a beat, and then the door creaked open. A red-headed girl with a face full of freckles peered out. Her eyes flicked anxiously from Ash to Chandra.

"Who are the people, Hope?" Her voice was a thin rasp.

"I don't know," Hope said. Then, with an attempt at a grin: "They shot Mac."

"Did they?" Mira pushed the door open wider. Behind her, Ash could see a small dim room with low ceilings, lit by scattered, flickering candles. A few girls were spread out across a bare mattress, dressed in sweats and oversize flannel shirts, playing cards. Another sat in front of a cracked mirror, trying to curl her hair with her fingers.

Mira considered Ash. "Are you our new pimp, then?"

"What?" Ash felt the backs of his ears flare. "No. *God* no."

"You shot Mac."

"Actually, *I* shot Mac," Chandra cut in. "Does that make me your new pimp?"

"Neither of us is going to be your new pimp," Ash said.

Mira didn't look convinced. "You shot Mac out of the goodness of your heart, then?" Her eyes traveled down Ash's body, assessing him. "Nobody does something for nothing."

"We're looking for someone. A girl. Small, with long, dark hair." Ash nodded at Hope. "Like her."

The corner of Mira's mouth twitched. "There are no other girls like her, my friend."

She started to push the door closed.

"Wait." Ash wedged his foot between the door and the frame, holding it open. He felt his heart beating in his throat. This couldn't be it. *Please.*

Mira's eyes softened. "We have all lost someone. I'm sorry."

Ash exhaled unevenly, half his breath releasing in a ragged spurt. His disappointment felt physical, like something had been carved out of him.

He'd been so sure she would be there.

He remembered the lift of hope he'd felt when he heard the guy at the bar's story. It had been nearly three weeks since Dorothy had disappeared. That was nineteen nights, each of them filled with hours and hours of darkness. Ash had spent every minute of that darkness staring at the ceiling above his bed, imagining ways he might've saved her.

The hope that she might be here had worked as a salve for a while, numbing his pain, giving him something to plan for. It was much easier to storm into a brothel with a gun than it was to face the truth.

And the truth was that Dorothy was gone. She'd been lost in time.

And Ash didn't know where to begin looking for her.

He slid his foot out the door. "Mac's bleeding pretty bad upstairs. If any of you are looking to make a run for it, now would be the time."

None of the girls moved. They looked at each other and then back at Ash.

Mira cocked her head. "But where else would we go?"

When Ash couldn't answer, she ushered Hope back inside and pushed the door closed.

3

DOROTHY

Three weeks ago, Dorothy had kidnapped herself.

Well. Her past self.

Time was a circle. She'd learned that a year ago, and she was still learning and relearning it, even now. When she went back to the 1990s to steal art from the Isabella Stewart Gardner Museum, she knew she'd be successful because she'd already *been* successful; the heist had gone down in history as the most impressive of all time. It was dizzying to think about, but, sometimes, the things one did in the past didn't really happen until the future, and things one didn't think had happened at all were already happening in someone else's past.

For instance, when Dorothy had first arrived in New Seattle, she'd heard about a mysterious girl named Quinn Fox. But it wasn't until she fell backward in time that she realized *she* was Quinn Fox. She'd always been Quinn Fox.

But she still had work to do. Certain things had to be put

31

into place in order for everything to happen the way it was supposed to. Roman needed to make sure Dorothy ended up with the exotic matter before she fell off Ash's ship, for one thing. And that meant that she and Roman had needed to kidnap her past self and plant the idea to go back in time in the first place.

It had been . . . elaborate. But Dorothy had been fully prepared for the tediousness of setting up clues for her past self to follow, of feeding Roman lines and planting hints and weaving suspicion—

She hadn't been prepared to see herself, though. That had come as something of a shock. She kept reliving the moment when it'd happened, the stuffy heat of the hotel room and the smell of mold and damp and something else, a lightly floral scent that had made her nose twitch, reminding her of her mother.

"What about our newest guest?" she'd asked Roman. The conversation had been staged, naturally. They'd needed Dorothy's past self to think they were going to kill her so that she'd steal the Professor's journal (which they'd conveniently left behind for her to discover) and jump out a window, thus delivering the journal to Ash and his friends. "Bring me whatever valuables you find, and get rid of the body. We need the room empty again by tonight."

Dorothy could still remember how terrified she'd been when she'd first heard those words. *Get rid of the body.* Like she was merely a thing to be disposed of, a chore. She'd imagined a single gunshot in her back as she was running away, a sudden numbness, followed by a thick, heavy darkness. Standing there, saying the words herself, she'd felt blood pumping in her palms and a bitter taste hit the back of her throat. She wasn't that girl any longer. She wouldn't be helpless again.

So maybe that was why she'd looked, to prove to herself that she'd changed. She'd heard the soft rustle of fabric behind her and she'd turned on instinct, inadvertently catching a glimpse of her own face.

It had been her old face, unravaged by a fall from a time machine, or a year spent with a vicious gang. Her skin had been clear, her hair dark and chestnut brown. The first thought Dorothy had, seeing her past self, was no wonder she'd kept getting taken: she'd looked more like a doll than like a person, and she'd been so much younger than Dorothy could ever remember being. And innocent.

As soon as she thought it, the word got stuck in her head, like a bit of a song lyric that she couldn't stop singing. *Innocent, innocent* . . . Had she ever been innocent? She'd been a thief and a con artist before she'd become Quinn Fox. She'd stolen money and hearts; she'd tricked men into believing she wanted them and then disappeared to leave them to tend to their wounds alone. *Innocent* was never a word she'd have used to describe herself, and she wouldn't have believed it if the proof hadn't been right there.

She'd felt a jolt then, as she realized that—innocent or not—the girl she'd once been was gone. Quinn Fox had killed her.

* * *

Now Dorothy tugged her hair loose, letting her white curls fall over her shoulders. She shrugged out of her stolen police uniform, exchanging it for her familiar dark cloak. She pulled the hood over her head so that it mostly hid her face, and tugged the sleeves down low over the harnesses that held her daggers.

Lips were next. She found a small pot in her cloak pocket and unscrewed the lid, revealing a deep bloodred mixture. She dotted it on her lips without bothering to consult a mirror. It was better if it was messy.

It wasn't real blood—it was carmine mixed with oil, like prostitutes in her time used to wear—but it looked like blood, which was the entire point.

Roman squinted at her, watching the transformation as he piloted the *Black Crow* over the choppy waters. They'd stopped outside the anil so they could switch places, him piloting the *Black Crow* while she changed in the passenger seat. He looked like he was holding something back.

"What is it?" she asked, pressing her lips together to make the red bleed onto her skin. She could see from her reflection in the window that she looked pale, almost dead. "Don't I look okay?"

"You look great," Roman said, and then paused, as though contemplating that. "No, I'm sorry, I meant that you look terrifying. I occasionally get those two mixed up."

Dorothy smiled. *Terrifying.* He meant it as a compliment. The two of them had worked hard to make her terrifying. Dorothy had seen a year into the future, but she'd never glimpsed Quinn Fox's face, and so she and Roman had spent weeks coming up with her disguise before deciding on her whitened skin and dark cloak and red lips. It had been the first part of their plan to take over the Black Cirkus. It was like a riddle. *How do you frighten frightening people?*

Easy. You become frightening yourself.

Her earliest days with the Black Cirkus were fuzzy now. She'd been badly injured, her face a mess of blood and mangled flesh. She remembered the suspicious voices that had buzzed around her when Roman first led her down the halls of the Fairmont. He'd wrapped her in his cloak, warning her to keep her injury hidden from the others.

"They can't know that you're hurt," he'd said, and Dorothy had been dismayed to hear the nerves in his voice and to see that his normally vibrant eyes were dark with fear. "They don't like weakness."

They. He was talking about the Cirkus Freaks, the notoriously vicious members of the gang that ruled the city. Dorothy could still remember the first time she'd seen them sailing over the waters of New Seattle in their motorboat, crossbows and axes strapped to their backs, howling as they aimed their guns into the sky.

They'd been terrifying, certainly—but Roman had been the worst of them all. They'd called him the Crow, and he'd been like the king of the thieves, charming and calculating and frightened of no one.

This Roman was nothing like that. He was good-looking, still, but skittish and thin, like a street dog used to scrambling for his food. His cloak didn't have its signature crow sketched across it yet. And then there was the matter of that sad, scraggly beard he was trying to grow . . .

Dorothy had grimaced looking at it. The beard would have to go.

"I am not weak," she'd said, her voice knife-edge sharp. "And neither are you. I've seen the future and, in it, you and I do not fear the Black Cirkus. We lead it."

The fear in Roman's eyes had turned bright and glittering then. For the first time he reminded Dorothy of the Crow she'd known.

He'd asked only, "How?"

Grinning, she'd told him.

She should've realized that night that becoming the notorious Quinn Fox would not be as simple as adopting a new name. There were things she would have to do to gain the Black Cirkus's trust. Terrible things.

"You're too small," Roman had often hissed at her, in those early days, when she still skittered through the Fairmont hallways with her head ducked, her shoulders clenched around her ears. "You look breakable."

She'd flinched at that word. *Breakable.* It reminded her of being kidnapped as a child by a drunken man in a bar. It made her feel helpless, and she'd sworn that she would never again feel helpless.

Still, she'd had to admit that Roman had a point. She was so much smaller than anyone else in the Black Cirkus. The other Freaks looked at her like she was something to be devoured. Like she was a *snack*. Sometimes she imagined she heard them licking their lips as she walked past.

It wasn't just her size. Her injury was taking longer to heal than she'd expected. It looked garish, red and raw and painful. It bled constantly. Dorothy had spent most of her time huddled in bathrooms, changing bandages and cleaning her shredded skin so it wouldn't get infected. At Roman's suggestion, she'd taken to covering her carved-up face with a low hood, so the other Freaks wouldn't know how badly injured—how *vulnerable*—she really was. But that only made them more suspicious of what she was hiding.

Worse than that, it made them curious.

There weren't a lot of girls in the Black Cirkus. Being female, Dorothy already drew far too much attention. The Freaks whispered about what she looked like beneath her ever-present cloak. Dorothy could feel the weight of their stares whenever she walked down the hallway, and she knew it would be only a matter of time before their curiosity got the better of them.

And then, one night, it did.

She'd been late sneaking back into the Fairmont, and some boy—a newer Cirkus Freak who she didn't recognize—had emerged from the shadows and grabbed her. For one dizzy moment, she'd thought it had been a mistake, that he'd been expecting someone else, perhaps, or simply bumped into her in his rush to get down the hall.

But then she heard the sounds of his friends hidden around the corner, laughing and cheering him on, and she knew that it'd hadn't been a mistake at all but an ambush.

They'd been waiting for her.

The boy was rough as he'd pinned her to the wall, one arm braced across her collarbone so that she couldn't move, the other gripping her waist, fingers jabbing painfully into her skin.

"Look at her wriggle," he'd said, his breath sour and too, too close. "Didn't I tell you she'd be fun?"

Fun? He thought this was *fun?* Dorothy hadn't been able to catch her breath. She knew that if she didn't do something now, this would happen again and again and again. She was small and weak and *fun.* Everyone at the Fairmont would see her as an easy mark, someone to be taken advantage of. Her new reality would be running from boys like this, fighting off grabbing hands and stinking breath.

And so she'd done the only thing she could think to do.

She'd bitten him. On the face.

She'd gotten a big chunk of his skin off, too, leaving behind a deep, ugly gash. The boy had dropped her and fallen to his knees, howling, as blood dripped from her chin.

She hadn't bothered to wipe the blood away but said only, "I don't like to be touched."

The boy was called Moon Face after that, in reference to the crater left in his cheek. And the whispers about Quinn Fox officially began.

Roman started most of them. He told people that they shouldn't get close to Quinn, that she enjoyed the taste of human flesh a little too much. It helped that she always smelled strongly of blood, courtesy of her still-healing injury. And then there was Moon Face himself, walking around with the shape of her teeth still imprinted on his face, a living warning.

Roman kept the rumors coming after that, making sure that each was ghastlier than the one before. He said that Quinn didn't know how to smile, that she'd been kept inside a closet until she was twelve years old and grew up without ever seeing another human face and it'd left her . . . wrong.

He said she could only mimic human emotions and she wore the hood low over her face to hide her empty facial expressions.

She could learn anyone's secrets by staring into his or her eyes.

She could kill a grown man with her bare hands.

With her finger.

With a *look*.

Dorothy felt foolish, that she hadn't thought of this earlier. Quinn Fox was a cannibal. It was one of the first things she'd ever learned about New Seattle.

Where I'm going, there are entire cities hidden underwater, and gangs that steal little old ladies on their way to the market, and a girl who lives off human flesh.

Ash had told her that, when she'd first met him in the clearing behind the church where she was supposed to be married. Only, then he'd been the handsome pilot with the gold eyes, smelling of campfire smoke and faraway places. She'd thought he'd been exaggerating. She'd never, in her wildest dreams, thought he'd been talking about her.

If Dorothy still had any lingering hope that she could return to Ash and his friends, it faded as the rumors about her grew stronger. She saw Ash once more but, by then, it was too late. She was already Quinn Fox, cannibal, leader of the Black Cirkus.

And he hated her.

4

ASH

The pea-green sky followed Ash and Chandra around to the back of the motel, where their boat was rocking on the black waves.

It hung above them ominously, as Ash tugged on the pull cord—once, twice, three times—and the motor growled to life.

It seemed to hold its breath as they climbed into the old boat and steered away from Mac's motel and down the narrow Aurora waterway, squat buildings bordering them on either side.

Not an omen, Ash told himself again, looking away from the sky.

They rode past a half-dozen motels just like Mac's. Dark, run-down places with boarded-up windows and armed guards at the doors. Ash made himself picture the faces behind all those windows. Broken, terrified faces. Most of them were underage. Most of them were working against their will.

But, hard as he tried, Ash couldn't see them. Dorothy's face kept creeping in instead. Dorothy scared and Dorothy laughing and Dorothy looking up at him, leaning in to kiss him . . .

He gave his head a hard shake, disgusted with himself. It should bother him more than it did. He shouldn't have been able to just walk away from those girls back at Mac's, just as he shouldn't be able to sail past these places without stopping, without trying to help.

Sometimes he felt that his capacity for empathy was a glass jar, that it had already filled to the brim with worry for Dorothy, for himself and his friends, and if he tried to cram anything else in there the glass would break.

He didn't like what it said about him, that he thought things like that. But he could feel the cracks forming already. So he kept his eyes ahead, and he held his breath until the motels were behind him.

They turned off the waterway and into a neighborhood that had once been called Queen Anne and was now, simply, West Aurora. Ash had just caught sight of the Space Needle in the distance, the massive, rusted saucer resting on top of the water, like a boat—

And then the ground trembled, sending a wall of steel-gray water arcing over him, momentarily hiding the structure from view.

Ash felt his stomach drop as water sloshed into their boat. Chandra grabbed his arm, her nails digging straight through the leather of his jacket and into his skin.

No, he thought. *Not now.*

And then the shaking stopped, abruptly, though the black and gray waves continued to swell.

Chandra loosened her grip. "Third one this week," she said, gasping.

"Fourth," Ash corrected. There'd been a quake in the middle of the night, small enough that it almost hadn't woken him up.

Chandra shook her head. "Freaky."

Ash swallowed but said nothing. Earthquakes were something they'd had to get used to over the years, ever since a massive earthquake hit the West Coast back in 2073, followed by an even larger quake in 2075. The 2075 quake caused a tsunami that'd left the city of Seattle underwater. The Cascadia Fault quake—or the mega-quake, as it was sometimes called—had been a 9.3 on the Richter scale, easily the most devastating earthquake the country had ever seen. Between the two quakes, the West Coast had been completely wiped out. Nearly forty thousand people had died.

The earthquakes had become more frequent since the mega-quake but, lately, it seemed that there was a new one every other day. They were always small, barely strong enough to send waves crashing up against the side of the schoolhouse where Ash and his friends all lived, or Dante's, their favorite bar. But, still, they made his nerves jittery.

"We'll be home soon," Ash told Chandra, tugging on the pull cord, again.

* * *

Professor Zacharias Walker's old workshop rose in the distance like a mirage. It consisted of a mismatched roof and siding made of old boards, tires, and pieces of tin. Ash watched the structure separate from the shadows and wished, as he often did, that he would find the Professor himself behind the rain-soaked windows.

Professor Walker had discovered time travel. He'd built two time machines—the *Second Star* and the *Dark Star*—and then he'd gone back in time and plucked Jonathan Asher, Chandrakala Samhita, and Willis Henry from various points in history and brought them to New Seattle in 2075, forming a team that he'd jokingly called the Chronology Protection Agency. They were supposed to travel through time together, uncovering the mysteries of the past.

And then the mega-quake destroyed the city. And, just a few months later, the Professor had taken the *Dark Star* and disappeared in time without telling any of them what year he was traveling to or why. Ash had spent months searching for him before discovering the Professor's old journal and, finally, learning exactly where he'd gone—to an old military base called Fort Hunter, in 1980. There, he'd planned to study the underlying causes of the earthquakes that had destroyed Seattle and killed the Professor's wife, Natasha.

Or he'd tried to. The Professor was killed not long after landing at Fort Hunter, executed by soldiers who suspected him of stealing valuable military secrets. Ash and his friends had tried to follow him back in time, but they'd failed. The trip had destroyed their only remaining time machine, the

Second Star, and nearly cost both Ash and Zora their lives. If Ash pressed his hand to the skin on his abdomen, he could still feel a piece of metal lodged just below his ribs. It was all that he had left of his old time machine.

Worse than that, Ash had found some of the Professor's notes back at Fort Hunter, and they seemed to indicate that two more massive earthquakes were coming. Only these earthquakes wouldn't just destroy a single city. They had the potential to destroy what was left of the West Coast. Maybe the whole country.

Light glimmered behind the workshop's windows, telling Ash that Zora was still awake. She rarely left her father's workshop anymore. She'd set up a cot in the back corner and had taken to washing herself with a rag and a pitcher of water instead of bathing. As far as Ash knew, she lived off cheese sandwiches and burnt coffee, and spent every waking moment going over her father's notes, trying to piece together his research, looking for some way of stopping the earthquakes he'd predicted before they occurred.

Seeing her light, Ash felt a deep twist of something like disappointment mingled with desperate hope. It was a new emotion, painful and optimistic at the same time. He wished Zora would just give up already, while, at the same time, he prayed for a breakthrough.

Or maybe it wasn't such a new emotion at all. Perhaps hope always made the disappointment that much worse.

The workshop door inched upward, water sloshing

around the wood as it moved—and then ground to a stop, gears crunching. Ash grimaced, punching the button on the remote control again. When the door stayed frozen, he piloted the little motorboat closer, so he could work the manual chain pull.

The only electricity in New Seattle came from the relatively few solar panels still left in the city. There weren't many that'd survived after the mega-quake, so they were incredibly valuable. Most of the people Ash knew had sold their panels years ago, in exchange for money or food, but the Professor had insisted they hold on to theirs. It'd helped that, until very recently, they'd been able to bring food back from the past.

Unfortunately, the panels had started to break down. They hadn't been made to last forever, and Ash cringed to think of what would happen when they stopped working entirely. The city was barely inching along as it was.

He docked his boat inside the garage. Zora was cross-legged on the dock, frowning down at a stack of her father's notes. The light he'd seen came from candles lined up along the walls, rather than the bulb hanging from the ceiling.

"Power's been spotty all day." She looked up, eyes flicking over Ash's boat, where there were still only two—not three— passengers. She seemed to hesitate before asking, "No luck at Mac's, then?"

"What do you think?" Ash didn't look at her but jerked the motorboat's engine off, perhaps a little too forcefully. Spitefully, he asked, "You?"

In answer, Zora merely balled up a piece of notebook

paper and threw it at him. It missed, and they were both silent as they watched it sink below the black water.

"I hope that wasn't important," Willis said. He was sitting on a stool in the shadowy corner just behind Zora, his pale skin and hair seeming to blend with his surroundings despite his massive size. He was whittling something. The hunk of wood looked like a toothpick in his monstrous hands.

"It was just a grocery list from two years ago." Zora shoved her black braids off her forehead. "Eggs, milk, and Toaster Strudel. God knows why he kept it."

"Toaster Strudel? Oh my God, remember before the earthquake when you could just go to the grocery store and buy Toaster Strudel?" Chandra crawled out of the boat, grunting as she sent it rocking beneath her. There were a few black-market stores and shops around, but they stuck to the necessities: drinkable water, fish, protein bars. If they wanted anything else, they had to seek out an official Center-sanctioned trading post, and they were expensive.

"I used to love those limited-edition maple brown sugar ones," Chandra continued. "God, they were so good. I'd sneak out and eat them after everyone else went to sleep."

Willis looked up, eyes narrowing. "That's why we were always running out."

"Don't look at me like you didn't steal extra cans of LaCroix from the kitchen and hide them under your bed." Chandra leaned over the side of the dock, staring forlornly at the spot where the shopping list had vanished. "You should really keep that stuff. It's history. Memorabilia from before the flood. Could be valuable someday."

Ash squatted next to Zora and stared down at the pile of mildewed paper that represented their last hope of saving this drowned and desperate city.

It didn't exactly instill confidence. Printouts from Roman's laptop lay stacked on top of old notebooks, all of it mixed up with lists and drawings from the Professor's office, pages torn out of his journal. It looked like Zora had been jotting things down, too. Ash recognized the slant of her handwriting on a scrap near the top of the heap and tilted his head to read what she'd written.

What the actual hell does any of this mean?!

He grimaced. That was disappointing. "No closer to understanding the math part, then?"

"Let's see, did I earn a degree in theoretical physics since I last saw you? No, I did not." Zora groaned and pressed her fingers over her eyelids. "What I'd give for *one single* textbook, but no. Old grocery lists I have in spades. But actual books?"

Ash knew he wasn't expected to respond to that. Zora had been complaining about their lack of books for weeks now. The Professor used to have shelves and shelves of old textbooks hanging around before the earthquake, but Zora hadn't been able to locate any of them with the rest of his notes. She'd never studied physics or calculus in school, and since their crappy, dial-up Internet had stopped working for good last week, she had no way of boning up on the subject now.

Unfortunately, that meant that most of her father's notes read like gibberish. Chandra had tried to help her out with some of the simpler equations but, as she liked to explain, medical science wasn't the same as time-traveler science.

"Call me if someone needs their kidney removed," she'd told Zora. "Otherwise . . ." And she'd shrugged, making a face at the nonsense equations.

"What kind of scientist keeps stacks of *trash* in his office, anyway?" Zora muttered, grabbing a few crumpled sheets of paper. "Receipts and old lists and doodles of tap-dancing ladybugs . . ."

Zora rubbed her eyes with two fingers, leaving dirt smudged across her nose. "I was crazy to think I could do this without him. The world is doomed. *We're* doomed. I should just . . . give up."

"Give up," Ash muttered, almost to himself and, all at once, he could feel the weight of the day settling over him.

Motel room windows, and Mac's leering smile, and Mira's cocked head.

But where else would we go?

He raked a hand over his face. *Seven days.* At most, he only had seven days left in this wretched, cursed place.

Oh, how he wished for more.

Rage tore through him—not there one moment, everywhere the next—and it mingled with the disappointment and the frustration and that damned hope, which he couldn't get rid of, even now. He stood and began knotting the boat up to the dock, his motions jerky and rough. It felt good to take out his aggression on something, even if it was just a rope.

He noticed, in a detached sort of way, that the others had

gone quiet. He looked up and saw Willis hunched over his whittling, knife gone still, and Zora staring down at one of her father's papers without reading it. Only Chandra was gaping at him openly. She'd never been good at subtle.

"What?" He didn't mean it to sound as harsh as it did, and he hated himself a little for it.

Zora sniffed. "You seem a little off."

"I'm fine."

Chandra snorted.

"We could all use a break," Willis said, placing his whittling on a small table beside him. Now that it wasn't hidden inside his massive hands, Ash could see a man's head and shoulders taking shape in the wood. "Dante's?"

Zora stretched her arms over her head, yawning. "I'd be down for a drink."

"And a shower," Chandra said, wrinkling her nose.

Zora shot her a look, and Chandra shrugged.

"When was the last time you washed yourself in the bathroom instead of out of that pitcher?"

"I wasn't going to say anything," Willis said quietly.

Ash was still holding the rope. He'd knotted it so tightly that individual fibers were beginning to unravel. There were rope burns on his palms.

The idea of going to Dante's, of sitting in their regular booth and drinking hooch and forcing himself to laugh at Willis's jokes or Chandra's sad attempts at flirting caused a dull ache to spread through his skull. He cringed and tried to rub away the pain.

"Ash?" It was Chandra, concern threading through her voice. "Are you okay? I know that you were hoping . . ."

Ash felt his muscles go stiff and shook his head. "I need some air," he said, zipping his jacket up to his chin.

Chandra's face fell.

"Come drink with us, Captain," Willis said. "It'll be fun."

"I'll just go around the block." Ash crossed to the door on the other side of the workshop. "I'll meet you all at Dante's or wherever. Later, though."

Willis started to say something else, but Zora lifted a hand, interrupting him.

"Let him go." Her voice was low, and she didn't look Ash in the eye. So, she was pissed. Zora tended to respond to people having emotions that she didn't approve of by getting pissed at them. It was a personality quirk that Ash wasn't interested in dealing with just now.

He pushed the workshop door open and stepped out onto the docks. Bitterly cold air bit at his cheeks and whipped his jacket against his body.

He thought of Dorothy's dark hair. Dorothy's eyes.

He needed some time alone.

He needed to think.

LOG ENTRY—JUNE 14, 2074
11:47 HOURS
THE WORKSHOP

Today marks the first time that I've stepped foot inside my workshop all week. I used to be in and out at least once a day but, lately, ironic though it may seem, I haven't been able to find the time.

There are daily training sessions with NASA and my new team of explorers, meetings with WCAAT, not to mention press conferences to inform the public of what we're up to. Most of today was taken up by a photo shoot. A *photo shoot*, of all things.

It's disappointing, to say the least. I'm a scientist, after all, and I'd like to be left to do my work. But the success of my past experiments has made me into a minor celebrity, of sorts, which was never my intention. I find myself longing for the days when no one knew who I was, when time travel was just a puzzle I couldn't stop thinking about.

You know, in those early days, a time machine wasn't even part of my plan. It's actually rather inconvenient to have to worry about an entire ship whenever you want to blip back in time, not to mention the time tunnel itself, and the exotic matter, of which there's a rather limited supply. I may have discovered how to travel through time much sooner, in fact, but I wasted years trying to figure out how to work around these problems, and those early attempts were all massive, messy failures.

And yet I can't help looking through my old notes now, wondering if I missed something. Perhaps time travel without a vessel, without an anil or exotic matter is possible....

All this has me thinking about Nikola Tesla, the Serbian-American inventor, electrical engineer, mechanical engineer, physicist, and futurist.

Tesla spent a lot of time and money attempting to develop the transmission of electrical power without wires—in other words, the coil.

You know the coil. It was that big copper ball that shot off sparks of electricity. Basically, it made Tesla look like some sort of crazy mad scientist, and, unfortunately, he never actually got it working correctly. A lot of his theories about how energy and electricity move through the earth's crust were based on faulty science, and he ended up pursuing this idea of "free energy" until all his funding ran out and his reputation was, basically, in ruins. It's a shame, too, because he was one of the smartest people the world had ever seen. A true genius.

In any case, I bring Tesla up now because he spent a lot of time observing the electronic noise of lightning strikes, and this led him to conclude that he could use the entire globe of the Earth to conduct electrical energy for free. He was super wrong, unfortunately, but the science itself wasn't bad. He was just wrong about how the earth would react to the science.

The anil, on the other hand, reacts exactly how he expected it to.

I won't bore you with the details. All you need to know is that Tesla was right; he just didn't know what he was right about. Most scientists working today believe that there are actually a great many more anils all over the world, but they're buried deep within the earth's crust. The working theory is that the Puget Sound anil was only made visible by the movement of tectonic plates and that, given another couple hundred years and further erosion of the earth's crust, more tunnels through time will appear. If that's true, it's possible that Tesla actually managed to connect his original experiments with some underground anil that he didn't even know was there.

So, in effect, Tesla was the very first time traveler. He's even quoted as saying that he's seen the future. Once, after being struck by a jolt of electricity coming off his coil, he said, "I saw the Past, Present, and Future at the same time."

If that's true, if he did see the past, present, and future at the same time, then he, somehow, managed to travel through time without access to an anil, without any exotic matter, and without a vessel.

It's imperative that I speak with him.

5

DOROTHY

The Fairmont's garage was dark when they landed, and empty. Roman and Dorothy gathered the stolen artwork from the back of the time machine and headed down the stairs in silence, stopping in front of a heavy, unmarked door deep in the Fairmont's basement.

Roman dug an old key out from under his coat, and Dorothy heard the click of metal in a lock. The door creaked open, revealing a deeper, velvety darkness beyond.

Another *click* and the room was illuminated.

As always, Dorothy felt her breath catch. It was hard to know where to look first. There was the stack of scrolls gathering dust in the corner, stolen from the Library of Alexandria moments before the siege in 48 BCE. The missing panels from the Bayeux Tapestry hung from the wall before her, showing William the Conqueror's Christmas Day coronation, in 1066. On a table below sat the long-lost crown jewels of King John.

Dorothy smiled as she looked at the jewels, remembering the week she and Roman had spent on the Wash in 1216. There'd been a lot of discussion throughout history about how the fool king had managed to lose his jewels, but it turned out that the luggage containing them had simply *fallen off* of the back of his carriage as he rode beneath the Sutton Bridge. Dorothy and Roman had waited for the king and his soldiers to gallop past, and then they'd taken the abandoned luggage for themselves. Roman had worn the magnificently jeweled crown the entire ride home.

"It's already half past nine," Roman said, interrupting the memory. "Are you ready for the broadcast?"

Ah yes. The broadcast.

Ironically, Ash was the one who'd given her the idea.

"The Black Cirkus wants to go back in time," he'd told her once. "They seem to think that's the key to fixing all our problems."

He'd said this like it was an idiotic thing to think, but Dorothy had found herself disagreeing. Because, really, what sort of problems couldn't be solved with *time travel*?

She'd started thinking about how she might go about changing some things. At the very least, the city needed power, access to medication and food. Too many people were hungry, and cold, and sick.

Dorothy had been a con artist before landing here. She'd never really been one for good deeds. But, for the first time in her life, she had all this power. And she knew how to fix this.

The problem was that the people of New Seattle disliked

the Black Cirkus. They remembered them as the violent gang of thugs and thieves who'd taken over the city in the days just after the mega-quake. But Dorothy knew they could be so much more and so, several months ago, she'd told Roman her plan.

"Let's speak to the people directly. We can have a . . . a broadcast." She'd stumbled over the word *broadcast*, which she'd only just learned. "The people in this city don't realize what's being kept from them. They don't know that time travel is still possible. Let me bring them to our side."

They'd built a makeshift studio in the corner of the Fairmont basement, with real cameras and spotlights, which Dorothy and Roman had stolen from a defunct television station in 2044, and a backdrop made from a tattered American flag that Roman had insisted made them look like rebels.

Dorothy, naive, had thought the campaign would be easy. Just go on television (another new word!) and tell the people what they could do. But, of course, it was much more complicated than that. Distrust of the Cirkus ran deep. It had taken over two hundred broadcasts—one every single night—and the better part of a year to plant the seeds. Now, though. Now, they were close.

Dorothy took her place before the flag. The sudden glare of the spotlights made her squint, but no one would see her eyes beneath the hood that hid her face. Roman stood behind the equipment, all in shadow, and she heard the telltale sound of buttons flipping and dials turning as he worked the switchboard.

"Three . . . ," said Roman, his voice cutting through the oppressive spotlights.

Dorothy took a deep breath.

". . . two . . ."

Here we go.

Roman held up a single finger, and then, after a beat, he pointed at her.

Go.

"Friends," Dorothy said, her heart beating hard and fast in her throat. "Do not attempt to adjust your television. Our broadcast has taken over every channel."

6

ASH

Ash usually avoided wandering around New Seattle at night. It was far too likely that he'd run into someone unsavory; a Cirkus Freak searching for an easy mark, or some jerk who recognized Ash from the days before the mega-quake and wanted to start a fight. The city was only safe for those who had the cash to pay off the thieves and lowlifes who prowled the docks after dark. Ash didn't have that kind of money, and, even if he did, he had far too much pride to pay for his own safety.

Besides, tonight was different. Tonight, he felt hyper-alive and also, strangely, like he was caught in a dream he couldn't wake up from. He practically salivated at the thought of throwing a punch, of feeling his knuckles connect with something hard and warm.

But there was no one around to fight with him. His skin tingled, uselessly.

He made his way to the end of the dock, stopping where it forked. One path led deeper into the dark water, bordered by ghostly white trees and mossy rooftops, while the other twisted toward the city. The buildings weren't lit up—the only electricity downtown was used to power televisions for the nightly broadcast—but Ash could make out the shape of them against the black sky.

He almost felt like laughing. It couldn't be any clearer than this: there was a good path and a bad path. He could turn right and wander around in the dark for half an hour, cool down before, eventually, making his way back to Dante's, where his friends would be on their second drink.

Or he could turn left and head downtown, where the Cirkus Freaks and the people who paid them off partied.

He heard the distant call of voices. It stoked his anger, the knowledge that there were some people in this town who could still walk around at night without being afraid.

Seven days, he thought.

Out loud, he muttered, "What the hell?"

Left. Definitely left.

He shoved his hands into his jacket pockets and lowered his head against the hammering wind. It was cold for November in the Pacific Northwest, but he found himself relishing the chill. It was a welcome respite from the burning inside him.

The voices grew louder as the buildings got closer together. A crowd of kids in nice coats stumbled out of a bar.

"No, *that* one," one of them was saying, his voice rising in exasperation. "She was looking at you, didn't you see?"

His friend snorted. "Not a chance."

"We could go back tomorrow," said the first. "Ask her."

Ash slowed to let them move past. They irritated him for reasons he couldn't name. Maybe it was that they clearly had money, or maybe it was just that they were obnoxious but not obnoxious enough to start a fight with.

They were just . . . happy.

Ash watched them, every muscle in his body wound tight. Their voices faded as they walked down the dock and, when they were gone, he pushed through the door of the bar they'd just come out of without bothering to glance at the sign hanging over it.

It was dark inside, with black walls and stainless-steel countertops and black leather barstools. There was a television above the bar, but it wasn't turned on.

A crowd of people milled around the cramped space, shoulder to shoulder in the dark. He thought he saw one or two look his way, but he didn't have the energy to worry about whether they'd recognized him or if they'd been Black Cirkus sympathizers before the mega-quake.

Before the Professor had disappeared, he and his time travelers had been a bit . . . controversial.

Some thought the Professor was a genius, the future of science and technology.

Others thought he was an out-of-touch intellectual, content to let the world around him fall to ruins while he focused on his books and experiments.

Neither side was entirely wrong.

Ash wove through the small, crowded room, keeping his head ducked, and found an empty stool near the bar.

A bartender appeared before him, staring for a beat too long before asking, in a resigned voice, "What do you want?"

"Beer?" Ash said, his eyes going wide as he read the chalkboard menu behind the bartender's head. "You guys got *beer*?"

Most bars in New Seattle hadn't had real beer since before the mega-quake. At least, the bars that Ash frequented hadn't had beer since before the mega-quake. Too expensive.

The bartender hesitated, and his eyes flicked to the crowd behind him. Ash resisted the urge to check over his shoulder, see whether anyone was staring at him, whispering. It had been a long while since he'd been inside a bar that wouldn't serve him.

"Come on, man, one pint," he said, digging around in his jacket. A pint of beer would cost him half the money in the envelope of cash he'd stolen back from Mac after Chandra shot him, but, just now, it seemed worth it. "I promise, I'll be good—"

The television hanging above the bar flickered on and Ash froze, hand still shoved down his pocket.

A shadowy figure appeared on the screen. She wore a hood that covered her face, and stood in front of a tattered American flag, a sketchy fox painted on the front of her coat.

"Friends," Quinn said, in her heavily distorted voice. "Do not attempt to adjust your television. Our broadcast has taken over every channel."

"You still want that pint?" the bartender asked.

Ash realized he'd frozen, one hand still gripping the cash envelope. He nodded and handed over a slightly damp bill, his eyes never leaving the screen.

Quinn continued. "I come to you this evening with happy news. For the past year, the Black Cirkus has been attempting to uncover the secrets of time travel, secrets that have long been kept from us by the scientist Professor Zacharias Walker.

"Tonight, I am glad to say that Professor Walker has been thwarted. Time travel is ours, at long last."

All talk in the bar ceased. Someone catcalled, while another called out, "About damn time!"

Ash realized he was holding the cash envelope so tightly that his fingers had started to cramp. He tucked it back into his jacket and began cracking his knuckles.

He'd known the Cirkus could travel through time. Or, at least, he'd suspected. He'd seen their time machine himself, and he'd thought he'd seen Roman and Quinn in 1980, at the Fort Hunter complex.

But he'd never been able to figure out *how* they were able to go back in time without any exotic matter and, over the last few weeks, he'd been able to push that question to the back of his mind. There'd always been other, more pressing things to focus on.

Not anymore.

"And now, we would like to invite you all to a revel of sorts." Quinn announced. "Tomorrow evening, the Black Cirkus will host a masquerade at the Fairmont hotel, at seven o'clock pm.

"Join us, and see how we will use time travel to build a

better present, a better future. Join the Black Cirkus, and we'll show you a new and better world."

The image froze, the broadcast over.

Conversations leaped back to life. Ash heard someone say, "Quinn Fox," but they sounded excited rather than terrified. A first.

Another added, tone casual, like they were repeating something they weren't sure they still believed, "But, she's the *cannibal*, right?"

And, "Didn't you hear her? She says she wants to help. To fix things."

Meanwhile, another conversation seemed to be going on at the same time, this one about the Professor and the Chronology Protection Agency. About him.

"Selfish," someone was saying. "The group of them, thinking they could keep all that technology for themselves."

"Time travel should be for everyone," said someone else. "Quinn Fox will make it right."

Ash bristled, tuning them out. How quickly people forgot. All Quinn had to do was dangle a carrot on a stick and, all at once, years of Black Cirkus violence was wiped away.

He lifted a hand to his face, remembering the heat of Quinn's blade on his skin. He'd spoken to her in person only once, while standing on a dock outside the Fairmont.

"We're leaving," he'd said, backing away.

And she'd responded, "It's too late for that."

And then she'd cut him across the cheek with a freaking dagger.

He could still feel the metal against his skin, the flaring of nerve endings, the way his heart had sputtered with shock, and then adrenaline. Not exactly a good first impression.

And yet, somehow, he was supposed to fall in love with her. Prememories didn't lie, and Ash had been seeing the same prememory every single time he'd entered an anil for the last year: a girl with white hair in a boat, water spread out around her, white trees interrupting the darkness. She would kiss him, and then she would kill him. He would love her, and she would betray him.

Quinn Fox had white hair. Quinn Fox was that girl.

He closed his eyes, swallowing the lump that had formed in his throat. His blood pumped hot and fast beneath his skin.

The prememory was real, as real to him as any memory could be. He could still smell the brine and salt smell of the water. He could taste the heat of Quinn Fox's lips.

He leaned forward without making the conscious decision to do so, one hand reaching for his back pocket. His fingers enclosed the creased and worn leather book and tugged it loose.

The Professor's old journal looked like hell. Ash must've thumbed through its pages a hundred times over the last three weeks, reading and rereading his mentor's entries, looking for hidden meaning behind the anecdotes and sketches and jotted notes. He no longer believed there was a way to keep his prememory from coming true, but he would have settled for something simpler. Advice, maybe. Or a promise that everything was going to be okay.

He exhaled through his teeth, wishing that the Professor were here, sitting on the barstool next to him.

But the Professor was dead. He'd died at Fort Hunter complex, on March 17, 1980. All that was left of him was this worn, leather journal.

Ash paused as he flipped through the book, finding a ragged edge of paper peeking out of the journal's binding. It looked like a page was missing but, when he looked closer, he saw that there were several sheets of paper ripped out, almost like someone had removed a whole entry. He ran his thumb through the torn pages, frowning. Had the Professor ripped them out himself? Why?

The bartender was suddenly before him, again, looking dubious. "Look, man, I let you have one, but—"

"I'll take another," Ash said, cutting him off. When the bartender frowned, he fished the cash envelope out of his jacket pocket and slammed it on the bar. What was the point of savings if he was going to die in less than a week?

Cautiously, like he thought it might contain something poisonous, the bartender opened the envelope, one eyebrow raising, appreciatively, as he counted the bills inside. Nothing made friends like good, hard cash. He slipped the envelope into his pocket and turned around to pour Ash a beer.

"Keep 'em coming," Ash said.

LOG ENTRY—AUGUST 27, 1899
16:24 HOURS
JUST OUTSIDE COLORADO SPRINGS

I have to write quickly, so this will be a rather short entry. Nikola Tesla has just run back to the house in the hopes of finding a bottle of bourbon, and I don't want to be scribbling away in a notebook upon his return.

He's a bit paranoid, Nikola . . . I don't want to give him reason to be suspicious.

I'm currently sitting on a wooden stool inside of his experimental station outside Colorado Springs. The main workspace is little more than a monstrous barn, dominated by the largest Tesla coil I've ever seen. There's other equipment, too. Generators and light bulbs, among other things, but very little in terms of what you'd call "creature comforts." I asked Nikola when he broke for meals or, indeed, what he actually ate, and he looked at me like I actually was a martian.

That's the other thing. He doesn't believe me about time travel. In fact, he seems far more comfortable with the idea that I'm some sort of extraterrestrial.

This, I believe, is my fault. I landed a bit too close to the workshop and, as such, Nikola saw my ship. Successful air travel isn't achieved until 1903, remember, so it's four years too early for me to go whizzing about in a flying machine. There's that and, of course, the fact that my ship is a bit advanced-looking for the turn of the nineteenth century. In any case, the jump to "alien" isn't totally out of nowhere.

Damn it, I think that's him outside now. I should really put this away before I'm caught—

7

DOROTHY

The spotlights switched off, leaving Dorothy blinking into spotty darkness. For a moment she heard only the plastic click of buttons, the dying whir of motors.

And then Roman, snickering. "*Revel?* Really? I'm afraid you're beginning to show your age."

Dorothy rubbed her eyes. "People don't say *revel* anymore?"

"Not for the last hundred years or so, no." Roman came out from behind the camera equipment, carrying the duffel bag containing their stolen artwork.

He placed it on the cart that already held the king's lost jewels and removed the Vermeer, tilting his head to study it.

He sounded awed as he said, "Just think, we're the first people in over two hundred years to see this painting in person."

Dorothy allowed her eyes to flick to the painting. It really was amazing. Not just the art, but all the beautiful things they were allowed to see, all the incredible places they were able to visit. Sometimes, they went back to a specific time or place out of necessity, and other times it was merely because one of them had wanted to see it.

The Vermeer, Dorothy had desperately wanted to see. A smile tugged at her lips as she pulled her gaze away.

She stopped beside Roman, lifting the king's scepter. "You know, I don't really understand the point of a scepter. Is it just a stick that you're supposed to hold? Or another place to put—"

Someone cleared her throat, interrupting her. Still holding the scepter, Dorothy turned.

The girl standing in the doorway was tall and broad-shouldered, with round hips and long red hair that she wore in a braid down her back. Her face was so freckled that it was hard to make out the color of her skin beneath, but her eyes were dark brown and vibrant.

"Mira," Dorothy said, surprised. Mira worked in Mac Murphy's whorehouse. Mac didn't usually trust women, but Mira had been with him since before the flood, and so he often allowed her a few small tasks outside of her usual duties.

But Mac always dealt with the Black Cirkus himself. Something must've happened for him to send Mira in his place.

Dorothy looked around, suddenly anxious. No one had seen the treasures down here except for Roman and herself. "Perhaps we should speak in the hall. . . ."

Mira cocked her head, amused. "I'm not here for any of

this," Mira said in her rasp of a voice. But her eyes lingered on the jewels, impressed.

"Then why are you here?" asked Roman.

"Mac was . . . unavailable this evening." She spoke coolly enough, but Dorothy thought she saw a flash in her eyes—humor, perhaps, or delight. There was a story there. "He sent me to collect your payment."

The Black Cirkus had been squatting in the Fairmont since the mega-quake flooded the city. It was a dilapidated mess, but it was also the only hotel in downtown Seattle that was still livable and, as such, it was incredibly valuable real estate. The Cirkus had managed to hold it for so long by paying off some rather unsavory people—Mac included.

Roman pulled an envelope out of his jacket pocket and handed it to Mira.

She nodded, lips pressed tight as she counted the bills inside. After a moment, she paused, glancing up. "I'm afraid you're a bit light."

"We'll make it up next week," Dorothy promised.

"Will you?" Mira pocketed the envelope, looking unconvinced. "This is the third time you've handed over less than the agreed-upon amount. Rumor has it you've been more interested in playing Robin Hood than making money lately."

A beat of uncomfortable silence followed her statement. Dorothy placed the king's scepter back on the table; Mira followed the movement with her eyes.

Dorothy wished this could be solved as easily as handing over the scepter—or any one of the other treasures—as payment. But, priceless though the items were, their actual *worth* here was very little. No one in New Seattle was flush enough to hand over money for jewels and gold.

Resources had always been slim in New Seattle. After the mega-quake destroyed most of the West Coast, the United States government moved the country's borders inland, leaving the remains of the devastated cities to save themselves. With all the nation's wealth consolidated to a dozen or so states at the center of the country, inflation along the coasts skyrocketed.

It cost a couple hundred dollars for a bag of grain large enough to feed one person for one week, a few hundred more for fresh water and a supply of vitamins to prevent someone from getting scurvy. Add to that the fact that most people in New Seattle had no way of making money or growing their own food.

Before Dorothy had arrived, the Cirkus had been a gang of petty thieves. They'd numbered hardly more than thirty members, all children and teenagers, most close to starvation. They'd been like stray dogs, nipping at each other, fighting over scraps.

Dorothy had organized them. She'd taught them simple cons, convinced them to work together. They made hundreds a week stealing from anyone stupid enough to be out on the docks after dark.

At least, they *used* to make hundreds a week. It was impossible to get a city to trust a gang of thugs when they robbed them blind each night, so Dorothy had urged the Cirkus

Freaks to lay off the thefts. Just for a little while.

It had not made her popular. The Freaks liked money, and that was running dry.

"Mac asked me to deliver the message," Mira said. "He'd like the rest of his money by tomorrow evening."

Voice toneless, Roman said, "And if we can't get it?"

Dorothy glanced at him, seeing only the lower half of his face beneath the edge of her hood. There was no possible way for them to get the money by tomorrow evening, but she wouldn't know it by looking at Roman's expression. The annoying thing about her partner was that he grew even more cool and collected the angrier he got.

Right now he seemed to be all calm, unworried confidence. But Dorothy noticed that a muscle in his jaw had gone tight. His only tell.

Mira considered him, head tilted. "Mac didn't say, but I can't imagine he'd be happy." She glanced at the broadcasting equipment in the corner, her lip twitching in a way that made Dorothy think she'd been watching from the shadows while Quinn Fox went on air to appeal to the people of New Seattle. "Perhaps he'll come by your little party and you can speak with him then."

Something prickled, uncomfortably, in Dorothy. Was that a threat?

The Cirkus Freaks were strong, but Mac was stronger. He made real money off his disgusting whorehouses, and that allowed him to procure certain things from the Center.

Firearms, for one thing. And bullets. The idea of going to war with him chilled Dorothy to her core.

Mira turned, and then she was out the door and gone.

"Well," Roman said. "That ruins everything."

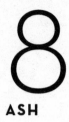

ASH

Ash wasn't entirely sure how he made it back home. One moment he'd been hunched over the bar, staring into the dwindling remains of his drink, and the next he was hauling himself through the window of the old schoolhouse, the taste of something sour clinging to his tongue.

Beer, he realized, grimacing. Lots of it. He didn't remember ordering, or drinking, a third (a fourth?). But he must've. He could taste it.

He stumbled down the hall, propping an arm against the wall to steady himself as he kicked off his boots.

Another step, and he stubbed his toe on a free weight that Willis had left in the middle of the floor. He swore and hopped around on one foot.

There was a sound, a shuffling of movement, and then Zora's voice calling, "Ash? That you?"

Ash lowered his injured foot back to the floor, cringing. He smelled coffee. Which meant she'd been waiting up for him. It must be later than he'd thought.

He hobbled the rest of the way down the hall, into the kitchen.

Zora leaned against the kitchen table, her ordinarily calm expression twisted into something troubled. Chandra sat beside her, spinning something that looked like a small, grease-covered gear with an inordinate amount of determination, and Willis was making tea, which seemed like overkill. Ash could already smell the coffee.

"You're all up late," he muttered.

Chandra wrinkled her nose and balanced the gear between two fingers. "You're drunk?" She said *drunk* like someone else might say *stupid*.

Ash frowned. Was he drunk? He didn't think he'd ever been drunk before, but it felt right. He was going to die this week. Getting good and drunk seemed like the sort of thing he should do during his final week of life.

"We were just talking about the broadcast," Zora said.

Ash sat, propping his foot on one knee so he could study his throbbing toe through his threadbare sock. "You saw?"

The teakettle began to whistle. Willis moved it off the burner. "The whole city saw, Captain," he said, pulling a chipped mug down from the cupboard above the stove. "It's all anyone's talking about."

"The Black Cirkus can travel back in time," Zora murmured, scrubbing a hand over her face. "I guess we already knew that, but now . . ."

She trailed off, but Ash knew what she meant. It felt

different to hear Quinn announce it to the entire city. A part of him had still been hoping what they saw at Fort Hunter had been a fluke.

Chandra looked up at Ash, pursing her lips. "Wait, where were you all night? You said you were going to meet us at Dante's."

Ash blinked, slowly, through his drunkenness. Every pair of eyes seemed to be on him, waiting for an explanation.

Hesitating, he said, "I . . . took a walk." And then he shrugged, like this might lessen the blow. "I sort of ended up in a bar near the Fairmont. . . ."

"You went over to the Fairmont?" Chandra flicked the gear she'd been playing with to the floor. "Why?"

Zora said, "He was probably looking for Quinn."

Chandra made a vague noise in the back of her throat. Willis's mustache twitched as he poured himself a cup of tea. Neither looked surprised by what Zora had just said.

"You told them?" Ash asked, annoyed. After Fort Hunter, he'd told Zora that Quinn Fox was the girl from his prememory, the one who was going to kill him. He had *not* told Willis and Chandra, and yet, it seemed, they knew.

Zora didn't even bother looking guilty. "Of course I told them. Secrets are stupid."

Ash was at a loss for words. He'd kept the truth a secret because he'd been embarrassed. Quinn Fox, the Black Cirkus assassin. The cannibal of New Seattle. How was he going to fall in love with *her*?

And now?

The anger left him at once. It had just been a flicker of feeling, not the real thing. It was impossible to be angry about something like a spilled secret when he had only a few days left to live. Besides, maybe Zora was right. Maybe secrets were stupid.

"So did you meet her?" asked Chandra.

Ash blinked. "What?"

"You went downtown tonight to find Quinn, right?" Her eyebrows lifted. "Well? Did you?"

"He would have told us," Willis said. But he didn't sound convinced.

"I would have told you," Ash assured him. "No more secrets."

"Right," Willis said, and Ash didn't think he imagined the relief in his voice. "You would've."

"So you still haven't met her?" Chandra asked.

"I still haven't met her."

"But you know she's going to be at this masquerade at the Fairmont tomorrow night, right?" Chandra gave him a sly look. "Does that mean we get to go?"

"Of course we're not going," said Zora, incredulous. "The point is to keep Ash from meeting the cannibal who's going to murder him, not deliver him like a present."

Ever since seeing Zora break down on the roof of Fort Hunter, Ash had an easier time hearing the small fluctuations in her voice, when her anger dipped into fear. He heard it now, and that's the only reason he was able to answer her calmly instead of snapping and starting a fight.

"Actually," he said, shifting his eyes away from her face. "I think it's about time the two of us were introduced."

Zora answered with a short, hard laugh, like he'd told a joke she didn't think was funny. "If you meet her, you'll *die*."

Ash noticed that she hadn't included the part about falling in love first. "I'm going to die either way."

Chandra coughed into her fist. Willis did something unnecessarily loud that involved a spoon clattering against the sugar bowl.

Zora was looking at him now, brow furrowed. Ash watched her swallow, trying to gather herself.

"I don't understand," she said firmly. "We talked about this. We were going to figure out a way to fix it. We were—"

"Fix what, exactly? How do you propose we go about changing a memory?"

"It's not a memory yet!"

"Zor— Jesus—that's what a prememory *is*. Didn't you read the Professor's journal? He saw the mega-quake before it happened. He saw it for months, and he didn't do anything because he *couldn't*." Ash raked a hand back through his hair. "If it was possible to change it, don't you think he would've? Don't you think he would've done anything to save—"

He broke off then, realizing he'd gone too far. Zora only stared at him, her expression chilly and blank.

Zora's mother, Natasha, had died in the massive earthquake that had destroyed Seattle, and the Professor had nearly ruined himself going back in time again and again, trying to find a way to bring her back.

Ash felt cruel, bringing it up like this. He looked at his hands. "Sorry."

Zora considered him and then nodded, and turned toward the window, her shoulders rigid.

"About this party," Chandra said, after a beat. "You feel like you have to go, right? Like it's destiny or whatever?"

Ash was quiet for a moment. He pictured Quinn staring out of the television set above the bar—or, rather, the darkness inside the cloak where Quinn's face should have been. He imagined walking up to her at this party, pulling his gun out, finger twitching on the trigger and—

It could be over, just like that.

He could live.

But he wanted something else, too. Maybe more. In his head, he threw back Quinn's hood and finally, *finally* saw her face.

His chest hurt with the wanting of it.

How? he thought. His heartbeat was cannon fire. *How do I ever fall in love with her?*

"I have to go," he said, looking at Zora. "I have to know how it happens."

Zora wouldn't meet his eyes, but a muscle in her jaw tightened.

"Okay," Chandra said. "Can't we all just go with you? We can make sure you don't do anything completely crazy, and if there is a way to keep your prememory from happening, it's more likely that we'll figure it out if we're all there together."

Ash frowned. This hadn't been part of the plan. "Wait—"

Chandra turned to Zora, hopeful. "You said that you needed your father's old textbooks to help you figure out the math in his notes, right? The ones he had in his office before the earthquake?"

Zora blinked, clearly surprised by this sudden shift in the conversation. "Yeah."

"Okay, well *we* can't go back in time to get them, but the Black Cirkus can, somehow. Either they've found more exotic matter or they've found another way to go back, and, either way, I think we should know how they're doing it."

She shrugged.

"Maybe it would help us figure out how to go back in time again ourselves."

"That's actually a good point," Willis said.

Chandra rounded on him. "Don't say *actually* like you're all surprised. I'm freaking smart."

"Wouldn't we be seen?" Willis asked. He lifted a teacup to his lips and blew gently. "Roman will be there, and the last time we saw him he was very much in a *shoot now ask questions later* sort of mood."

"The whole city's going to be there," Chandra said. "We're lucky it's a masquerade, otherwise everyone would recognize us."

"*I'm* not fading into any crowd," Willis said.

"You might have to stay behind for this one," Zora said. Ash glanced over at her and saw—unbelievably—that she was considering this.

He sat up straighter. "Zor—"

Willis cut him off. "And I'll just, what, sit at home darning my socks while the rest of you attend the party of the year?" Willis sniffed. "Why, yes, that sounds like my idea of the perfect evening."

Chandra said, "Darning your socks?"

"It used to be a thing," muttered Willis unhappily, sipping his tea.

Zora leveled a heavy gaze at Ash, and he could see the two sides of her brain going to war. She didn't want him to go anywhere near Quinn. But Chandra had made a convincing argument.

"You don't have to do this," Ash rushed to say. And then, turning to Willis and Chandra, he added, "*None* of you do."

"If you're going, we're going," Chandra said simply, and Willis nodded.

Zora remained quiet, chewing on her lower lip. After a moment, she said, "If I do this, if I help you meet her, will you at least try to change things?"

Ash swallowed. He'd gotten so tired of waiting. There were only seven days left. Seven days to fall in love with the enemy, seven days for her to betray him. It didn't seem like enough time.

A small part of him still hoped for a miracle. The curiosity was stronger, but it didn't mean the hope wasn't there, too.

But if there was nothing he could do to change the future, at least he could meet it face-to-face.

He took a deep breath.

"Of course," he said.

Zora stared at him for a beat longer. "Then, I guess it's settled," she said.

9

DOROTHY

"I wish you'd take that stupid thing off," Roman said, as they climbed the stairs to the Fairmont's main floor. "You look like the Angel of Death."

Dorothy didn't have to push her hood back to know that Roman was scowling at it. She lifted a hand without meaning to, fingers brushing gnarled skin. The wound was a year old, but the memory of the pain was still fresh. She dreamed about it most nights. She'd often wake with her heart racing, certain that her fingers were still coated with blood, her face still split open.

She adjusted the hood so that it covered more of her face. "Can you imagine the stories people would tell?" she said. "The cannibal of New Seattle is missing half her face. The rumors about me are bad enough already."

"I'm serious. Tomorrow night we're planning to convince the people of this city that we're their saviors. We can't do that if they think you're a monster."

There was a pause. Dorothy could feel Roman's eyes on her, and she knew he was debating whether to apologize for calling her a monster, or push her harder.

This was the paradox at the heart of her new identity: she had to be utterly terrible if she was going to keep the Black Cirkus in line. But the rumors about her made the rest of the city wary of trusting her.

It was an impossible role to play: savior and monster, devil and saint.

"Don't be so dramatic," she said, trying for casual. "I enjoy being the city's monster."

Roman looked at her and then away, saying nothing. He would see through her nonchalance, she knew. He had a way of reading a person's thoughts with a glance, which was doubly infuriating since she was never able to guess his own. His eyes were always flat and black and distant, his expression infuriatingly blank. Unlike her, he seemed to easily control the members of the Black Cirkus without ever wandering over the line marking him as a monster. He could charm an old lady and terrify a Cirkus Freak all in a single breath.

Dorothy turned away, nose twitching. It hardly seemed fair.

The Fairmont's main floor was perpetually damp, slicked with the sludgy water people carried in from the docks on the soles of their boots. The furniture and walls were covered in creeping black mold.

Still, the old hotel was beautiful, even in its dilapidated state, with its oak columns, brocade walls, and intricately tiled floors. There was a swimming pool, although it was, somewhat ironically, underwater, the top of the domed skylight peeking out from below the black waves. The rest of the hotel centered around a courtyard, also underwater, but morbidly beautiful, nonetheless, with plush armchairs and ornate lamps forever drifting on the still water.

Best of all were the Fairmont's garages. Half-hidden below the waves, they looked flooded from the outside, making them the perfect hiding spot for a very large time machine. Dorothy didn't know of another place in New Seattle quite like it. And, if Mac called in their debts, they would lose it all.

"We could always go back to the way things were before." Roman shook the damp from his boots as he stepped into the hall beside her. "We could send a group of Freaks out tonight."

Dorothy was quiet for a moment, turning this over in her head. Roman was right, if they sent out a group of Freaks to the docks, they could probably steal enough money to satisfy Mac by morning. But that would undo all the goodwill she'd been trying to build with the broadcasts. They'd be right back where they were a year ago.

"No," she said finally. "We can't do that." The open hallways surrounding the flooded courtyard weren't crowded at this hour, but Dorothy saw several Cirkus Freaks standing at the other end of the room. She felt the shift in the air as they caught site of her in the doorway. She heard the murmured rush of whispers as they leaned toward one another.

Did you see who just walked in?

Her lips curved into a practiced smile. This was a different smile than the one she'd cultivated with her mother. That had been demure and pretty, designed to attract. This smile was like the sharp edge of a knife. It would cut someone if they came too close.

Turning back to Roman, she instinctively lowered her voice, adding, "Besides, I think he's bluffing. Mac doesn't care about the money, he's just using it as leverage to get something else."

"Perhaps," allowed Roman. He glanced at her and it looked like he was going to say something else. But he just shook his head and started across the hall, toward the others.

Dorothy watched him for a moment longer. She didn't have to ask what he was holding back. She'd been thinking it, too. Whatever Mac Murphy wanted from them wouldn't be easy, and it wouldn't be something they'd want to give up.

The Freaks were in the middle of a conversation. Though she was still across the room, the acoustics were such that Dorothy could hear what they were saying as she walked toward them.

"Did you actually see him?" a Freak named Eliza was asking, skeptical. Eliza was beautiful, in a ferocious sort of way, with eyes like shards of ice beneath heavy, black brows, and skin so pale it read at a distance as pure white. "Or did someone tell you he'd been there?"

"I *saw* him," said her companion, Donovan, his voice slow and thick. Dorothy had always thought Donovan had far too much in the way of shoulders and torso, and far too little head sitting on top of it. He adjusted the gun at his waistband with a grunt. "He wasn't even doing nothing, just drinking his beer. And the way he was sitting there, it was like he owned the place. Asshole."

The third Freak, Bennett, smiled, teeth white against his dark skin. He was smaller than Donovan and, though his head was normal-size, he'd never given Dorothy reason to believe that he had anything impressive going on inside of it. Still, he was a hard worker and loyal.

"I don't believe it for a second, man," he said to Donovan. "You got it wrong. They all drink at that grimy bar near the old campus—"

Bennett stopped talking, glancing up, nervously, as Dorothy joined their circle.

"You're back," he said, a little stiffly, Dorothy thought.

Donovan's eyes looked anxious as they flicked to her, like he'd just swallowed something foul. "Evening, Quinn."

"Evening," Eliza echoed, cold but polite. She smiled but, paired with those icy eyes, the expression didn't exactly come across as friendly.

In her first frightened days at the Black Cirkus, Dorothy had hoped Eliza might be a friend. But the girl had always kept her distance.

Like the others, Eliza tolerated the cannibal who hid her face. But that didn't mean she liked her.

It used to bother Dorothy that Roman was her only true ally here, that every day she put her life in the hands of people who didn't seem to care much whether she lived or died. Now, she took it in stride. It was just another irony that came with her life as Quinn Fox.

They loved Roman. Her, they feared. She'd long ago decided that was close enough.

"Who's on duty tonight?" she asked, her voice chilly. The Fairmont was under armed guard at all hours.

"Quentin's team," said Bennett. "We all go on in an hour."

"Good," added Roman. "Pay particular attention to the basements. We can't afford a robbery before tomorrow night."

He and Dorothy turned to go, and Donovan picked up the conversation where he'd left off. "I'm telling you, it was one of them time travelers, the pilot, I think. Before the mega-quake, I'd see him walking across campus to meet that damn Professor, acting all superior because he got to sleep up in that fancy college while the rest of us were in the tents." Donovan scratched the back of his neck, big lips twisting. "Only I don't remember his name. Ashy? Or Ashes?"

"Asher?" Roman said, turning back to them. Dorothy felt everything inside of her go very still.

Ash? Here?

She wasn't prepared for that. When she thought of him—and she tried not to think about him, not often, not anymore—she always pictured him in the pilot's seat of the *Second Star*, skin flashing blue and purple in the light off the anil, gold eyes crinkled.

He didn't make sense in this small, dark space, surrounded by these people.

Roman asked, "He was here?"

"Not here, down at the Dead Rabbit," said Eliza. "Donnie says he left about half an hour ago."

"Did he speak with anyone?"

Donovan shrugged. "Not that I saw."

Roman glanced at Dorothy, frowning distantly. She knew he expected her to do something, or say something, but everything she thought to do or say seemed . . . insufficient, somehow. Her pulse fluttered.

It had been a year since Ash had kissed her. For her, at least, it had been a year. She'd seen him since then, but only once, and she'd been Quinn then. She'd cut his cheek with a dagger, but that hadn't exactly been romantic. And now he was here. Or he'd *been* here.

"I'm headed to bed," she said. She felt suddenly and abruptly exhausted.

Or, perhaps, she just wanted to be alone.

To Roman, she added, "You should sleep, too. Tomorrow's a big day."

Dorothy's room was on the fifth floor of the Fairmont, but it looked exactly like the one she'd been kept in when she was kidnapped the year before. Two beds, each covered in a white quilt. Wooden furniture. White curtains. Blue chair. She hadn't bothered trying to personalize it, like Roman and the other Freaks had done with their rooms. Maybe it was all those years of traveling across the country with her mother, but she'd grown used to living out of suitcases, staying in nondescript hotel rooms, ready to move at the drop of a hat. She felt most at home in rooms where it looked like no one lived at all.

The only item in the room that was actually hers was the small, silver locket hanging from her mirror. Her grandmother's locket, the one thing she still had from her own time period. She touched it with one finger, like she always did when she came into the room.

She'd sometimes wondered when or where she'd originally come up with the name Quinn Fox. A year ago, she'd said it was her name because she knew that a girl named Quinn Fox had landed in New Seattle around that time. But if time were a coil, then somewhere along the line back and back, she must've thought up the name herself.

The only clue she had came from the locket. There was an animal of some sort carved on the front, but the years had worn it down until it was no longer recognizable. Dorothy's first thought was that it was a dog, or a cat, but now she believed that it was a fox. Her mother's grandmother's maiden name had been Renard, which was French for *fox*. So that fit.

But where had *Quinn* come from? Dorothy turned the locket over, studying the name engraved on the back. Like the fox, it'd been worn until only a few lines, and a curve remained. It could read "Colette" or "Corinne" as easily as "Quinn" and Dorothy would never know for sure. Her grandmother's name had been Mary, and it clearly didn't say that. So it hadn't belonged to her, originally, but to someone else.

Dorothy sighed and turned away. If the locket hadn't belonged to her grandmother that meant there was some other woman who had passed it down, a great-grandmother or a distant aunt whose name—or a twisted version of whose name—Dorothy now used as her own. It was so strange to think that there was an entire line of family she would never know, a family whose legacy she carried on, hundreds and hundreds of years later.

Would they be proud of how far she'd come? She'd never worried about that before. She'd been so concerned with survival that it had been impossible to think about whether she was dutifully carrying on her family's legacy.

Now, she wondered.

She removed her cloak and draped it over the back of her faded, blue chair. Beneath, she wore thin, black trousers, a slim-fitting shirt, and knee-high leather boots. They were simple clothes, but even simple clothes were hard to come by in New Seattle, especially if they were new. Most people had to scour the thrift stores downtown, hoping to find things in their size with few holes, unworried about whether they matched or had any semblance of style.

Dorothy could've brought something back from the past, obviously, but she'd wanted something from this time period, something modern, and so she'd bribed border security to get a few basics shipped in from the Center. The clothes had been expensive, but, at the time, she'd thought they were worth it.

Now, with money as tight as it was, she felt guilty about the extravagance.

Dorothy only ever removed her hood when she was in this room, alone, and now she stopped before the full-length mirror that hung from the back of her bathroom door and stared in open fascination at the horror that was her face.

The gash curved from her hairline to her chin like a great, twisted snake. It cut straight through her left eye and arced over her cheekbone, leaving the skin twisted and raised in its wake.

She lifted a hand, tracing the scar with her finger. It felt warm and smooth to the touch. The scar marked her as *other*, separating her from everyone else as effectively as the rumors about her did. *Monster. Cannibal.*

Turning, she caught sight of the gown she planned to wear the next night hanging from her closet door. It was a floor-length evening dress made of floaty, ice-blue chiffon, with a fitted bodice and spaghetti straps. Dorothy had seen Grace Kelly wear the dress while watching *To Catch a Thief* and had insisted they go back for it.

She took the thin fabric between her fingers, frowning. She'd had a thin, silver mask custom-made to cover her scar, and she'd planned to wear it with her hair pinned up, to show off her long neck. She would look beautiful again. The city's savior.

She'd told Roman that her injury was the reason she'd wanted to make the party a masquerade. She'd long used the same reasons to explain why she still wore the hood, and they leaped easily to her lips:

She didn't want to give the people of New Seattle any more reason to fear her. She couldn't save them if they thought she was a monster.

And that was all true. But it wasn't the whole truth.

With a deep sigh, Dorothy looked back at her reflection, her eyes moving over the twisted scar, the ruined skin.

And, beneath all of that, her face. It was different from the face Ash had known, but still familiar. If he saw her, if any of her old acquaintances did, they'd recognize her at once.

And there was the real reason for the masquerade. Dorothy had insisted on the mask because of Ash, because she knew he'd be there and she didn't want him to find out who she really was.

LOG ENTRY—JUNE 14, 2074
04:53 HOURS
THE *SECOND STAR*

I've only just returned home, and I'm afraid I'm the tiniest bit tipsy. Nikola and I talked about physics long into the night. We made it through most of his bourbon.

Nikola explained his brush with time travel to me, and I'm sorry to say that I now believe it was nothing more than his brain short-circuiting after a near-death experience, much the same as when people claim that they've seen "a tunnel of light" and interpret it as the entrance to heaven. Nikola has not traveled through time, of that I'm certain. I'm no closer to learning the secrets of traveling through time without an anil or exotic matter than I was before all this madness began.

Which isn't to say that my trip was a complete failure. Far from it. Nikola has gotten me thinking about all sorts of scientific queries I could work on to solve using time travel. Most particularly, he has me ruminating on the future.

Roman and I have taken several trips into the future, but, to be honest, I've found them mostly fruitless. Unlike the past, the future doesn't appear to be fixed. It changes every time I visit. Sometimes the changes are slight, while, other times, they're monumental.

Of course, I, like everyone, have often wondered how my own actions might change the course of the future. But Nikola pushed me to consider this on a deeper level. He was intrigued about my journeys, asking about specific experimentation I might have done to study my own personal ability to effect change.

He got a strange, puzzled look on his face when I admitted that I hadn't pursued that line of study very far. It really got me thinking about how I might design a series of experiments to delve deeper into these questions. My mind is on fire.

More soon.

10

ASH

NOVEMBER 6, 2077, NEW SEATTLE

There was a door in the old schoolhouse that they never opened. It was just past the kitchen, across the hall from the Professor's office. It wasn't so much what the door led to but what it contained.

Boxes, all carefully taped shut and labeled *Natasha*.

Natasha Walker had been Zora's mother. A historian, she'd provided the team with period-specific costumes and quizzed them on historical trivia whenever they'd traveled back in time. She also made the world's best grilled cheese sandwiches and had a weakness for twentieth-century British rock singers (she used to play David Bowie on repeat). But she'd died in the mega-quake, and now all that was left of her were these dusty old boxes.

Most days, Ash pretended the door and the boxes inside didn't exist. But, today, he and Zora stopped in front of it, preparing.

"You sure you're okay?" Ash asked.

Zora rolled her eyes, but Ash knew this was a front. The muscles in her shoulders had tensed. If she'd been anyone else, he would've done the comforting thing—hand on her shoulder, tight squeeze—but she was Zora, so he just reached past her and opened the door so she wouldn't have to do it herself.

She released a low exhale, almost a sigh. "Thanks."

"Don't mention it." Ash squinted into the darkness, waiting for his eyes to adjust. The closet had an overhead light once, but they didn't have enough solar panels to keep it working, and the bulb was broken, and, anyway, the boxes were stacked all the way to the ceiling, so it's not like the light would've done them any good. They'd been packed in tight, angled and arranged to fill every spare bit of space.

Natasha, 1920s cocktail dresses, read the label on one. Another said, *India, 500 to 600 BCE.*

"That's from when we picked up Chandra, remember?" Ash said, nodding at the box.

Zora didn't say anything. Ash glanced over in time to see her flick a hand across her cheek, blinking.

He looked away. It seemed wrong to watch her cry.

"I didn't think it would feel like this," Zora said. "To see her things . . ."

"We don't have to do this right now."

"It's a masquerade. We need costumes." Zora cleared her throat and stood up a little straighter. "Let's take them all."

They dug the boxes out of the closet and then carried them into the kitchen, where Willis and Chandra were waiting.

Chandra was blinking very quickly. Willis ran his fingers

over Natasha's faded handwriting but said nothing.

Ash's throat felt tight as he dug through the old clothes. The last time they'd played dress-up like this had been the morning of the earthquake. The Professor had laughed as they'd all tried on loose-fitting T-shirts and faded denim. Roman had pulled on a pair of bell-bottoms and asked Ash what he thought while, behind him, Zora had snorted into her fist. Natasha had joked that none of their hair was the right length to be in fashion.

"Sideburns!" she'd shouted. "No one will believe you're children of the sixties without sideburns."

The memory hurt to think about. Ash grabbed one of the Professor's old suits without looking too closely at it and stalked from the room to get ready alone.

It wasn't a bad suit, as far as suits went. It was charcoal-colored wool, and closer-fitting than anything he'd ever worn. It looked like it was from the turn of the century, early 2000s, but he'd never been an expert on fashion, so he couldn't tell for sure. The tie was black silk, and it stubbornly refused his attempts to twist it into something resembling a knot.

Zora appeared behind him, head cocked to the side. "You look alarmingly like my father."

"I don't think I ever saw your dad wear anything except for that tweed jacket with the elbow patches."

"He used to dress up to take my mother out." Zora touched the sleeve of Ash's jacket, her expression wistful. "Long time ago."

Ash pulled the tie apart, again, starting over. His eyes

drifted down. Zora wore a floor-length sequined cocktail gown with a plunging neckline. Strands of pearls dripped from her neck.

He whistled through his teeth.

She was holding a mask attached to a long, thin stick in one hand, and she lifted it, hiding her face behind peacock feathers and rhinestones. "You like?"

"I don't see how you're going to fix a motor in that getup."

"It's possible that the ladies of the 1920s weren't terribly interested in fixing motors."

Dorothy would have been twenty-three in 1920, Ash thought. He gritted his teeth, pulling the tie apart a little too violently.

"Stop, you're going to strangle yourself." Zora came up behind him and deftly tied the tie with just a few twists of her hands.

"How'd you learn to do that?" Ash asked.

"Hmm . . . Mom taught me." Zora dug out a top hat and a pointed black mask from the open box beside Ash's feet and handed them over. "Here. We wouldn't want anyone recognizing you."

Ash pulled the mask over his face, finding himself grateful when the black fabric hid his expression.

What he wanted to say but couldn't because Zora wouldn't understand, was that he was afraid. He was afraid of meeting Quinn even though, at the same time, he wanted to meet her—*needed* to meet her.

He was afraid of the next six days—afraid to die but equally afraid of standing still.

He settled the hat on his head, jerked the knot of his tie to the center of his neck, and took a step back, considering himself.

"Now you look perfect," Zora said.

Perfect wasn't the word he would've used. The person who stared back from the mirror wasn't like any version of himself he'd seen yet. He looked . . . grown up.

He looked ready.

People filled the docks outside the Fairmont, dressed in a wide array of thrifted ball gowns, mismatched suits, and handmade masks, chattering excitedly. There were more people than Ash had seen in one place since the earthquake. He felt his breath catch as his boat tore past, rounding the dock and slowing to a stop around the back of the hotel, where they parked beside a line of others. Zora had already pulled up on her Jet Ski, and she was leaning over to help Chandra climb off.

"I should've made you take me in the boat," Chandra muttered, ringing the water out of her skirts. She was dressed like a Renaissance woman, with a corset tightening her waist and a massive powder-white wig balanced on her head. She wobbled on ridiculously high heels.

"Ack," she muttered, pulling at her skirts. "How do people walk in these?"

"You didn't need to wear heels," Zora said.

"No, *you* didn't need to wear heels," Chandra said. "You're nineteen feet tall. I'd like to dance with an actual human man, not his knees."

"I like dancing," Willis sniffed. He wasn't joining them inside but had opted to come along anyway and stay with the boat in case they needed a quick getaway.

Ash couldn't help but notice that he'd glanced longingly at the entrance to the Fairmont and was tapping his foot in time with the music drifting through the hotel's windows.

And now Willis's eyes traveled up the sides of the Fairmont's outer walls, and he frowned slightly. "I wonder how difficult those would be to climb."

"Don't even think about it," Ash said. He switched off the engine, but it took a moment for his ears to adjust to the sudden stillness left in the wake of the motor. Distantly, he heard voices talking and laughing.

"I wouldn't go to the party," Willis murmured. "I'd just . . . poke around a little."

"You'd just dance around the halls like a crazy person," Chandra pointed out. "And you can do that out here."

Willis made a face at her but didn't press the point.

Ash readjusted the long, pointed mask on his face. "Are we ready?"

They were.

A line of people snaked around the side of the hotel, waiting to get inside. Ash and his friends lowered their masks as they plunged into the crowd so they wouldn't be recognized. Here, especially, Ash didn't want to be challenged to defend the Professor's stance on time travel.

But no one seemed particularly interested in them. Everyone was murmuring excitedly, admiring each other's masks and craning their necks to see inside the hotel. The line moved quickly and, soon, they were off the dock and through the Fairmont's doors.

As soon as Ash stepped inside the hotel, he saw light.

It was real light, like they used to have before the flood. A massive chandelier dangled from the ceiling above him, lit up like Christmas morning, golden light reflected in the crystals that dripped from its brass arms. Sconces lined the walls, and ornate lamps stood beside armchairs and love seats. They didn't flicker with candlelight. They buzzed with electricity.

Ash wasn't the only one staring. All around him people had stopped in place, mouths hanging open, eyes wide with wonder. There hadn't been power in this part of town since 2073. To restore electricity to the old hotel now would have taken a miracle.

Ash was still gaping when a tray of food whizzed past on a silver platter. He blinked, not quite trusting his eyes.

The tray held *fruit*. Plump, pink strawberries and shiny apples and . . .

"Bananas!" Chandra shrieked. She grabbed a piece of fruit off a passing tray and began peeling, as though she expected to see something else beneath the thick, yellow peel.

Ash stared, his mouth watering. The closest things they had to fruit in New Seattle were the chalky vitamin bars sold in Center-sanctioned outposts. He hadn't eaten a banana in over two years, but he could still remember the sweet, almost creamy taste.

"Quiet," Zora said, dropping a hand on Chandra's arm. "We're supposed to be keeping a low profile, remember?"

"But, Zora, *bananas*." Chandra took an enormous bite, her eyelids drooping in pleasure. "Oh my God . . ."

"Let's keep moving," Zora said.

The crowd was slowly making their way toward a wide doorway at the far end of the lobby, their chattering growing louder and more excited. Ash could feel the energy radiating off them as they inched across the room. It sent nerves prickling over his skin.

Something was on the other side of that doorway, and he had a feeling it was a bit bigger than fruit and electricity.

"What do you think is going on up there?" Zora asked.

Ash shook his head. He had no idea.

The lobby opened into a grand ballroom, with high ceilings and cocktail tables scattered about. There were more guests in ball gowns and masks, more waiters carrying silver trays. A full brass band had been set up near the front of the room. Ash caught the glint of light off their instruments from the corner of his eye. He heard a deep voice croon:

"Oh, the shark, babe, has such teeth, dear. And it shows them pearly white . . ."

The hair on the back of his neck went up. He knew that song. It had been one of his father's favorites. He craned his neck, trying to catch a better glimpse of those instruments.

And then the crowd began to thin. Ash could make out the shapes of strange objects over the tops of people's heads.

The golden corner of a gilded frame. A propeller. A gleaming, black statue.

Something cold hit the back of his throat. He stopped walking.

It was as though time had folded over itself so that objects from all different periods, things that never should have been in the same room together, suddenly . . . *were*.

There was a row of pinball machines set up against the far wall, lights flashing. Between them stood black onyx statuettes of Egyptian gods. A massive, white tusk hung from the ceiling.

Mammoth? Ash thought, frowning. It looked too large to belong to an elephant. He glanced down and saw a man hunched over what looked like a small, leather box a few feet away, squinting. It appeared to be some sort of camera.

Another silver tray drifted past them. This one was covered in snack cakes—Twinkies, Ho Hos . . . Little Debbie fudge brownies covered in nuts.

"Those brownies," Zora muttered, turning to follow the silver tray with her eyes.

Ash swallowed, his throat feeling suddenly tight. The Professor used to love them, but they'd stopped making them after the flood.

A bell clanged, quieting the crowd. Ash inched toward a gap in the people. Through it, he could see that the brass band had stopped playing. Someone else stood in front of the microphone. Ash felt a strange, cold anger move inside him.

Roman wore a tuxedo. His dark hair was slicked back

from his face, and he had a white mask perched over one eye and cheek.

Ash's hands curled into fists. Before he'd joined the Black Cirkus, Roman had been the Professor's assistant and one of Ash's best friends. And then he'd betrayed them all by stealing the Professor's research and joining the Black Cirkus.

"What's happening?" Chandra murmured, pushing up beside Ash. "I can't see anything."

"Quiet," muttered Zora. "I want to hear what he has to say."

Roman raised both hands. He grinned, but his eyes stayed cool. "Good evening," he said.

Ash's eyes passed over him and landed, instead, on the figure standing beside him on the stage. Quinn Fox.

For the first time that Ash could remember, she wasn't hidden beneath her dark cloak or mask. Instead, she wore a floaty blue gown with loose skirts. She had her head tilted toward the back of the room, tangled white hair cascading over her bare face.

Look at me, Ash thought.

". . . want to thank you for coming," Roman was saying. "I hope you're enjoying the refreshments. We spent hours this morning going back in time to bring back all that fruit."

A ripple of laughter moved through the crowd, like he'd told a joke. Ash shouldered through the people just ahead of him. Someone said something, but the voice barely registered. This moment didn't feel real.

Turn, damn you.

Quinn tucked a lock of hair behind her ear. Now, Ash could see the corner of her scar. The line of it cut through her eyebrow and twisted over her eye before curling into the skin at the top of her lip.

Roman continued, ". . . have brought back luxuries from the past, items most of you might only ever dream of."

Quinn's lips curved. They were red, just like the rumors said they would be.

Blood, Ash thought, and he felt something sour hit the back of his throat.

Turn and look at me.

Quinn lifted her head. She turned.

For a moment, Ash didn't understand. It wasn't Quinn Fox standing onstage at all. It was, unbelievably, Dorothy. Her skin was paler than he remembered it being, and her hair had turned white. And, of course, there was that awful scar twisting down the side of her face. But it was her.

Ash's lip twitched and for a moment he wasn't sure whether to smile or frown. He felt an instant jolt of ecstasy—she was *here*; he'd found her, finally—but it was followed immediately by confusion. Why was she pretending to be Quinn Fox? He looked around, waiting for someone else to notice.

Roman was talking again, and the crowd around Ash had started to cheer. Dorothy whispered something into Roman's ear.

Ash started shaking his head. Something was taking shape in the back of his mind. A memory.

He was lying in bed after they'd crash-landed in New

Seattle, and Zora was tucking a white braid behind her ear.

I think it has something to do with the energy in the anil, she'd said . . . *Strange, right?*

Ash blinked, absently reaching for his own lock of white hair, just below his ear. If someone had fallen *through* an anil, would all of her hair turn white?

He took a sudden step backward as the realization grew larger and larger in his head.

Dorothy wasn't pretending to be Quinn Fox.

Dorothy *was* Quinn Fox.

His mind still felt sluggish, struggling to catch up with what his eyes were telling him. Dorothy couldn't be Quinn Fox. Quinn Fox was supposed to kill him, and Dorothy would never kill him. None of this made any sense—

"No." He said this out loud, but the crowd was cheering again, and he doubted anyone heard him. He said again, "*No.*"

He felt a hand on his arm. Someone was saying his name but Ash couldn't form the words to answer. He didn't think he could move.

He wasn't going to fall in love with Quinn Fox tonight.

He was already in love with her.

He'd been in love with her all along.

11

DOROTHY

Dorothy stood on a platform at one end of the massive ballroom, trying very hard not to look as uncomfortable as she felt. She wasn't wearing her mask. She'd made the impulsive, last-minute decision to leave it behind.

It was meant to be a statement, a way of facing the paradox at the heart of her identity head-on.

Beautiful and hideous. Devil and saint. Monster and savior.

Both. She was, and always would be, both.

And, perhaps, there was some small part of her brain that thought Ash might be here tonight, that he might see her and realize that she'd never needed him after all. She'd become the most powerful person in this city all on her own.

Petty though that might be, it had seemed brilliant when she'd thought of it. Now, though, she was beginning to wonder if she'd made a terrible mistake. Her fingers twitched as she pictured the slight silver mask, lying on the dresser back in her hotel room, where it was little use to her.

She lifted her chin, trying to regain her confidence. The overhead lights were bright, almost blinding, and she felt rather than saw the crowd of people surrounding her. Watching her.

All those eyes were making her fidgety. Even before she became Quinn Fox, Dorothy had never liked standing before a crowd. Con artists tended to avoid being the center of attention, as a rule. It was too easy to be spotted, for one person to point and say things like, "Hey, I think that's the girl who stole my wallet," which, generally, led to more people pointing and realizing and . . .

All in all it was better to stay out of the spotlight. And yet here she was now, standing beneath a very literal spotlight. She wanted to pull her hood low over her face, but, of course, her hood wasn't there. She felt exposed. Vulnerable.

Smile, she told herself.

Even she had to admit that the display they'd put together was impressive. It'd been her idea to decorate their masquerade with all the amazing things throughout history that no longer existed. All this time she and Roman had been looting the past so that they might dazzle the people of this city with what they'd managed to bring back.

"It's important to open a con with a show of strength," she'd explained to Roman, in the beginning. "People naturally trust the rich and powerful. If we want to bring them over to our side, we'll need to do something impressive."

"But this isn't a con," Roman had told her in return. "We

really do want to fix the city."

It might not have been a con in the strictest sense of the word but, structurally, it was similar enough. First, they created a need, and then they made it clear that they were the only ones who could fill it.

It had taken the better part of a year to plant the seeds. And, now, everything was finally ready.

The sound of applause crashed over her, and then Roman was taking her hand, beaming. She snapped back to attention just in time to hear him finish the speech they'd prepared together.

"Those of you who've lived here long enough will remember that Seattle was broken long before the mega-quake flooded the city. The 2073 earthquake had already wiped out our power, ruined our homes, and killed thousands. Some of us lost everything."

The crowd fell silent, their attention rapt.

Roman went on. "I was just a child when the earthquake of 2073 destroyed my family's home and killed my parents. Like many of you, I was forced to take refuge in an emergency pop-up tent on the grounds of the old university while the people in power promised me that they had things under control."

Dorothy was quiet, listening. She'd heard about the pop-up shelters that people had once called Tent City. It was in those shelters that the Black Cirkus had started.

"But we were lied to," Roman continued. "People died waiting for much-needed medication, and food, and electricity that was never restored. As of tonight, there are new people in power. And we're here to tell you that it's time to rebuild our city."

The crowd reached a fever pitch, their roar thunderous. Roman had to raise his voice to be heard over the cheers. "Tomorrow morning, the Black Cirkus will go back in time, to the year 2073, to the days just before the earthquake took out the solar grids in the University District. We're going to take those grids back and bring them here, now. After five years of darkness, we're going to restore electricity to New Seattle!"

Dorothy felt a grin split her face as she looked out over the ecstatic crowd. They were cheering for them.

For *her*.

She turned to smile at Roman, but his eyes had landed on something at the far end of the room, and his grin had gone stiff.

Dorothy followed his gaze to a boy with dusty-blond hair. He wore a charcoal-gray suit and black tie, but she could easily imagine him in a leather jacket and white T-shirt, skin slightly reddened from the sun.

She felt everything inside of her go still as the boy lifted a hand to remove the black mask covering his face—

And then it was Ash staring back at her, his expression stormy. His eyebrows were low on his forehead, his gold eyes blazing. The muscles in his jaw stood out in sharp focus.

Dorothy swallowed. She knew what he saw when he looked at her: Quinn Fox, the monster, the villain.

But she saw the boy hunched over the airplane in the clearing behind a church. She saw the boy who'd kissed her in a time machine.

Her lips burned where they'd long ago brushed against his, and her palms felt suddenly clammy. What was she doing? Why was she standing here? Why hadn't she gone to him?

She was staring. She knew she should stop, but she couldn't turn her head. It was like fighting gravity.

She heard herself mutter, "Excuse me."

And then she was walking off the stage, calmly, like this had been planned, her head held high. There was a door just behind the platform. She pushed through it and, immediately, the noise of the crowd dimmed, muffled by wood and walls.

She could've stopped there; she could've leaned her head against the door and breathed, but her skin still buzzed with nerves so, instead, she made her way down the long, twisting hallway as quickly as her skirt-bound legs would carry her. The hallway ended in a door, which turned out to be a bathroom.

Thank God.

Her heeled boots echoed off damp tile. There were no lights, but candles flickered at the walls, their flames reflected in the windows and mirrors.

Dorothy stopped in front of the sink and switched on the faucet, forcing herself to breathe as she watched the water circle the drain. When the basin was full, she took a handful of water and splashed it onto her face. Handful after handful to her face, her neck.

I'm fine, she told herself. It had just been too many people. She didn't like being in front of a crowd. She didn't like everyone staring at her, wondering where she'd gotten the scar. She felt better when her face was hidden, when she could control what people saw when they looked at her.

Not people, a voice at the back of her head whispered. *Ash*.

She closed her eyes, breathing hard. It was foolish to pretend this wasn't true. She never should have let Ash see her standing next to Roman, see her scar. Why hadn't she worn her damn mask?

She went still, fingers curling around the sink. Water dripped from her nose.

She'd thought she was over it. Over *him*.

She'd chosen this.

Dorothy switched off the faucet without lifting her head. She heard a stir behind her, almost an exhale, and she jerked around, water dripping from her face. Her pulse surged. But there was no one there.

She shook her head, grabbing a towel from the rack beside the sink. She dried her face roughly and tossed the towel into the sink. Then she made her way to the door, throwing it open—

She stopped breathing.

Ash stood in the hallway outside of the bathroom. He had a hand raised, as though he'd been about to knock, but now he froze, his eyes fixed on hers.

"Oh," Dorothy said, on an exhale. She would've said more, but her lips felt like they might crack if she moved them.

Ash was here.

The air shivered. Her legs wobbled.

His eyes were blazing, and, when he spoke, his voice was low and aching.

"It's you," he said. "I found you."

12

ASH

Dorothy's expression was raw beneath the curtain of her white hair. Ash felt a crease knit his brows. He didn't know what had happened to make her face look like that, but he could imagine. Instinct rose inside of him, to touch her cheek, to comfort her. His hand twitched—

Then something in her face shuttered. It was as though a door had slammed shut, hiding her emotions from view. She straightened, her shoulders going stiff.

"Ash," she said. "What are you doing here?"

Ash flinched, her voice hitting him like a slap. It was so familiar, so instantly, achingly familiar.

"What am I doing here?" he repeated. He felt numb. "I saw Quinn—I saw *your* broadcast, and I came to see how the Black Cirkus was able to travel back in time."

It wasn't the whole truth, but Ash didn't know how to say the rest of it. *I came to find Quinn. I came to meet the woman who would kill me. I didn't know it would be you.*

Dorothy cocked her head. Ash had seen her do this before, and it made something inside of him ache.

"Surprised?" she asked.

Surprised?

"You could say that." He'd imagined this moment many times, although, of course, he'd never imagined it like this. He choked out, "I thought you were dead."

He hadn't let himself dwell on this, but he'd thought it. It'd been the thing that haunted him in the dark, as he was trying to fall asleep. That Dorothy was dead. That he'd killed her.

And now . . .

His eyes moved to the scar twisting down the side of her face. "What happened to you?"

She seemed taken off guard by the question. "I was hurt," she said, her hand moving to the scar. "In the fall."

Ash fisted his hand, not sure if she'd let him touch her. "I'm sorry."

"It was a long time ago." Now her brows were drawn, her eyes fierce. "We didn't know what would happen, did we?"

No, Ash thought, studying her. *We didn't.*

He remembered how she'd been when he'd first met her in the churchyard: the mischievous curve of her lips, the laughter in her eyes when she teased him. Now she just looked hardened. Angry. The change was startling.

He asked, "How long have you been here?"

"A year," she said flatly.

"A *year*?"

"You're wondering why I didn't come find you."

Ash shook his head, but he couldn't dismiss it. She *didn't* come find him. He would've searched every whorehouse in the city, would've shot every pimp and followed every lead. He had only a few days left to live, and he would've wasted them all trying to find her.

And she'd been here, all along. There hadn't been anything to stop her from coming to him.

"Why didn't you?" he asked. "I could've helped you. I could've—"

"You said you were going to take me back," Dorothy said. "Don't you remember?"

Ash swallowed. He remembered.

It was just after they'd left the Fort Hunter complex. They were in the anil, on their way back to 2077, and Dorothy had crept into the cockpit to ask him if she could stay.

"I could be one of you . . . ," she'd said. "I could be with you."

He could picture how she'd looked then, as easily as if it had happened a moment ago. Her dark curls had frizzed around her face, falling loose of her braid. Grease and sweat had covered her cheeks. She'd been the most beautiful thing he'd ever seen.

But he'd told her no.

I can't had been his exact words.

Oh, how he wished he could take them back.

"It wasn't that long ago." Now, Dorothy's voice was bitter. "For *you*, at least. For me it was longer."

Ash's throat felt suddenly thick. He could tell her now, he realized. He could explain about the prememory. He'd told her that she couldn't stay with them in the future because he'd known he was falling for her. It seemed foolish now, but he hadn't thought it was fair to Dorothy to be with her when he knew he would fall for Quinn.

Oh, the irony. He'd never imagined *this*.

"Dorothy," he started. "I—" He started to reach for her, but she shrank away from him, her hands going to her neck, where she'd worn a small silver locket once. Now her neck was bare.

His hand fell, and he looked away, losing his nerve. "I should go."

There was a beat of silence. And then: "You should."

Was that disappointment in her voice? Ash couldn't tell, and he couldn't look at her again.

He hurled himself down the hall and was gone.

13

DOROTHY

Dorothy hunched over the sink, eyelashes fluttering as she tried to hold back tears. She wasn't breathing. She felt slapped. She felt . . . undone.

She'd been fine until he'd said her name—*Dorothy*—and then it felt like someone had reached into her chest and squeezed the air from her lungs.

She hadn't been ready. Over the past year, she'd been so careful to avoid the school, and Dante's, and anywhere else she might see him. But she couldn't avoid him forever, and now, finally, he'd found her. He'd just been *standing* there, staring at her, and he'd seen her face, her scar. He knew who she was.

He knew everything.

Her heart was pounding. How often had she imagined this moment? She must've pictured it a thousand times, standing before Ash and telling him that she'd moved on. She had a new home, new allies. She didn't need him.

She hadn't realized it would be a lie.

And—*God*—now, she couldn't stop seeing the expression on his face when he'd looked at her. The twitch of his lips, the narrowing of his eyes . . .

He'd been revolted by her. In her darkest moments, Dorothy had never imagined Ash would look at her like that. She flinched, thinking of it.

She curled her fingers around the sink, hating herself for thinking it could be any other way.

It's happened. It's over.

Dorothy closed her eyes and took a deep, uneven breath, letting the truth of this settle over her. She might not have wanted Ash to find out like this, but she'd always known he would find out. They were on different sides now. There was nothing to be done about that.

She breathed in, and she breathed out. She had to control this.

Whatever she'd felt for Ash once, it was over now.

She *needed* it to be over.

But when she opened her eyes, she saw him reflected back at her from the mirror above the sink.

She felt a jolt as their eyes met. "What—"

"I forgot something." His face was tense, and his voice sounded thicker than it had moments ago. Time seemed to still as he crossed the room and took her face in his hands.

Those hands. Dorothy's eyes fluttered. They were just like she remembered, his skin rough and warm and smelling, slightly, of smoke. Heat flared through her.

She tilted her head back as he leaned down to kiss her.

PART
TWO

My mind misgives some consequence yet hanging in the
stars shall bitterly begin.

Romeo and Juliet, *Act 1 Scene 4*

14

ASH

Ash remembered an early morning flight during his first month at the academy. Flat, gray sky and hard winds and the smell of ozone burning through the air. The plane had felt like a toy, its engine a metal scream that rattled his teeth and crawled into his bones.

And then the engine sputtered; Ash was falling.

It hadn't felt like he'd expected it to. Terror and panic and terror again. No, there'd been only a sudden stillness and the vague awareness of sun bleeding through the clouds. Ash had closed his eyes and breathed.

The engine roared back to life a second later, an animal reawakening. The fear hit then, white hot and raging. Ash's hands didn't stop shaking until after he'd landed. His soul kept shaking long after.

Ash had never been in love before but he'd been told that it felt the same. Like falling.

Dorothy released a short gasp of breath when he took her

face in his hands. He kissed her and, for a second, he forgot all about black water and dead trees and white hair. He forgot the feeling of cold steel sliding through his skin, and heartbreak ripping through his chest.

Instead, there was this: Dorothy's lips, warm against his own. Her fingers touching the back of his neck and then snaking up through his hair. Her chest pressing into his.

He was falling again and, just like before, there was no terror or panic. Only stillness, and sunlight in the clouds.

It ended, abruptly, with a knock.

"Dorothy?" Roman's voice came from the other side of the bathroom door, muffled by wood. "Dorothy, are you in there?"

Ash opened his eyes, and the rest of the world rushed back in.

"He can't find you here," Dorothy said, her eyelids still lowered, her voice low.

Ash curled a hand around hers. He didn't want to think about what it meant that Roman had come looking for her, that he knew her real name.

"Come with me," he whispered, urgent. He wasn't leaving her again.

Dorothy eyes opened. "I—"

"*Please.*" He could hear the desperation in his voice. It made his cheeks burn, but he didn't look away. "I was wrong, before, when you asked if you could stay. You belong with us, Dorothy. Come back with me."

Another knock. "Dorothy?"

The doorknob rattled.

"I—" Dorothy's eyes moved to the door, her expression complicated. "I can't."

The words hit him like a slap. He glanced at the door. Was she staying behind for *him*, for Roman?

It was too much to consider, and so he pushed the thought away. "I'll come back," he said, squeezing her hand. "Soon."

And then he crossed the bathroom and threw open the small window, dropping into the black water below.

15

DOROTHY

Dorothy stood, breathless, one finger hovering near her mouth. She could taste Ash's lips on hers. She could feel the warmth of his hands wrapped around her waist.

He'd asked her to go with him. He'd seen what she'd become and, still, somehow, he'd wanted her.

Why hadn't she gone with him?

She closed her eyes and, though her head was full of Ash, he wasn't what her mind lingered on just now. Instead, she thought of his time machine, the *Second Star*. She thought of Zora and Willis and Chandra, and the feeling she'd had when she was sitting among them.

Belonging. Never in her life had she felt that, not before and not since. She'd thought she'd found a place there, with Ash and his friends. She'd been so sure that she'd finally found a home.

But even as her mind lingered on Ash and the *Second Star*, other, fresher memories rushed in:

The people crowded inside of the Fairmont's ballroom, cheering for her.

Roman's voice, strong and sure, as he told them of their plan to save the city.

The feeling of power she got when the things she'd read about in history books became real.

Tomorrow, she was going to change the world. Why did Ash want her *now*? When it was too late?

Dazed, Dorothy opened the door.

Roman stood in the hallway, elegant in his black tuxedo and white tie. It was the same tuxedo Clark Gable had worn in the 1936 film *Cain and Mabel*, Dorothy knew. Roman had stolen it out of the actor's dressing room once the film finished shooting.

For a brief moment she remembered the boy he'd been just a year ago—thin and hungry, with darting eyes and a wispy beard—and felt a jolt of pride. A year ago, he would've looked ridiculous in a tux but, now, he looked dashing. *This* Roman was someone the people of New Seattle would follow.

Unfortunately, the moment of pride was fleeting. Roman wasn't alone. Mac Murphy stood beside him, short and squat as ever. He wore an ill-fitting suit with a fat tie, an unlit cigarette behind one ear. He had crutches wedged beneath each of his arms, and a thick bandage wrapped around his upper thigh. A spot of blood had already begun to seep through the gauze, staining the bandage brown.

Dorothy had to bite back a smile at the sight of it. From the look of the bloodstain, that was a bullet wound. She had imagined shooting Mac many times, herself, and she would've loved to know who'd been lucky enough to pull the trigger.

"Mac," Dorothy said, swallowing her glee. "To what do I owe the pleasure?"

Mac hobbled forward, and now he was too close, invading her personal space. Dorothy wanted to back away, but she thought he might take it as a cue to enter, and she could think of nothing she wanted less than to have Mac Murphy crowded inside of the tiny hotel bathroom with her.

And so she stayed where she was, close enough to Mac that they were nearly touching. She could smell the cheap cologne on his skin. When she didn't move aside, he clumsily grasped her hand and brushed his thick, chapped lips against her knuckles. Beside him, Roman grimaced.

Be thankful he didn't feel the need to kiss you, she wanted to snap at him. But she kept the thought to herself.

"Charmed, as always, Miss Fox," Mac said, grinning horribly.

"Likewise," Dorothy said. She was careful not to yank her hand away too quickly.

Roman pulled at the knot of his bow tie so that the silky fabric came loose around his neck. He seemed nervous, or at least uncomfortable. "Mac has something he'd like to discuss with us."

"Does he?" Dorothy turned back to Mac. "Mira gave us the impression that you'd be sending your goons over to break our legs if we couldn't pay your bribe."

"Don't be silly, girl." Mac flicked his hand, and Dorothy

bristled. *Girl.* "What's a few dollars here and there? I value our relationship too much to let a little thing like that get in the way."

Something prickled, uncomfortably, in Dorothy, though she kept her expression impassive. She didn't like to think that she had a relationship with Mac at all.

"Then why are you here?" she asked.

And now Mac's gaze seemed hungry. "You're having cash-flow problems, sweetheart," he said, and Dorothy opened her mouth to respond, but he lifted a hand, stopping her. "Don't bother lying. I know it's not just me you're in debt to. I hear you owe Graham Harvey and Chadwick Brunner a few hundred dollars each, too." Mac paused, studying his fingernails.

Roman glanced at Dorothy, eyebrow twitching. Dorothy suspected the Black Cirkus was strong enough to hold the hotel by force, if it came to that, but they'd never had to test that before. It would be foolish to start now, when there was so much else at stake.

Eyeing Mac, she asked carefully, "What do you want?"

Mac flashed his teeth at her, attempting a smile. "I'd like to fund your little expedition."

"Why?" asked Roman, blunt.

"Call it my good deed for the year. I'll cancel your debts to me, and I can help you pay off Chadwick and Graham, maybe even throw a little extra your way to cover whatever else you need to keep going." Mac balanced on one crutch, digging a half-empty pack of matches out of his pocket. "Your Cirkus Freaks eat, don't they? And it can't be cheap to keep that time machine running."

He pulled the cigarette from behind his ear and stuck it between his teeth, smiling thinly. When neither Dorothy nor Roman answered, he shook his head, lighting a match. "Look, I know what you used to bring in looting little old ladies on the docks. How you've kept this enterprise going for over a year is beyond me. Chadwick and Graham have already been whispering in my ear about running you out of your hotel, and, personally, I think that would be a damn shame." He said this with a hand pressed to his heart, a sympathetic expression twisting his toad-like face. "You need a backer, darling. Someone with deep pockets and a little additional security to help you keep the rats from crawling all over you."

Mac brought the match to his cigarette, nostrils flaring. Dorothy had to work hard to keep the grimace from her face. She hated the smell of smoke.

He was right, unfortunately. The Cirkus had barely been keeping their heads above water for a while now. It would be a relief to have some more money coming in. Getting it from Mac meant that Dorothy wouldn't have to sully her new reputation by stealing it, and she wouldn't disappoint her Freaks by letting them go hungry.

But forming any kind of official partnership with Mac felt . . . dirty.

"What would you expect in return?" she asked.

"In return? Are you kidding? You kids are aiming to fix my city." Mac shook the flame out with a jerk of his hand. "What else could a man want?"

Roman lifted his eyebrows, quiet as Mac took a deep drag from his cigarette. Roman knew how to let a silence stretch and grow in a way that made people intensely uncomfortable. Often, they wound up saying things they shouldn't be saying.

Watching him, Mac smiled. "All right, all right. You got me. There is one thing." Mac studied the red tip of his cigarette. His expression was blandly curious, like he'd never seen a lit cigarette before. Shrugging, he asked, "You ever been to the future?"

Dorothy frowned. She hadn't been any farther into the future than she was now. It had always taken on a deeply dreamlike property in her mind, the possible and impossible blending until she couldn't tell the two apart. Sometimes she found herself forgetting that her time machine was capable of moving in two directions.

"The future isn't like the past," Roman said, interrupting her thoughts. "It hasn't happened yet, so it's not fixed. Many different versions of the future exist side by side, and you never actually know which one you'll visit."

"So you've been?" asked Mac. "To when? A few days from now? A year?"

"I took a few trips forward when I worked with the Professor," said Roman. "But the future changes so frequently that it's impossible to say whether it will remotely resemble what we saw."

Mac released a sigh as he leaned forward, cigarette ash flaking from between blackened fingers. "Come on now, how much could things really change?"

"More than you might think," Roman said. He spoke casually enough, but there was tension in the corner of his lips, like he was holding something back.

Dorothy frowned. How odd. He'd always talked about his visits to the future easily enough with her.

Mac dropped his cigarette onto the tile floor, crushing it out with the tip of one of his crutches. "You know what my family was before the earthquake?" His eyes rested on Dorothy's, waiting for an answer. When none came, he said, "You follow my family tree back as far as it'll go and you'll find Mafia, pimps, criminals, grifters. I may not come from fancy folk, but we've survived wars and recessions and every natural disaster you can name, and we did that by being smart." He tapped his temple with one finger. "My granddaddy used to compare us to cockroaches. Nuclear holocaust could hit tomorrow, and we'd find a way to make it out alive."

The comparison to cockroaches was a little more self-aware than Dorothy expected of Mac, but she didn't point that out.

"I'm not going to beat around the bush with you two," he continued. "I'm on board with your little missions back in time, saving the city and all that. But I want to see my future. I've got to be smart about this, you see. I've got a few . . . business ventures in the works, and I want to get a sense of how everything's gonna turn out." He scratched his chin, frowning. "Does that sound like something you two might be able to help me out with?"

Business ventures. Dorothy could imagine what he meant

by that. She stared back at Mac and waited for the usual revulsion to rise, but it didn't.

A few trips into the future—that was nothing.

"Think about it," Mac said, interrupting her thoughts. He turned, awkwardly, on his crutches and began hobbling down the hall. "We'll talk again, soon."

Dorothy opened her mouth to speak when she thought Mac was out of earshot, but Roman lifted a hand, stopping her. He was silent until Mac had rounded the corner at the end of the hallway, and then he entered the bathroom and closed the door with a soft click.

"What—" Dorothy started, but Roman moved past her, his gaze sweeping over the chipped sinks, the small, dark windows, the graffiti-covered stalls. There was something jerky and restless in his movements, like he was only just holding back his anger.

Dorothy frowned. "Are you all right?"

"Is he gone?" Roman asked. His voice was casual enough, but several degrees colder than it had been a moment ago. He lifted his eyebrows, unsmiling. "Or have you hidden him in some stall?"

"Who?" Dorothy asked, and Roman cut his eyes at her, nostrils flared.

"Don't bother," he spat, and Dorothy felt anger ripple through her.

How *bitter* he sounded, as though he had any right to judge who she spent time in bathrooms with. How many times had she seen him leave the bar at the end of a long night, arm in arm with some pretty girl? And she'd always known well enough to mind her damn business, thank you very much.

She drew her shoulders back, meeting his gaze. "Were you following me?"

A short, hard laugh. "Don't be absurd."

"Then what—"

Roman made a noise in the back of his throat, interrupting her. "I saw him standing in the crowd. The nerve of him, coming into my hotel—"

"You were following *Ash*?"

"And imagine my surprise when I found him with you."

Dorothy felt herself begin to waver. She still didn't think she had anything to apologize for, but she could see how, to Roman, this might look like a betrayal. Not that she'd been hiding in the bathroom with someone, but that she'd been hiding in a bathroom with Ash.

"You're acting like you caught us with our clothes around our ankles," Dorothy said. "We talked, that's all."

Roman cut his eyes at her. "Did he ask you to leave with him?"

So that's what was bothering him, the thought that she might choose them over him.

"Yes," she answered, wary. Roman made a sound of disgust and she added, "And I told him no. Obviously."

There was a moment of tense silence. And then Roman's shoulders drooped, the anger seeming to drain out of him.

"You don't know them like I do," he said, rubbing his eyes. "You weren't here during the mega-quake. Everyone thought the Professor was some sort of genius. But, when the earthquakes hit, he was content to let the people of this city die rather than do something to try to help them."

"I know all that," Dorothy said.

"You don't know all of it." Roman looked up, imploring. "Did you know that, after his wife died, the Professor went back again and again to try to save her? He did that for months, but when I asked him to—"

He shook his head, mouth snapping shut.

This interested Dorothy. In her year of knowing Roman, he'd never spoken to her about his life before the earthquakes. It was as though his life had started the day the Professor recruited him to be his assistant.

"Asked him to what?" Dorothy asked, taking a step toward him.

Roman ignored her. "I know you don't think Ash and the others are bad people, but they stood by the Professor; they defended him. The only reason Ash came here tonight is to stop us from going back. They still think that this, all of this, is theirs."

"You don't have to worry about that. He left."

"Did he?" Roman asked, his tone brittle.

Dorothy studied him. It was strange, but there'd been a second—not even a full second, but a fraction of one—when something suspiciously like disappointment had snapped across Roman's face. And then the irritation was back, and anyone else might've doubted that the hurt had been there at all. But Dorothy knew what she'd seen.

"Roman—" she started, reaching for him.

He swallowed, audibly, and turned away from her. "If you'll excuse me, I think it's time I head to bed." He was being careful now, weighing each word he spoke, like he worried they might betray him. "Tomorrow's a big day."

And then he slipped down the hall, and was gone.

16

ASH

Ash sank deep, deeper. The water had the effect of a cold shower, calming his skin, clearing his thoughts. He saw only black, felt only the reverberating echo of his heart beating in his chest.

Dorothy was Quinn. Quinn was Dorothy.

In less than a week, Dorothy was going to kill him.

Dread built in his chest, crowding out these terrible thoughts. There'd always been some part of him that'd expected to have a choice, when the time came. He'd already accepted that he would fall in love with Quinn Fox, and he knew she would eventually kill him. But he'd still been waiting for something . . . for a moment, perhaps, when he could make the decision to walk into this future willingly.

But this . . . this was no choice. Or, if it was, it was one he'd made long before he'd fully known what he was choosing. He'd already fallen for Dorothy. He couldn't change that now. The future felt like a vise slowly closing around him.

With the questions still pounding in his head and his lungs burning, he kicked to the surface and swam back to the docks.

Zora was waiting by the Fairmont's back entrance, their agreed-upon meeting spot should they get separated. She was on her tiptoes, one hand shielding her eyes, and seemed to visibly relax when Ash appeared.

"*There* you are." She snatched his arm, dragging him around the corner. "I thought—"

She broke off with a rough shake of her head. She didn't have to tell him what she thought.

They walked down the dock in silence, Zora steering Ash to the garage, where the boat was parked, instead of back to the party. Ash didn't know why they were leaving and didn't think to ask. His head was still full of Dorothy: Dorothy *here*, Dorothy alive, Dorothy's lips pressed to his.

Zora, watching him, asked, "Are you okay?"

He exhaled through his teeth. "You saw her?"

"Oh, I saw her, all right." Zora's voice was venom. "Our little con artist was standing beside Roman dressed up like a murderous ghost. I guess that explains how the Black Cirkus is able to travel through time, at least." She glanced at Ash, sideways. "She had the exotic matter when she fell, remember?"

Ash felt this knowledge in his gut a second before it made its way to his head. *Of course.* He should've put that together, but he'd been too distracted by everything else—*Dorothy was alive. Dorothy was Quinn. Dorothy was going to kill him*—and hadn't had a chance to think it all through. Dorothy had betrayed them.

Zora stopped walking, abruptly. There was a restless energy in her, her eyes flicking from his face to the water and back again. "So?" she asked. "What now?"

Ash frowned. "What do you mean?"

Zora, voice cracking, said, "Are you in love with her?"

Ash swallowed and looked away.

"Damn it." Zora stared at him. "We said we would stop this. We came here to figure out how to keep you from falling in love with Quinn, not so that you could make puppy dog eyes at her!"

"I know—"

"I actually thought it was possible, back when you didn't know her. But now." Her eyes were wide and bright, but she wasn't crying. She wouldn't, not Zora. "It's *Dorothy*."

Ash said, again, "I *know*."

"I was the one who told you to go after her. Back in Fort Hunter, I told you that if you fell for her instead of this girl with the white hair . . . Do you remember?"

Ash remembered. "That's not why this happened. None of this is your fault."

"You don't understand." She began to pace, that restless-ness taking her over. "I was *so* sure it would change things. That you could just fall in love with someone else." She released a short, fierce laugh. "Easy, right? Just pick another girl and everything would be okay. But that's what made this happen. If you hadn't fallen for Dorothy, things could've been different. Maybe . . ."

She trailed off, staring out over the black waves, her brows furrowed.

"None of this is your fault, Zora," Ash said again. He wasn't sure what else to say.

Zora didn't appear to be listening. "I never understood before, how impossible this was. All this time I just thought you could make a different decision, change your future. But that decision is what brought you here. It's like . . . it's like fate." Her eyes flicked back to him. "How do you stop a memory?"

Ash looked up at the Fairmont, eyes skimming over the lit-up glass. *How do you stop a memory?*

Maybe this moment right now was always the only one that'd mattered, this choice the only one he'd ever be given. Dorothy was waiting behind one of those windows. Finally, *finally*, he knew where she was. He knew she would kill him. He knew how and when.

He supposed he could choose to walk away. But that felt impossible, like choosing not to inhale.

And so he said simply, "You don't."

"Oh my God, *finally*. Do you have any idea what time it is?"

That was Chandra. Ash and Zora had just gotten back to the schoolhouse and found her sitting at the kitchen table, still dressed in her Renaissance-woman costume, though her makeup was smudged and she'd removed her wig, leaving her black hair flattened and sweaty against her scalp.

On the way back to the schoolhouse, Zora explained that there'd been an incident at the Fairmont: she and Chandra has been recognized by a Cirkus Freak and had left in a hurry before the entire Black Cirkus could chase them out. Zora had sent Chandra and Willis home in the motorboat while she'd stayed behind to find Ash.

Now, Willis was leaning against the wall, holding Chandra's powder-white wig in his massive hands. He'd been gently finger-combing the curls back into place, but his eyes lifted when Zora and Ash walked into the room.

"We thought you'd both left us to join the Black Cirkus," Chandra said.

"We did *not* think that," Willis said. "But we were starting to get worried. It's late."

"Sorry," Ash muttered, pulling out a chair. He felt them both watching him, waiting for an explanation.

A muscle in his jaw clenched. They knew about Dorothy, too. He dropped his head in his hands so he wouldn't have to meet their eyes.

After a moment, Chandra cleared her throat. "What do you mean we didn't think they'd join the Cirkus? *You* said you expected Zora to defect for the brownies alone."

Willis sniffed. "They were very good brownies. Or, at least I dimly recall that they were good. I haven't had one in a very long time."

"Come on . . . I already told you I'm sorry I didn't bring you any, will you get over it?"

With a grunt Ash reached into his pocket and pulled out two mushy chocolate brownies still in their cellophane wrappers, which he dropped onto the kitchen table.

"They got a little wet," he muttered. "But they're still chocolate."

Willis's eyes lit up. He put down Chandra's wig and picked up a brownie, carefully unwrapping the cellophane.

Zora took a bottle of Dante's moonshine from the fridge, slamming the door a little too aggressively.

"What crawled up your butt?" Chandra asked.

"Don't start with me," Zora said, scowling. She swigged moonshine straight out of the bottle.

"I don't see why everyone's in such a bad mood. It was a great party. Good snacks, good dancing, good *company*." Chandra wiggled her eyebrows at Ash.

Good company. She was talking about Dorothy, he knew. He glared at her.

"Too soon?" Chandra asked, all innocence.

Now Zora was staring at her, her face incredulous. She wiped her mouth with the back of her hand and said, "What the hell, Chandra?"

Chandra shrugged, unapologetic. "I refuse to be upset that Dorothy's alive. I like Dorothy. And, yeah, okay, she's working for the enemy now, which isn't *awesome*, but it's better than if she'd gotten lost somewhere in time and Ash fell in love with a soulless monster we didn't even know." Turning to Ash, blinking. "Well? Isn't it?"

Ash hesitated. Nodded.

Chandra chewer her lower lip. "I'm . . . well, I'm a little surprised that she didn't . . . you know . . ."

Willis said, blunt, "She didn't want to come back with you?"

"No." Ash fell back into his chair, suddenly exhausted. "She didn't."

"Oh. Well that makes sense, she has the big mission tomorrow morning, right?" But Chandra didn't look convinced. She hesitated, glancing at Willis. "Now might be a good time to tell them about the other thing."

Ash felt a flicker of interest. "The other thing?"

Willis took a small bite of brownie. "I was going to make you wait until tomorrow, as punishment for not letting me come to the party. But the brownie has put me in a better mood."

Zora set the moonshine down. "You were going to make us wait for what?"

"It turns out I was right about the Fairmont walls. Easy to climb, and some fool on the fourth floor left his window open." Willis took another bite of brownie, giving his head a slow shake.

He was enjoying this, Ash could tell.

"After that, it was a relatively simple matter to find out which room belonged to Roman. I ran into a young Cirkus Freak in the hallway, and you'd be amazed at how helpful he was." He licked chocolate off his fingers. "Given a little incentive, that is."

"What did you want from Roman's room?" Ash was

leaning forward in his seat now, drumming his fingers against his knee.

"The Professor's textbooks went missing around the time Roman left, didn't they?" Willis said. "We always thought they were lost in the earthquake, but seeing as Roman stole a bunch of other stuff from the Professor's office, I didn't think it was that much of a stretch to assume he'd steal these, too."

With a flourish, Willis stepped aside, revealing a small stack of moldy-looking textbooks.

There was a beat of silence.

"They won't turn you into a genius overnight," Willis said to Zora apologetically. "But I thought they might help you with some of the math in your dad's journal."

Zora pressed her hands together. She looked like she might cry. "Willis . . . ," she said in a strangled voice. And then, as though she no longer trusted herself to speak, she crossed the kitchen and took his giant face in her hands, planting a kiss right on his mouth.

Willis's face went red.

"Well," he said, clearing his throat. "That was completely unnecessary."

According to Greek myth, a woman named Cassandra was gifted with the ability to see the future when the god Apollo caught sight of her and determined her to be of extraordinary beauty.

When Cassandra rebuffed Apollo's advances, he cursed her with something particularly cruel in punishment: Cassandra would be able to see the future, but no one would believe what she saw.

I feel a bit of camaraderie with Cassandra just now, and so I feel it only fitting to name this mission in her honor.

I give you:

Mission: Cassandra 1

Objective: Attempt to alter the future.

For my first experiment, I think it wise to start small. I want to look into the idea of personal choice as it relates to predestination. Or, put colloquially, I'd like to determine whether I can change my own choices.

I believe that proving or disproving this will be relatively easy. I will simply travel one day into the future and observe myself as I make my way through my day-to-day life. I'll keep careful notes of what I do and where I go, and then I will return to my present timeline. I will have twenty-four hours to change just one thing from what I previously observed.

Just one choice.

I'll update on my return.

I'm writing this from the "future"—one day in the future, to be exact. I traveled twenty-four hours forward, and landed the *Second Star* a few blocks away from the workshop so that present me wouldn't see future me arrive.

That's already a contradiction. Because the present me that exists in the future would already know that I'm here, wouldn't he? Because I already went back?

That line of thinking is making my brain hurt, so back to the task at hand. I stayed out of sight and observed what "I" did over the last hour so that I might intentionally make a different choice when faced with the same options tomorrow (that is *this*) morning. This is what I discovered:

07:00 hours—Woke up and ate normal breakfast of black coffee, one orange, and a bowl of oatmeal with brown sugar. Have small argument with Natasha, who's annoyed that I've been working so diligently over the winter holiday.

07:30 hours—Get Zora up for school and make her breakfast.

08:30 hours—Drive Zora to school. A car accident on I-5 caused major delays, which resulted in us being twenty-five minutes late for Zora's first class. I promise her a milkshake if she "forgets" to tell that piece of information to her mother.

09:45 hours—Return to the workshop, where I spend the next several hours going over my notes from the previous day. I admit that this is a little strange to watch. The "notes" I'm going over are the notes that I'm writing right now. I'm watching myself go over the same notes in the future, even as I move my hand to write them. Extraordinary.

14:23 hours—Break for lunch. Natasha has informed me that there's leftover roast chicken in the fridge, but I leave the workshop to get a burrito from the taco truck down the street instead. Shh.

... And that brings us to where we are now. I have to admit, it's excruciatingly boring to watch myself live an entire day. It's occurring to me that I'm not a very interesting person.

In any case, I have enough data now to continue with my experiment, and so it's time to go home.

Or, rather, to my past home. Present home? It's impossible to keep all of this straight.

UPDATE—
JUNE 21, 2074
15:06 HOURS

Okay! I've returned to the present timeline with my notes, and I'm ready to proceed with the current experiment. My mission was to change one small part of the day that I just witnessed my future self living.

I've seen that I chose to eat a burrito for lunch. Tomorrow, though, I'm going to change my mind and have pizza instead. Will I be successful? Only time will tell.

UPDATE—
JUNE 22, 2074
14:51 HOURS

Here we go! I'm back in the future, trying to live my life as though I don't know that my past self is hiding outside of the window directly behind my head, watching my every move and recording it in the very notebook I'm currently writing in. My plan was to choose something different for lunch: pizza instead of a burrito.

I imagine that whoever is reading this is at the edge of their seat with anticipation, so I won't make you wait much longer. I successfully ate a slice of pizza.

I referred to the journal as soon as I ate the slice of pizza, half expecting to see that the entry had changed. But there, in black in white, in my own damn handwriting, was the word *burrito*.

Cassandra 1 was a success. Humans have free will. We are indeed capable of changing the future.

17

DOROTHY

NOVEMBER 7, 2077, NEW SEATTLE

Dorothy was not prepared for the crowd that awaited them on the docks the next morning. She saw them from the air as she and Roman flew toward the anil, and they had a magnetic hold on her gaze. Hundreds of people, standing shoulder to shoulder, cheering and holding signs, faces upturned to watch the time machine fly overhead.

Her heart leaped in her throat. She could hear their voices through the thick glass of the windows. If she squinted, she could read their signs:

The past is our right!

A flare of pride.

She had done that.

And then she wasn't just scanning the crowd, she was *searching* it, looking for dirty-blond hair and wind-chapped skin and a familiar, beat-up leather jacket. Heat flickered through her as she realized what she was doing, who she was looking for. Was he there now? she wondered. She thought he might be. She imagined she could feel his presence radiating below her. She lifted a hand to her face, finger grazing her lips.

"You're awfully quiet," Roman said, and Dorothy tensed, wondering if he'd guessed that she'd been thinking of Ash. She'd often thought Roman capable of reading minds, but, when she glanced at him, she saw that his eyes were trained on the window and the crowd beyond it.

"Incredible, isn't it?" he said, sounding awed.

"It is," Dorothy said. "I didn't realize there were this many people in the city."

"New Seattleites can be difficult to impress," Roman said. "We only show up for something truly spectacular."

He looked at her, smiling fully now. He hadn't mentioned what had happened the night before, and so she didn't, either. But, this morning, she'd found a cup of coffee waiting for her outside of her hotel room door, and she'd suspected it had been his way of apologizing for his outburst.

She studied him for a moment longer, wondering if she should say more.

She'd never actually told Roman what had happened between her and Ash but, of course, he'd figured it out. In order for everything to work out as it had in her past, Roman had needed to go back in time to 1980, help Ash and his friends escape from Fort Hunter, and make sure that Dorothy ended up with the exotic matter before she fell off the *Second Star*. All of it had been planned, perfectly, to make sure she would land at Roman's feet in 2076. Dorothy knew there wasn't a chance of anything going wrong. She'd already lived through it, and it would've created a paradox if things hadn't gone exactly as she remembered. So she wasn't worried.

But Roman had been living through it all for the first time. And, when he'd come back from the past, he'd seemed . . .

Changed.

"You never told me you'd fallen in love with him," he said to her, once, and Dorothy had been so shocked to hear him say it that she hadn't thought to deny it.

"I-I'm not anymore," she'd said, instead. Roman had held her gaze for a moment longer, and she'd half expected him to tell her to prove it, to choose.

But he'd done neither of those things, and Dorothy found herself remembering a conversation they'd had long ago. She'd asked Roman why he'd betrayed Ash and the Professor and everyone else, and he'd responded, "I'm afraid we haven't been acquainted long enough for that story. . . . Maybe one day, I'll let you in on all my secrets."

That had been a year ago now. Roman knew all of Dorothy's secrets and, yet, his were elusive as ever. Dorothy knew that Roman didn't display emotions easily. Always, his feelings were buried beneath a sly smile or a sharp joke so that she was constantly wondering what he really thought, why he guarded himself so closely.

She stared at him for a moment longer, the question already on her tongue. *What happened to you? What haven't you told me?*

But darkness fell over the ship before she could ask it, and they were inside the anil and it seemed, once again, like an opportunity had passed.

NOVEMBER 29, 2073, SEATTLE

When they exited the anil, they were in a strange, new world.

Well, strange to Dorothy, at least. *This* Seattle hadn't been flooded. The trees were monstrous and leafy green, not white and dead. Buildings towered into the sky, nearly blocking out the sun, and they huddled so close together that Dorothy had a hard time imagining how cars made their way between them—

That is, until they descended below the cloud cover, flying the *Black Crow* low enough for Dorothy to actually see the cars zooming down narrow streets, before disappearing farther into the concrete jungle.

Extraordinary, she thought, leaning close to the window as they flew over it all, their time machine hidden by the day's heavy fog. Electronic billboards flashed dizzily in the gray, and the huge concrete arc that Dorothy had seen in New Seattle—*highway*, it was called—was now loaded with cars and trucks and motorcycles.

In just two short years it will all be destroyed.

Something sour hit Dorothy's throat. She leaned back in her seat, looking away from the window. Many people wouldn't even have to wait two years. The first earthquake would hit the next day. She'd heard about this earthquake before but, for the first time, it felt real.

People were going to die. Half the city would lose their homes and have to move into tents. The power in entire neighborhoods would be knocked out and never recovered; hospitals would be overrun; children would go without food and water.

She felt suddenly sick.

Roman glanced at her sideways, seeming to read her thoughts. "It was four years ago."

His voice was strange, and Dorothy bristled, thinking he meant to scold her for getting emotional over something that had already happened, something they couldn't change. "I know that—"

"No," Roman cut her off. "I meant that it really wasn't that long ago, when you think about it."

There was a brief silence, and then Roman said, "*Black Crow* preparing for landing." He switched a button on the control panel and pulled down the yoke.

They began to descend.

18

ASH

NOVEMBER 7, 2077, NEW SEATTLE

A tremor moved through the city as the *Black Crow* disappeared into the anil.

Ash tightened his hands around his coat, shivering in the early morning fog. He and Zora had gathered on the docks to watch, along with a few hundred others, some holding soggy signs, the paint bleeding in the damp. Some were even chanting.

"The past is our right! The past is our right!"

Ash felt fidgety, all too aware of the eyes in the crowd. He saw a man standing a few feet away, staring, head cocked like he was trying to work out how he knew him. Ash turned away, pulling his collar up to hide his face.

He'd been hoping for some sign of Dorothy, but she hadn't left the time machine, hadn't even stuck a hand out the window to wave at her adoring fans.

This feeling—the sudden hope followed by crushing disappointment—was so great that his hands curled into fists.

He glanced at Zora and saw that her eyes were glued to the swirling mess of colors churning in the middle of the sea. The skin between her brows creased as she reached for his arm.

"Does it always do that?" she asked.

Ash focused on releasing the tension in his hands. "Do what?"

"That tremor—"

Before he could answer, the anil lit up. It was no single color, but all colors, shifting and unknowable. The ground below them began to shake.

The *Black Crow* was returning.

19

DOROTHY

NOVEMBER 29, 2073, SEATTLE

Dorothy hadn't spent a month planning this con. It'd been easy. All they'd needed were a few props.

Roman landed the *Black Crow* in a thick copse of trees near the edge of town, next to the white-and-blue SolarBeam delivery van he'd procured on an earlier trip back in time.

"Damn thing took forever to find," he'd complained bitterly. "I had to hack into old Craigslist ads going back over two years before I found someone looking to unload one. *Craigslist*, Dorothy. The user interface alone made me want to kill myself."

Dorothy had rubbed her thumb and forefinger together. "Do you know what this is?"

Roman's face had darkened. "Don't."

"It's the world's smallest violin playing just for you."

After the van, everything else was relatively easy. Uniforms were ordered from a wholesale retailer with same-day delivery, and they'd picked up the clipboards while they were in the 1990s, from a place called Target, which had delighted Dorothy endlessly (they sold bananas and arm chairs and trousers *all in the same place!*). And then it was simply a matter of storing their finds in a safe place until they needed them.

Now, Dorothy unbuttoned her cloak and tossed it in the back seat, revealing her SolarBeam uniform: navy-blue polo shirt, dark trousers, and silver windbreaker. She hid her hair beneath a head scarf, and then slid a SolarBeam baseball cap on top, lowering an eye patch over her ruined eye.

"They're going to think you're a pirate," Roman said, tucking his own polo into his trousers.

Dorothy checked her appearance. The scarf hid her white hair, but Roman was right, the eye patch was a problem. It made her memorable. Memorable was bad.

"Next time, we should try pulling off the glim dropper." She pushed her door open and a blast of chilly, November air swept over her, raising the hair on her arms.

Roman's eyebrows went up. "Excuse me?"

"It's like the fiddle game, only it involves a man—or woman, in our case—looking for her glass eye. My mother and I never tried it because it requires a one-eyed person to pull it off." She adjusted her eye patch. "Now, that wouldn't be an issue."

Roman only shook his head, snickering.

They loaded up the SolarBeam van and drove to Beacon Hill, a neighborhood south of the city that had been hit hardest by the earthquake. Everything they stole today would've only been destroyed in the aftermath of the storm, so it wasn't *really* stealing at all.

It was more like . . . misplacing.

At least, that's what Dorothy told herself as she knocked on the door of the first house.

An older woman with white, dandelion-puff hair and a bulbous nose answered. "Can I help you?"

"Hello, ma'am, my associate and I are from SolarBeam. We've had a few complaints in the neighborhood about panel failure. Would you mind letting us in to check your units?"

Dorothy nodded at her clipboard. Smiled. Behind her, Roman was making some very manly noises as he loaded a few large boxes into the back of the truck.

The boxes were empty. They'd unloaded them just seconds before, figuring the whole con would seem more believable if they were already packing up a few "faulty" units in need of repair.

Sure enough, the woman squinted at Roman and fumbled for the glasses hanging from her neck. "Oh dear. What seems to be the problem?"

Roman had finished loading up his empty boxes. He wiped the nonexistent sweat from his brow, and said, "It's hard to say, ma'am. If the panel's failed in a way that still allows an electrical current to pass through, the other panels on that string won't be negatively impacted whatsoever. But if one of its bypass diodes has been affected, well, then the current can't flow through it, and the bad panel might actually take down its entire string."

It'd taken him hours to memorize the most boring section of the SolarBeam instruction manual they'd found online, but his hard work paid off.

The woman just stared at him, blinking. "Oh?"

"It would be best if you let us take them in to be . . . recharged," Dorothy finished. She thought she saw Roman cast her a look—the word *recharged* must've been incorrect—but she didn't bother meeting his gaze. The old woman noticed nothing.

"By all means," she said.

She led them out back, to where the SolarBeam units were propped up in her yard. The units were very small, about the size of paperback books, and there were twelve of them in total, gathering sunlight that they would turn into enough electricity to power her small house for a month. Roman and Dorothy gathered all but two.

"Those should keep your power running until we return," Dorothy explained, nodding at the solar panels they'd left behind.

"Good thinking, dear," the woman said, too kindly. "And when do you expect to return?"

Dorothy opened her mouth to deliver the prepared line and then closed it again, staring at the woman's face.

Emelda Higgens, she thought. The name had just popped into her head. She and Roman had spent the last few weeks preparing a list of the residents of this neighborhood so they'd know exactly who to hit. They had photographs and bios, but

Dorothy couldn't remember all of them.

But Emelda . . . Dorothy remembered her. Emelda was seventy-two years old. She was going to die in eight hours, as the initial shocks of the earthquake sent her home of twenty-five years tumbling down around her. She'd be found in the debris, curled around her tiny, white dog, which she'd inexplicably named Pumpkin.

Dorothy couldn't breathe.

Roman's hand was suddenly at her back. "We'll be back bright and early tomorrow morning, Ms. Higgens," he said. Something in his voice had changed. He cleared his throat. "Thank you for your time."

Ms. Higgens smiled, vaguely, before turning around and shouting, "Pumpkin! Where are you at, boy?"

The door closed behind her.

Dorothy was already shaking her head as they hurried back up the street, where the delivery van was waiting. "I'm sorry," she said. "I don't know what happened, I just thought of the earthquake and how all these people, how *she*—"

Dorothy fell abruptly silent as a screen door screeched open, and a little girl raced outside.

The girl was all knobby limbs and scabbed knees, black hair escaping from an already messy ponytail, cheeks rosy from the cold.

The girl cupped her hands around her mouth. "Hey, gearhead! Mom says that if you don't come in now we're feeding your dinner to the cat."

"I'm finishing the tree house!" called a voice from the trees.

"Mom says the tree house isn't a priority!"

A boy dropped from the tree a moment later and raced into the house after his sister.

Watching them, Dorothy felt her stomach turn over. She didn't remember seeing a single children's photograph or bio on any of their lists but, of course, there would be plenty of them living here. Had Roman left them off deliberately? Had he thought she'd lose her nerve when she realized who they were stealing from?

She'd been telling herself this theft wasn't a big deal. The solar panels would've only been destroyed in the earthquake, after all. By taking them now, they were actually *saving* them, for the future.

But . . . couldn't they have at least tried to save the people, too? Couldn't they have discussed it?

"Come on," Roman said, his voice altered. Dorothy glanced at him and saw that he was staring at the door of the house where the two kids had just disappeared, his gaze sharp. He cleared his throat, and looked away. "Next house."

They gathered 240 solar panels by the end of the day, enough to power a ten-block radius. It was more power than New Seattle had seen in over four years. It was, by any measure one could name, a success.

But Dorothy didn't feel successful. She watched Roman

from the corner of her eye while they stacked the panels into neat rows at the back of the *Black Crow*.

A dozen questions rose up in her throat, all some variation of *What happened to the children?*

But she couldn't ask that question because she knew the answer already. An earthquake was going to hit this city in less than eight hours. Every house in this neighborhood would be reduced to rubble. By this time tomorrow, the little girl with the braids and the boy building the tree house would most likely be dead.

Roman slammed the door to the cargo hold shut, his eyes shifting to the horizon. "We should head back," he said. "Before . . ."

Dorothy nodded, following his gaze to the sky. The edges of this world had already turned orange and pink. It looked like the city was on fire and Dorothy had to remind herself that it wasn't yet. But it would be.

"Right," she said, and she climbed into the time machine after him.

LOG ENTRY—JUNE 27, 2074
05:49 HOURS
THE WORKSHOP

Now that we've determined that humanity has free will, and that the future is not predestined, I'd like to take a look at how far that free will extends. In other words, I want to know if my personal ability to make choices different from the choices I've seen myself make in the future could change more than what I have for lunch tomorrow.

I'm once again going to travel one day into the future only; this time, I'll pull up a local news site and read about the terrible things that are going to happen today, and then I'll attempt to use free will to see if it's possible to change them. As always, I'll update on my return.

UPDATE—06:24 HOURS

After scanning the news, I've decided to focus my energies on this story:

Motorcyclist seriously injured in hit-and-run crash near Renton.

The motorcyclist in question is an eighteen-year-old kid with his whole life ahead of him, and the crash wasn't his fault, it was the fault of some jerk-off who didn't even stop to make sure he was okay. He has some pretty serious injuries, too, so if I can keep this from happening, I can change this kid's entire future. I did a quick search of the kid's name, and it looks like he lives in Redmond, which is just a half hour drive from here.

Here's the plan: I'm going to stop by this kid's house and tell him that I'm Professor Zacharias Walker (there was a special on me last year ... I'm fairly well-known at the moment) and that he's going to be in a car accident today, and so he should avoid his motorcycle for the next twenty-four hours. Wish me luck!

UPDATE—18:56 HOURS

I've just returned, and I'm afraid I don't have good news.

The mission started out well. I got into my car and drove to this young man's house and told him exactly what I'd planned to tell him, that I'm a time traveler and that he's going to be in a debilitating accident if he chooses to ride his motorcycle today.

Unfortunately, he did not believe me. Perhaps this is something I should've expected, but I have to admit that I was quite surprised by his reluctance to accept my story. I thought that, even if he wouldn't admit it to my face, he would take my warning to heart and stay off the damn bike.

I've been glued to the news site all afternoon, hoping that my warning had worked.

And then, at 18:45 hours, the news story appeared. Motorcyclist seriously injured. I'd failed.

This is the Cassandra Complex at work, I'm afraid. Cassandra was gifted with the ability to see the future, and then cursed because no one believed what she told them to be true.

I just can't accept that. There has to be some way to make them listen.

That kid was planning to go to WCAAT in the fall. I feel like I'm responsible for his death.

20

ASH

NOVEMBER 7, 2077, NEW SEATTLE

One moment, the anil looked like it always looked: a glimmer of light dancing over black. A swirling mess of mist and smoke. A crack in time.

Then, the *Black Crow* was there.

Ash flinched at the ship's sudden appearance, nearly knocking into the person crowded onto the dock behind him. The ship didn't arrive, exactly. It was simply *not there* one moment and very much *there* the next.

Wind blew through the screaming crowd. The ground bucked. Zora said something, her fingers clawing at the damp leather of Ash's jacket, but Ash couldn't hear her and, anyway, his mind was somewhere else.

Was this how time travel looked from the other side? he wondered. He wouldn't know. He was always inside the cockpit of the time machine when it exited the anil, hands wrapped around the yoke, heart pounding in his throat.

The fact that he wasn't there now caused a deep, sucking

sadness to open up inside of him.

The guy he'd noticed earlier, the one who'd seemed to recognize him, was standing closer now, watching him with a quizzical smile on his face. He'd been one of the ones shouting *The past is our right!* and pumping his fist at the *Black Crow*.

Ash felt his muscles begin to knot. He could picture how a confrontation might go. The guy would say something rude or ignorant or both. And he—unable to help himself—would throw the first punch.

He leaned over, speaking directly into Zora's ear so she would hear him over the still-cheering crowd. "I've seen enough. Should we find the others?"

Zora nodded distantly. She was staring very intently at the time machine, forehead creased in concern. And then she blinked, shaking her head.

"They're already at Dante's," she said, her voice sounding very far away. "Yeah, let's go."

"Okay . . . so I think this number is the primary wave . . . which means *this* must be the secondary wave, see?" Chandra said, squinting. She had the Professor's old textbooks and a thick pile of his notes spread out on the table before her, and she was looking back and forth between two rows of scribbled digits, pencil tapping her chin. "So you can measure the interval time of the S-P to find the distance from the seismometer to the epicenter. Hey, that makes sense."

"*That* makes sense?" Zora snorted. "Is your definition of

that word different from mine?"

"Well, it's just how he ended up with this digit here, see? No *here*. Look at where I'm pointing."

Zora shot her a murderous look.

They were at Dante's, a cramped, dirty bar with mismatched chairs and tables covered in sticky layers of Dante's famous homemade hooch. Strings of half-busted café lights hung from the ceiling above them, but Ash couldn't remember the last time they'd actually emitted anything like light. Instead, there were drippy candles lined up against the walls, their flickering flames doing very little to illuminate the vinyl booths and wobbly café tables.

It wasn't much. But no one here stared at them. Ash blinked at the textbook sitting open before him. His brain felt slow and soupy, and he hadn't been able to follow a word of what Chandra was saying. Willis seemed to have given up, too. He'd quietly closed his book ten minutes ago and was currently folding his cocktail napkin into an origami swan.

Only Zora was still trying to follow along, and it didn't appear to be doing anyone any good. She dug her fingers through her hair. "I'm a *mechanic*," she said, teeth gritted. "I could build a time machine out of the stuff lying around this bar."

Chandra blinked at her, eyes monstrous behind her thick glasses.

"What I'm trying to say is I'm not an idiot." Zora flipped the textbook closed, irritated. "This doesn't make any sense."

"It does," Chandra insisted. "You can learn it if you try."

"I *really* can't."

"Okay." Chandra closed her textbook, too. "Maybe it's time for a break. Get another drink, take some of the pressure off?"

Zora dropped her head to the table, groaning loudly. Willis quietly placed the cocktail napkin swan next to her.

"Maybe we should try looking on the bright side," Chandra said, sliding a glass of something thick and brown across the table. "New Seattle is going to have electricity again. Remember electricity? It powers televisions and computers and turns on lights and helps with fancy things like *heat*. We like electricity."

She lifted her thick, brown drink to her mouth, slurping loudly. Ash frowned at her for a moment before deciding he didn't actually want to know what the drink was, or how she'd convinced Levi to make it for her.

"We already have electricity," Willis said. "And we didn't have to sell ourselves to the Black Cirkus to get it."

"Please tell me you aren't talking about the Professor's old solar panels, because they've been acting up for weeks." Chandra's eyes brightened. "We could finally watch the rest of *Buffy the Vampire Slayer*. I've only seen the first four seasons."

"Come on, Chandie, *Buffy*?"

Ash turned his glass with two fingers, watching the clear hooch slosh up along the sides. Back at the docks, he'd wanted to be here, surrounded by his friends, drinking Dante's terrible liquor and going through these textbooks, finally feeling like they were accomplishing something.

But, now, he found himself longing for the docks shifting beneath his feet and the cold bite of wind on his cheeks, the sound of the crowd chanting around him. He looked around this bar, and all he could think about was how he'd brought Dorothy here, the way her eyes had gone wide when she'd first stepped into this room.

He wondered if she would've spoken to him, if she'd seen him standing on the docks just now.

And then he hated himself for wondering.

And then he hated himself a little more because, to be honest, he would've been perfectly satisfied if she'd walked past him without a word, as long as he got to see her face.

It was kind of ironic, if he thought about it. For the last year Quinn Fox's face had haunted him. Or, rather, the darkness under her hood had haunted him. The absence of a face. He'd scowled and turned away whenever it flashed on his television screen.

Now, it was all he could think about.

He wanted to laugh. Or scream. He wanted to kiss her again. His lips burned with the wanting.

He glanced at the door, his knee jumping below the table. Could he go to her now? Would she see him?

"What did you think of that tremor?" Zora had a glass of water sitting in front of her, and she was absently tracing the lip with one finger.

Ash blinked, refocusing his attention on her. "Tremor?"

"There was a tremor when the *Black Crow* entered the

anil, and another one when they returned." Zora frowned. "You didn't notice?"

"There are always tremors," Ash said. "There was one when Chandie and I were coming back from Mac's the other day."

"Nearly drowned us," Chandra added, slurping.

Willis had another cocktail napkin in front of him, and he was folding it into something that had fins. He lifted his eyes. "Did you think it was something else?"

"No. Ugh, I don't know." Zora took a pencil out from behind her ear and tapped it against her bottom lip. "It just seemed weird to me."

Ash felt guilt twist through his gut. *This* was what he should be thinking about. Tremors and earthquakes and saving the world. *Not* Dorothy's lips. Heat shot up the backs of his ears. What was wrong with him?

"Another?" Willis asked, nodding at his now-empty glass.

Ash dropped his eyes to his textbook. The numbers looked like gibberish, but he doubted another drink was going to get him any closer to understanding what they meant.

He was feeling restless. He needed a change of scenery. He needed to go somewhere that didn't remind him of Dorothy.

He pushed back his chair, tucking the textbook under his arm. "I'm going to take a walk," he told his friends. "Clear my head. I'll see you all back at the school."

21

DOROTHY

"Friends, do not attempt to adjust your television," Dorothy said, blinking into the glare of spotlights in the Fairmont basement. "Our broadcast has taken over every channel.

"I'm happy to announce that our trip back in time was successful. We returned early this morning with two hundred and forty solar panels, all in working order. That's enough to power all of downtown Seattle, more electricity than our city has seen since before the mega-quake."

Dorothy paused, eyes flicking to the darkness beyond the spotlights. She thought she'd heard a door open. Footsteps. And was that Roman's voice, murmuring to someone she couldn't see?

Her hands felt suddenly clammy. "Th-this is only the beginning," she continued, faltering. The broadcast was live; she couldn't just stop. "Those of you who lived through the devastation of the earthquakes will remember that the hospitals were looted back in 2074, and important medications were stolen. Many people died, not because of the earthquake itself, but because of lack of access to medication and medical attention. Many people are dying, still.

"Tomorrow, at dawn, we will go back in time again. We will return to the day the hospitals were looted, and take the medication before it can be stolen. And then we will bring it back here. For you."

A small burst of static, and the broadcast was over.

"Marvelous, as always," Roman said, but his voice sounded stilted.

Dorothy shielded her eyes, squinting past the spotlights. "Is someone else here?"

She could make out black shapes moving behind the recording equipment, the squeak of shoes on concrete.

No, not shoes—crutches.

And, then, the sound of soft, slow clapping.

"Bravo," Mac called out, hobbling into the light. He was wearing the same ill-fitting suit he'd had on the night before, though it was quite a bit dirtier now than it'd been then. The bandage at his thigh was fresh and no longer bloodstained.

"You were watching?" Dorothy asked, standing. She didn't like the idea of Mac in the darkness just beyond her spotlights, watching her when she didn't know he was there. There wasn't a single other person in this city who'd have come to the Fairmont without invitation.

"The whole city was watching," Mac said. "The two of you are heroes." He said the word *heroes* lightly enough, but there was something unpleasant threaded through his voice.

Dorothy suppressed a shudder.

"But I didn't come here tonight just to catch the show." Mac readjusted the crutches beneath his arms. "I got something to show you. Come on."

He started hobbling toward the door.

Dorothy glanced at Roman, frowning, and Roman shook his head. He didn't know what Mac was up to, either. That didn't bode well.

"Well, come on," Mac said, hesitating at the door. "It's a gift. It ain't going to bite you."

Dorothy chewed her lower lip. Gifts were manipulative. They nearly always came with strings attached.

And there was the matter of his offer. She and Roman hadn't had a chance to discuss it yet. Foolishly, she hadn't expected Mac to show up again so soon.

You would've, said a voice inside her head. The voice sounded alarmingly like her mother, Loretta.

In your old life, you wouldn't have given a mark time to think and second-guess. You'd have struck while his greed was fresh.

Which, Dorothy had to admit, was true. Back when she'd made her living as a con artist, she'd been careful never to leave a mark to his own devices for too long, lest he talk himself out of whatever it was that she was trying to get him to do.

But she could see no way out of seeing what Mac had brought them, and so it was with some reluctance that she and Roman followed him out of the basement and up the stairs, to the Fairmont's main halls.

There, she spotted a group of Freaks gathered around the bay windows that served as the hotel's main entrance, studying something that she couldn't see and murmuring excitedly. Dorothy hesitated, uneasy. If Mac had presented this gift to her and Roman alone, she might still have found some way of refusing it. But, now, they had an audience.

A *growing* audience, she noticed, as more members of their gang emerged from hotel rooms and hallways to see what had caused the commotion. Mac had planned this intentionally.

Her eyes darted over to him, wary. "What is that?"

Mac, balanced on his crutches, twisted around to face her. "Like I said, it's a gift." He smiled, thin and sharp.

It was a *big* gift.

A few of the Freaks fell silent as Dorothy approached, leaving her to wonder whether they'd been whispering about her, perhaps pointing out that she rarely brought them gifts. She felt her lip twitch and tried to keep her face impassive as they parted, revealing nearly a dozen wooden crates piled onto the damp carpet.

Eliza was kneeling before an open crate while Bennet hovered over her, one end of a crowbar wedged beneath the crate's lid. The rest of the Freaks were huddled tightly around them, and it seemed to Dorothy that they were holding their breath, waiting to hear what she and Roman might say.

Roman turned to her, one eyebrow cocked, and Dorothy knew that he, too, wanted to see what Mac had brought them. If she were to take the gift back now they'd all hate her more than they did already.

"Well, go on then," Dorothy said, and the tension seemed to leak out of the air. Ben popped the lid off the crate. Eliza reached inside.

"Holy . . . ," she murmured, removing a tin can without a label. "Is this . . . food?"

An excited murmur went through the crowd of Freaks. Food was scarce in New Seattle. It was one of the reasons the fruit at their masquerade had gone over so well. *Actual* food like Dorothy remembered from her time period—fruit and bread and milk—was a luxury only the very rich could afford. It had taken her and Roman hours to gather enough from the past for their party guests and, once they'd brought it all back to the Fairmont, they'd needed to keep the room where it was being stored under armed guard to keep their own gang from looting, the rest of the Freaks muttering, annoyed, that they might've liked some fruit for themselves.

"I think that one is canned peaches." Mac nodded at the can in Eliza's hands, clearly delighted. "But you might need to open it to find out."

Excited now, Eliza began digging through the crate in earnest. There was more food. A lot of it was dried goods: bags of grain and flour, beans and rice. But there were also tins of soup and vegetables. Sugar. Eggs.

Liquor.

"Bourbon?" Ben said, hooting as he leaned over Eliza and pulled a bottle filled with brown liquid out of the crate. "I haven't seen this since before the earthquakes."

"*We* could have brought back bourbon, if you'd asked,"

Dorothy said, sour. They could have brought back canned peaches and sugar and eggs, too, but they hadn't. There never seemed to be enough time, space, or money for such luxuries.

"Now, you don't have to," Mac said, scratching his chin. "It frees you up to bring back more important things, doesn't it? We have food here."

Dorothy pressed her lips together, considering how to respond. She felt like she was playing a game of chess and Mac had just moved a pawn forward and easily knocked her queen to the side, smiling at her as he did so. She felt foolish, a little girl playing a grown-up's game.

Donovan and Ben were fighting about the bourbon now, talking over each other as each of them tried to remember how it tasted.

"It's smoky, isn't it?" Donovan was saying, turning the bottle so that amber liquid sloshed up the sides of the glass.

Ben shook his head. "No, no that's Scotch."

Dorothy bristled, tuning out their argument. How easy would it have been for her to purchase a bottle of bourbon during one of their trips back in time? It had never seemed important—they had alcohol here, after all, crappy though it was—but now that she could see how much it was doing for morale, she realized her misstep. Perhaps such a luxury hadn't been necessary, but it would've been smart. Mac had seen that, so why hadn't she?

She glanced at Mac, lips pursed. And now *he'd* been the one to provide it for them, and who knows how much he'd spent to get it shipped from the Center. A lot, surely. There was a reason no one had good liquor this far west.

"This is too much," Roman said. He met Dorothy's gaze and held it for a moment. "We couldn't possibly accept."

Donovan and Ben stopped fighting over the bottle, their faces falling. Ben opened his mouth, but then Dorothy turned her dark eyes on him, her expression severe, and he stayed silent, looking like a scolded child. She saw Donovan and Eliza exchange looks from the corner of her eye. This would not go over well.

"Don't be silly." Mac released a short laugh. "It's a *gift*."

Gift, gift, gift, Dorothy thought. Funny how every time Mac said that word it sounded more like *bribe*.

"We wouldn't know how to repay you," Dorothy said. It was as close as she dared come to rejecting his offer outright, but Mac's lips drew back over clamped teeth, and Dorothy knew he understood her meaning.

No, our answer is no.

Then, from behind them, a sharp gasp.

Mac's smile grew triumphant. Dorothy felt suddenly cold. She knew, even before she turned around, that something had changed.

Eliza was holding a long, narrow package. Like the food, the package wasn't labeled or marked in any way, but she'd opened one end and dumped its contents out to find—

Bullets. They lay on Eliza's open palm, shiny as beetles. Staring at them, Dorothy felt something inside of her coil tight.

Guns were easy to find in New Seattle.

Bullets were trickier.

"Figured you could use 'em to hold the Fairmont," Mac said, eyes glinting. "In case Graham or Chadwick give you any more trouble."

Nothing in his words hinted at a threat, but Dorothy heard it anyway:

Look how easily I'm able to get bullets, he seemed to be saying. *Look how I'm able to put them into the hands of your people, people whose loyalty can so easily be bought, people who don't even like you. . . .*

And now Dorothy was seeing Mac's gift in an entirely new light. He hadn't meant to win her and Roman over at all. He'd meant to win over the Cirkus Freaks.

The hair on the back of Dorothy's neck stood up. Without the Black Cirkus, she and Roman were just two people. They didn't have any particular power or strength. The only thing that set them apart from everyone else in this wretched city was their time machine—and that could be taken.

She swallowed, hard. For the first time, she realized what a precarious position she was in.

She glanced at Roman. His expression was impassive as ever, but he'd lowered his hand to hers and he didn't seem to notice that his fingers had clamped vise-tight around her wrist. Dorothy cringed slightly, as her skin crushed against bone.

"How far into the future do you wish to go?" he said, voice hushed so the other Freaks wouldn't overhear.

Mac's eyes flashed. "Let's start with something easy. How

about five years from now?"

For an instant, Roman seemed to forget to keep his facial features so carefully arranged, and Dorothy saw a brief glimmer of the anguish he must feel inside.

A moment later, his face looked so perfectly at ease that it was hard for Dorothy to remember it was a lie. Dorothy felt a cool dread crystallize inside of her.

"Very well," Roman said.

He paused for a moment and then added, "Although, I should warn you . . . you're not going to like what you find there."

MAY 2, 2082, NEW SEATTLE

They exited the anil into a world of perfect dark. There were no stars to illuminate the ghostly white tree trunks, no distant oil lamps flickering through the black like fireflies, no far-off buzz of electricity, no moon. It was as though someone had painted the outsides of the *Black Crow*'s windows black, leaving only the faint green of the control panel.

Dorothy could just make out the silhouette of Roman's face in the eerie glow. His lips were drawn in a tight line, the muscles in his jaw tense.

"I thought we were going to land in the afternoon," she said, and Roman looked at her, and then away.

"Local time is 3:02 p.m.," he said.

Then, hesitating, he added, "The sun's been blocked by volcanic ash."

"What?" Dorothy was quiet as the horror of this washed

over her. There was no *sun?* Her hands grew clammy.

How could all this happen in just five years?

It felt like surfacing from deep water to find the world on fire. For just an instant, she wanted to turn around, go home, pretend she'd never seen this.

Mac's voice came from behind them. "This ship still has light, doesn't it?"

Roman said nothing but flipped on the time machine's headlights. A steady, white beam cut through the darkness like a knife, splitting the world in two.

Bits of black dust hung in the air before the ship's headlights, giving the world the appearance of a television set that couldn't quite focus. Through the dust, Dorothy saw that the sky above their time machine was dark as oil, and starless, mirrored in the waters below so that she couldn't tell where one bled into the other. She scanned the horizon for a city. But there was no city. Instead, a single jagged structure rose from the waters, covered in layers of craggy black rock and ash.

Dorothy's eyes narrowed as she stared at the structure, something tugging on her memory. It seemed to have been a building once, but it didn't look like one anymore. The *Black Crow*'s headlights bounced off the bits of broken glass still clinging to its windowsills, brick walls covered in thick layers of ash. It didn't have a roof, and a huge gaping hole had opened up in the middle of its walls, looking for all the world like an open mouth.

Still, though, there was something familiar about the columns out front, the position of the windows . . .

Oh God. Dorothy pressed her mouth so firmly closed that she could feel the imprints of her teeth against the backs of her lips. She suddenly realized what she was looking at.

It was the Fairmont. In just five years, it would go from the most sought-after hotel in the city, to this ruin of burnt bricks and broken glass.

"Check out your castle, princess," Mac said, chuckling beneath his breath. "Doesn't look so impressive now, does it?" He leaned forward in his seat and tapped his window with one finger. Dorothy had the impression of a child shaking a snow globe.

This world will not change if you shake it, she wanted to snarl.

"I guess it seems a little silly that we were all fighting over that." Mac's lip curled as he turned to her, grinning. Disgusted, Dorothy looked away.

Mac might think of the Fairmont as nothing more than a prize. But she'd lived in that old hotel for a year now, and it was the closest thing to a home that she'd ever known.

She wanted to scream. She wanted to throw her hands over her eyes and demand that Roman turn off the headlights. She wanted to unsee everything that lay before her, even as she knew it was impossible.

She would remember this forever. She would see the imprint of it on her eyelids every night as she tried to fall asleep. The blackened, broken-down Fairmont would be the last image that haunted her on her dying day.

"Remember," Roman said. "This is just one possible future. It's not definite."

"What the hell happened to make it look like this?" asked Mac.

"We . . . don't know for sure." Roman seemed to weigh his words carefully before adding, "Before I left the Chronology Protection Agency, the Professor was theorizing that another earthquake could hit the city in the next five to ten years. Possibly more than one earthquake. He thought that the movement of tectonic plates might be so great that they would set off a wave of volcanic activity."

Dorothy turned to him, frowning. "An earthquake can cause a *volcano* to erupt?"

"Yes," said Roman. "The Professor predicted the eruption of Glacier Peak, Mount Baker, and Mount Rainier for sure, but those might not be the only ones to blow. There's also the Yellowstone Caldera, the supervolcano. Maybe even the Aira Caldera, in Japan."

Mac laughed, the sound low and bitter. "Explain to me how the hell we're going to avoid all of *that*?"

Roman stared out the window. "It's just one possibility," he said again.

Mac shook his head, peering into the black for another long, searching moment.

"I've seen enough," he said. "Take me back."

Roman flew them across the barren landscape and back into the anil. The tunnel of stars and purple clouds and black sky spun around them, and then Roman piloted the time machine through the tunnel walls, and the air around them thickened, growing heavy and wet. Water pounded against the windshield, making the glass creak—

NOVEMBER 7, 2077, NEW SEATTLE

—and then, a second later, they were surfacing, and New Seattle's familiar skyline lay before them. Milk-white fog hung over the surface of the sound. Choppy waves rose to greet them, slamming over the *Black Crow*'s windshield as they hovered above the water. The city looked like nothing in the distance. Like darkness layered over more darkness. It was only when a far-off boat wove through the buildings that she could see the shape of the skyscrapers cutting into the night, the glimmer of light off windows.

Roman lifted his head and sniffed the air. Dorothy smelled it, too: brine and salt and the sweet, dank scent of mold. It was the smell of New Seattle, and it crept in through the time machine's thick windows the second they exited the anil.

Home sweet home, she thought, numb.

Roman flew the *Black Crow* to the Fairmont garage and, landing, cut the engine. Dorothy's eyes moved, restlessly, over the clouded windows and rusted pipes. It seemed strange, she thought, that this place should look so normal after everything she'd seen.

Behind them, Mac gave a deep, satisfied sigh. "Well. That was certainly illuminating."

Dorothy let her eyes close for a fraction of a second.

"I'm glad you . . . enjoyed it," said Roman, voice cool.

"Although we shouldn't go so far next time." Mac threw open the back door. He maneuvered his crutches out of the time machine first and then, grunting, hauled the rest of his body out, too. "Maybe just two years. I want to know exactly when this big earthquake is supposed to hit."

From the corner of her eye, Dorothy saw Roman's hands tighten around the *Black Crow*'s yoke.

He said, "Next time?"

Cackling, Mac said, "Don't worry, I'll make it worth your while." He winked at Dorothy and headed toward the parking garage's back exit, crutches creaking. Neither she nor Roman had made a move to get out of the time machine.

Dorothy had never considered leaving their current time period before. But now there was a wild, unhinged part of her that wanted to grab the wheel and fly them somewhere— *anywhere*—else.

Paris in the 1920s. Rome at the height of its empire. Somewhere they could put an entire lifetime between themselves and the horrors of the world she'd just seen.

"We could go," she said, thinking out loud. "If that's—"

Roman cut her off firmly. "No. We can't." He kept his eyes trained on Mac's retreating figure. It wasn't until the parking garage door closed behind him that he tore his eyes away and added, his voice softening, "At least, *I* can't leave here. This city, this time period, it's my home. It's the last place I . . ." He scrubbed a hand over his face, trailing off.

"But, if you wanted to go to some other time, I could always drop you off."

Dorothy waited for him to elaborate—*"the last place I"* *what?*—but he stayed silent and, eventually, she shook her head, too. Neither of them would be running away. Roman was the only real friend she'd managed to make in over two centuries. She couldn't just leave him here.

And Ash is here, said a voice at the back of her head. She gritted her teeth, heat rising in her cheeks. As much as she hated to admit it, she couldn't imagine putting a lifetime between her and Ash. Which meant that she and Roman would need to find a way to change the future they'd just seen. Somehow.

"How does it happen?" she asked, dumbfounded. "Do you know?"

"Not here," Roman said. He looked, suddenly, very old. "I need a drink for this conversation."

LOG ENTRY—JUNE 30, 2074
07:09 HOURS
THE WORKSHOP

There are car crashes every day and I'm going to stop one, if it's the last thing I do.

Today's headline: *Four confirmed dead after fiery crash on I-5.*

Warning the boy from yesterday didn't work, so I'm going to take a new tactic. I'm going to delay the driver.

According to the story I found, this crash is going to occur when a semi slows for traffic, thus causing another commercial vehicle following directly behind to slam into him. I'm not going to get too emotionally involved with the victims in this one in case... well, in case it doesn't work out, but if I can keep this from happening, four lives will be saved.

A witness claims to have seen the driver of the first truck at a roadside diner about an hour before the crash. My plan is to intercept him before he can leave the diner. If I can delay him for even five minutes, then the second driver will pull ahead of him on the road, and the crash will never happen.

UPDATE—12:56 HOURS

I successfully found the driver of the first vehicle and delayed him for approximately fifteen minutes past the original time he'd been determined to leave the diner. This should be a sufficient amount of time to allow the driver of the second car to pull ahead of him on the highway, preventing the crash entirely.

UPDATE—15:46 HOURS

The story just popped up on Seattle's news site. *The exact same story.*

Four dead. Fiery crash on I-5. Every word on the site is exactly the same. Nothing I did prevented anything.

I can't for the life of me figure out what I'm doing wrong.

22

ASH

NOVEMBER 7, 2077, NEW SEATTLE

Ash hadn't realized he was making his way back to the bar near the Fairmont until the buildings bordering the dock began to look familiar and the soles of his boots hit good, clean wood instead of damp and moldy boards. There were fewer trees out here, and more voices—louder, laughing voices—and then he saw the familiar black door at the end of the dock, and he knew where he was going.

He still didn't know the name of the place, but there was a small sign hanging above the door: a black rabbit, lying on its back. Morbid. He shoved the door open with his shoulder and went inside.

It wasn't as crowded as it'd been when he came through the other night. A group of kids wearing black hovered around a table in the back, talking loudly, but none of them looked up as he walked past. A girl with her hair tied back in a bandanna stood behind the bar. She was building a tower out of cardboard boxes of matches.

"Nice," Ash said, nodding at the matches. The tower was three stories high.

The girl shrugged. "I've had a lot of practice," she said. The little cardboard boxes of matches were something they had in bulk around here. The Center sent boxes and boxes of them, as though a book of matches might help solve problems like lack of heat and light and power.

The girl flicked a pack of matches between her fingers. "What are you drinking?"

"I'll take a pint," Ash said.

She placed the beer in front of him, but when Ash went to reach for his wallet, she waved him away. "On the house."

Ash lifted his eyebrows. "Really?"

The bartender leaned in closer, cupping a hand around her lips. "I recognize you. Jonathan Asher, right? You were the pilot who worked with that scientist guy back when he first discovered time travel."

Ash shifted in his seat. "That doesn't usually get me free drinks around these parts."

"Yeah, well, I like to keep an open mind." She nodded at the group of guys in black sitting in the back of the bar. They were talking over each other now, getting rowdy, drunk. "Unfortunately, *they* aren't quite as evolved. Once they figure out who you are, they're going to beat the crap out of you." She shrugged. "You may as well have a drink first."

Ash started to stand. "Maybe I should—"

She rolled her eyes. "Oh, sit *down*. I'm messing with you. They're all too drunk to care who you are."

Ash wasn't sure whether that was true, but he slowly lowered himself back down to his barstool, still feeling uneasy.

"Besides, things are different now." The girl turned back to her matchbook tower, and one of her sleeves pulled back to reveal a smudgy, black tattoo in the shape of a circus tent, the words *the past is our right* scrawled below it. "Now that Quinn and Roman can go back in time, everyone thinks this is all going to change. This morning on the docks, I heard someone say they were going to try to reverse the damage from the mega-quake during their next trip back in time." She cocked an eyebrow and said, her voice almost challenging. "Even *you* have to admit that would be amazing."

Ash didn't know what to say. It would be amazing; he just didn't think it was possible.

"I had a big house out in West Seattle before the mega-quake," the girl said, almost to herself. "I was supposed to start college in the fall." She gave her head a shake and added, with a small laugh, "Who knows? If they really do fix things, maybe I still can."

Ash raised his glass. "I hope it works out for you."

Ash figured it'd be easier to concentrate on the textbooks without his friends around distracting him, and he was surprised to find that he'd been right. There was a rhythm to the numbers that was immediately familiar, like an old song he didn't realize he remembered all the lyrics to. Poring over them, he could almost imagine he was back in the Professor's workshop at WCAAT in the days before the earthquake.

Ash had always loved that workshop. It hadn't looked like how he might imagine a professor's study should look, all old leather and heavy wooden desks, but had more of an artist's studio vibe. A massive drafting table stood in the middle of the room, surrounded by easels where the Professor would prop oversize notebooks filled with scribbled equations and sketches and theories. One entire wall was taken up by bookshelves, a vintage ladder standing before them so the Professor could reach the highest shelves.

Ash could still remember the smell of that place—the cigarettes the Professor swore he didn't smoke and the charred scent of burnt coffee—him and Zora and Roman lying on their stomachs on the faded rugs that Natasha had thrown over the concrete floors to keep out the chill. The gentle rustle of turning pages and sunlight melting through the windows, the Professor's footsteps pacing the floor between the three of them. He used to tell long, rambling stories about Stephen Hawking and Nikola Tesla, or lecture them on the different time traveler's paradoxes. *But if what you do when you go back in time* actually *influences what you do in the past, then the solution to the theory is far more interesting. . . .* Roman glancing at Ash from across the room and rolling his eyes dramatically. Ash snickering, trying to cover it up with a cough.

After all that, Ash would've expected that *some* of what the Professor had told him might've stuck. But the equations meant nothing to him. He'd read over them and his mind would snag on some small detail—*didn't the Professor say something about energy acting differently in an anil?*—but the thought would be gone a moment later, drifting through his head like smoke.

Ash couldn't say how long he'd stayed there when the bartender appeared before him and slid a hand over his textbook. He looked up and saw that the blood had drained from her face.

"Something wrong?" Ash asked.

She shook her head. "I wasn't going to say anything because you don't look like you want any trouble," she said, her voice low. "But you, uh, might want to be moving on."

Ash regarded her uneasily. "Yeah?"

"Roman made us all promise we'd tell him if you came back." The bartender's eyes caught on something behind Ash's head, and she swore, under her breath. "And, well, he just walked in."

23

DOROTHY

The Dead Rabbit was a hole. Black walls and black barstools and dim lights made the place look smudgy and rotten, like wood that'd been left wet for too long. The floors were perpetually sticky, and the smell of smoke hung thick in the air, courtesy of the few people rich enough to afford cigarettes and rude enough to smoke indoors.

Dorothy noticed all this in a detached way as she scanned the space for a place where she and Roman could talk in private. She had her hood pulled low, the stiff fabric covering her eyes and most of her face, so she could see only her own boots, and a few feet of dirty floor.

A cheer went up from the back of the room, and Dorothy lifted the edge of her hood.

"Blast," she said, stiffening. Eliza and a few other Cirkus Freaks had already gathered at their regular table. They looked like they'd been drinking for a while and planned to continue for a good while longer.

"We'll get rid of them," Roman said.

"To toilet paper!" Ben was saying, toasting the others with a glass of Mac's bourbon as Dorothy and Roman approached. "And sugar! And real liquor."

Eliza and Donovan both echoed, "To real liquor!" and clinked glasses, sending bourbon sloshing over the sides.

Beneath her hood, Dorothy frowned. She'd been thinking of the dead, black world they'd just returned from, and it took her a moment to remember what they were celebrating. It came back to her quickly: wooden crates stacked on damp carpet, dozens of Cirkus Freaks watching as Eliza unloaded bourbon and peaches and bullets, courtesy of the very man who'd stared out into that black, dead world and smiled. She felt vaguely ill.

"We need the table," she said with a sigh, and lifted her hands and pushed back her hood, revealing her scarred face.

Ben didn't move but stared at her, huge-eyed. He didn't seem to realize that he was still tipping the bourbon toward his mouth until he'd poured it all over himself.

"Watch it," Roman snapped, as Ben muttered, "Damn," and slammed his glass back down on the table, grabbing for a stack of cocktail napkins. He apologized and started to stand, but Eliza put a hand on his shoulder, stopping him.

"We just got here," she said, and lifted her drink to her mouth. "We hoped to celebrate your great success and enjoy a little of Mac's liquor."

Dorothy felt the corner of her lip curl. It had been a long time since any of the Freaks had disobeyed a direct order from her.

And now Eliza was staring back at her, head cocked, like she was daring Dorothy to argue.

"Celebration's over," Dorothy said in her best Quinn Fox voice. "Get back to work."

Eliza released a small chuckle and looked from Ben to Donovan, eyebrows raised in disbelief.

Ben seemed less inclined to argue. "Quentin and Matt's team are on duty tonight." He was still sopping up the spilled bourbon now and sending vaguely disgusted glances at Dorothy's face that he seemed to think she didn't see. "We don't have anywhere else we need to be."

"Are you saying there's no work to be done in the Fairmont?" Roman asked, cool. "Nothing that could use your attention?"

Ben's ears turned red. Donovan was already standing.

But Eliza stayed seated. Her eyebrow twitched as she added, "Mac's men get a day off now and then."

"Is that what you want?" snapped Dorothy, her anger getting the better of her. "To work for Mac?"

"Why the hell not?" Eliza said. "Being a Freak hasn't gotten me anywhere."

"Mac doesn't generally allow women in his employ to carry firearms," Roman reminded her. "I'm not sure you'd enjoy the work he'd expect you to do."

"Better than this Robin Hood crap," Eliza said, and pushed her chair back hard, its legs squeaking against the sticky floor.

Dorothy heard her mutter something under her breath as she and the others made their way to the door.

Dorothy bristled. A better leader would go after them, restore the peace, but she couldn't bring herself to move. Her mind was occupied with other things just now. She was suddenly aware of each minute that passed, each *second*. She could feel that nightmare world she'd just seen creeping closer and closer, a wave that was going to crash over them.

She dropped into a chair and reached for Eliza's discarded drink, downing the remains of her bourbon in a single swallow. She wanted an explanation for where they'd just been. The Freaks she could deal with later.

"So what was that?" she asked, voice hoarse.

Roman looked toward the door. "The beginning of a mutiny, I think—"

"You know I'm not talking about them."

He lifted Ben's glass of bourbon to his mouth and then seemed to think better of drinking it and placed it back on the table instead. "*That* was our future," he said.

"It was the real future, then? Not some trick to freak out Mac?"

Roman lifted his eyes. "How would I go about creating a *trick* future?"

His sarcasm struck a nerve. "Don't," Dorothy warned. "Don't you dare turn this into a joke. All this time you knew what was coming, and you never told me. Why?"

She punctuated the question by slamming her hand against the table, causing the remaining bourbon to tremble and slosh against the glasses.

Roman leaned back, his gaze trained on her. The bar's

dim lights caught his eyes, turning them a deep, stormy blue. "Why do you think?"

Looking back at him, Dorothy felt the anger go out of her. It hadn't been real anger, anyway, but a mask for everything else she was feeling and, now that it was gone, waves of fear and despair crashed over her in full force. She saw the Fairmont's blackened brick and broken windows, the mouthlike hole in the middle of its walls.

She curled her hand into a fist to keep it from shaking. "You told Mac that it wasn't set, right? It's not like the past. We can still do something."

"I don't know." Roman seemed to weigh his next words carefully before continuing. "I haven't told you the whole truth about my trips into the future with the Professor. The Professor went into the future once, without me, and he found it like . . . well, he must've found it like that. Everything dead. He wouldn't tell me exactly what he saw, just that there was still time to change it. He was very upset."

Roman looked down at his hands.

"What happened next?" Dorothy urged when he didn't continue.

"Well, I wanted to know what he'd seen, so I took his journal and read about it. It sounded awful. I didn't believe it. So I took the *Second Star* on my own. I guess you'd say I stole it after the Professor had gone to sleep. I wanted to know what our future was going to be, and I wanted to believe him, that it could be changed. But it's been like that every time I've gone forward."

"You think he was lying?"

"No." Roman frowned. "No, I don't think so. I think that whatever butterfly effect—"

"Butterfly effect?" Dorothy interrupted.

"In chaos theory, the butterfly effect is a phenomenon whereby a minute localized change in a complex system can have large effects elsewhere."

"English, please."

"In the next five years, something is going to happen, probably something that seems small at the time. That small change will lead to bigger changes and bigger changes and so on, until—"

"The world becomes what we just saw."

Roman nodded. "Exactly."

Dorothy was still for a moment, processing this. She remembered walking around this city for the first time, with Avery. She'd spent much of her childhood wandering the dusty little frontier towns of the Midwest, and Seattle, in contrast, had seemed glorious, a city of the future, with its ferryboats and electric lights and charming university. She could've wandered through the narrow, meandering downtown streets for hours, neck craned back and eyes wide, taking in the sights.

She may not have wanted the life that came with becoming Mrs. Dr. Charles Avery, but oh how she'd loved this city.

An ache gripped her heart. "So we do something," she said, on an exhale. "We figure out this butterfly moment, or whatever it is, and we change it."

Roman lifted an eyebrow. "You think it's that easy? To

find one moment, one *second* in years and years of seconds? And even if you did find it, what then? How would you know that whatever choice you were making was the right one?"

Dorothy couldn't believe what she was hearing. "You propose we do nothing?"

He couldn't be saying that, surely, and yet he didn't argue.

Dorothy had to work to keep her voice steady. "For the last year we've been planning to save this city. What was all of that for if you're just going to stand by and let it be destroyed?"

"We have a few years left." Roman still wouldn't look at her. "And, because of what we did this morning, those years will include heat and electricity—"

"What does any of that matter if we're all going to die?" Dorothy leaned forward. "I thought you'd left the Professor for this, so that you could change our past and give this city a chance—"

But that wasn't exactly true, was it? Dorothy didn't actually know why he'd left the Professor. He'd never told her.

I'm afraid we haven't been acquainted long enough for that story.

She looked up at his face and saw that he looked younger than he usually did, his face softened by fear. It made it easier for her to imagine him as he must've looked when he'd worked with the Professor. She pictured him sneaking out in the dead of night to steal the old man's time machine. Traveling into the future again and again. Staring out at that desolate, black landscape, hoping it might change.

Something twisted in her chest. She couldn't imagine

how lonely that must've been.

She felt a lump form in her throat. "Roman—"

Roman stood, abruptly, and made a show of tugging his jacket straight. He wouldn't look at her. "It's getting late."

"You aren't *leaving*." Dorothy sat up taller. "We need to talk about this."

"Later," Roman said, glancing at her. He looked on the verge of saying something else but only shook his head and took up a glass of bourbon, downing it. He jerked his chin in goodbye and started for the door.

The nerve, Dorothy thought. She stood to follow him, noticing as she did that the guy at the bar had twisted around on his stool and was watching her. Her eyes landed on him as she made her way to the front of the bar, and she froze, feeling slapped.

Ash.

Ash was sitting at the bar, staring at her. His expression was stormy, eyebrows pulled down low on his forehead, gold eyes blazing. Electricity seared the air between them.

Dorothy's heart was doing something complicated inside of her chest.

What was he doing here?

He was the one who broke their gaze first. He stood and wove his way to the door at the back of the bar. He lingered for a moment and, though he didn't look back at her again, Dorothy understood.

He wanted her to follow him.

LOG ENTRY— JULY 2, 2074
06:32 HOURS
THE WORKSHOP

Today's crash: Dog darts across the street, causing a mother of three to swerve and drive her Chevy Avalanche into a tree.

No one dies in this one—not even the damn dog—but I'm going to keep this mother of three from having to replace her windshield if it's the last thing I do.

Don't even wish me luck. I don't need luck. I'm a man of science, for Christ's sake.

UPDATE—12:33 HOURS

This is almost comical at this point. Seriously, I'm sitting here laughing hysterically because I honestly don't know what else to do. If I don't laugh, I think I might cry.

I found the dog. I figured this time, it might be easier to deal with a dog than a person, you know? How hard is it to control a dog?! All I was going to do was get the dog on a leash and keep him from running across the street as the woman's Chevy Avalanche drove by.

But the dog hated the damn leash. As soon as I clipped it onto his collar, he started freaking out, thrashing and barking and pulling. I tried to keep hold of him, but he was too strong. He knocked me off my feet and darted into the road—

Right in front of the Avalanche. Which swerved. And hit a tree, cracking its windshield.

You know what this means, right? It means *I* caused the crash. I grabbed the dog and put him on the leash, and that's why he freaked out and darted across the street.

Did I cause the other crashes, too? Did delaying that driver at the diner cause him to drive more recklessly to make up for lost time? Did I put the idea to get on his motorcycle that day into that kid's head, just by showing up and telling him not to?

Is all of this my fault?

24

ASH

Ash moved down the hallway in a daze, his heart hammering in his ears. Black Cirkus posters blanketed the walls—THE PAST IS OUR RIGHT!—and any other time he might have ripped them down. But not now. Now, he barely saw them. His mind was focused on only one thing:

Would she come?

He hoped she would. It embarrassed him how much he hoped for this, but there it was. He felt like he was lit from within, like there was fire blazing in his chest, eating away at his skin and muscles and bones.

The hall grew cooler as he made his way toward the bathrooms, and a shiver passed through him. Distantly, he heard the sound of water sloshing against the docks on the other side of the bar's thin wall, wind pushing into the side of the building.

There was an extra door at the end of the hallway, an exit.

Ash glanced over his shoulder. Would Dorothy know to follow him?

He pushed the back door open—

Dorothy was just outside, waiting. Ash stepped onto the dock with her, letting the bar door close behind him. "You're already here," he said, surprised.

"I thought you . . . wanted me to come," Dorothy said, hesitant, fingers twisting around the braid hanging over her shoulder. It was messy, white curls escaping and frizzing in the damp. There were already a few strands plastered to her forehead and her neck, like she'd been out in the wet for a long time instead of just a few seconds.

"I just meant that you got back here quicker than I expected."

"I know a shortcut." Moonlight caught the silver locket at her neck. "I used to come out here a lot."

Ash waited for her to say more, and, when she didn't, he crossed the dock, hesitantly. His skin felt alive. Was it out of the question to reach for her? He didn't know. She seemed so different than she had the night before, at the masquerade.

He rested his hands on the wooden banister just beside her, close enough that his thumb grazed her hip. He could feel the heat radiating off her body. It made it hard for him to think. He couldn't remember what he'd wanted to talk to her about.

"I looked for you this morning," he said, and something dark passed over her face.

"You looked for Dorothy," she said. "I'm not Dorothy anymore."

He frowned. *Is that what she thought?* "A new name doesn't make you a new person."

"It's not just the new name, though, is it?"

"You mean . . ." He brought his hand to the scar that cut across her face, but she inhaled, sharp, before he could touch her. He froze, fingers hovering above her skin. "Is this . . . okay?"

She closed her eyes and was quiet, dark lashes trembling against her pale skin. "Yes."

He lowered his hand to her scar. Every nerve in his palm flared so that all he felt was spark and heat, and it was a long moment before his fingers processed the texture of her skin. He didn't know what he'd expected. The scar looked like it would be rough to the touch, but it was soft and warm and familiar. It was *her*.

She'd been holding herself stiffly but, the moment he touched her, she released a breath that was almost a sigh and seemed to melt into him. "Ash."

Ash lowered his forehead to hers. Her damp hair stuck to his skin, and he could feel the shape of her locket press into his chest. He was instantly transported back to the *Dark Star*, to the first time he'd touched her, the first time he'd kissed her. Had it really been only three weeks ago?

No. Not for her. Dorothy had lived a year between that moment and this one. The realization opened up a deep hole inside of him. Because of him, she'd spent a year here, alone.

"Come back with me." Ash hadn't realized what he was going to say until the words were already out of his mouth. "Please, you don't belong here."

"I wish I could." She pressed a hand to his chest, frowning. "But that's not why I came. There's something I need to ask you."

"Can it wait?" he murmured into her hair. She still smelled the same, like soap and lilies. How was that possible?

"It's important. I need you to think back. Did the Professor ever mention Nikola Tesla?"

The words were so strange that Ash frowned and leaned away from her, caught off guard. "What?"

"The Professor was doing experiments with Nikola Tesla." Dorothy cast an anxious glance at the door behind Ash and then shifted her gaze back to his face. "Did he ever say anything about that to you? Anything at all?"

"I don't think so." Ash frowned. "What—"

Dorothy cut him off. "They would've had to do with traveling through time without a vessel. Does that sound familiar?"

It didn't. Ash scratched the back of his neck. "It isn't possible to travel through time without a vessel. A few people tried, back before the Professor built his time machines, but the anil is too volatile, and they were all badly injured."

"Yes, but the Professor went on experimenting with it, to see whether he could find a way." Dorothy fiddled with the locket hanging from her neck, her fingers anxious. "Think.

Maybe he wrote something in that journal of his? Have you read the whole thing?"

Ash was already shaking his head when he remembered the ragged edges he'd found poking out of the binding. "Wait a minute," he said, almost to himself. "There were entries missing. I don't know where they went, but—"

He was interrupted by the sound of wood creaking, a footstep on the other side of the door, and he shifted into the shadows, his skin humming. A second later the back door swung open and the bartender walked onto the docks. She brought a cigarette to her lips, withdrawing a pack of matches from her coat pocket.

Ash turned to Dorothy—one hand lifting to point down a narrow dock that twisted back toward Dante's—and froze, heart pounding.

She was already gone.

I've made a huge mistake.

I—I don't know what I was thinking, really. I wanted to see it again, I suppose, to see what, if anything has changed.

But I never expected this.

I should explain. This morning, I once again took the *Dark Star* forward, into the future. But, instead of going just a few days ahead, this time I went one hundred years ahead.

I suppose I wanted to see how our world was going to turn out.

I exited the anil, and the world I saw before me was changed beyond my wildest nightmares.

I've been here for only a few hours, so my findings are rudimentary, at best. Everything is black. Ashes cover the ground and block out the sun. It's nearly ten o'clock in the morning, but it's still as dark as night. There's no vegetation, no animals, no people. I flew past WCAAT and found little more than a pile of rubble frozen in ice.

My heart hurts, writing that down. The most advanced school of technology the world has ever seen, and it's been reduced to nothing, to ashes.

This can't be happening . . . something catastrophic must've happened to have left the world like this. I have no way of knowing what it was, but I can only hope there's still time to change it back.

25

DOROTHY

Dorothy moved down the docks like a shadow, ears pricked, listening for any sound besides the shuffle of her own feet. There was none, though something musty-smelling rose up from the water, making her nose twitch. She didn't think she'd ever get over the smell of this city. How the perpetual damp left everything reeking of mold and rot.

She paused beside the door to the Fairmont's back stairwell, glancing over her shoulder to make sure she hadn't been followed.

The darkness twitched, and Dorothy steeled herself.

But no one came.

A moment passed and she still didn't move. It wasn't until she realized she was waiting for Ash to materialize in the darkness that she swore at herself and turned around.

Come with me, she remembered. And she pictured Ash's face as it had been the night before, his cheeks flushed pink, his eyes searching hers.

She couldn't go to him. Of course she couldn't, it was madness, his even coming here. It was better that she find Roman and try to talk some sense into him. But her heart felt heavy as she slipped through the Fairmont's door, and Ash's voice stayed with her long after she tried to push it away.

The door to Roman's room was open a crack, and a thin line of yellow light dribbled into the hallway. Dorothy lifted her hand to knock—

And then paused, frowning.

Roman was talking to someone.

Dorothy had never spied on Roman before. For the last year, he'd been her greatest ally, her friend, even. She trusted him, as much as she was capable of trusting anyone, and so she'd always extended him the courtesy of privacy.

But, for the first sixteen years of her life, she'd been a con artist. A sneak and a thief. Her mother had been the only family she had, and Loretta believed that someone was a fool if she bothered with things like friends.

Dorothy chewed on her lip. She knew perfectly well what her mother would do in this situation.

And so, holding her breath, she crept closer and pressed her ear against Roman's door.

"Higgens looks just like I remembered," Roman was saying. His warm tone surprised Dorothy. Usually he sounded like that only when he was speaking to her.

She leaned in closer.

"Thank God, I didn't see that horrible dog of hers," Roman continued. "I'm not sure I would've been able to resist giving it a good, hard kick. Do you remember when it got into a fight with Freddie and he came back with this huge chunk taken out of his fur? And then Higgens tried to pretend like her precious Pumpkin would *never* do something like that."

Dorothy frowned. *Higgens? Pumpkin?* She searched her memory for where she'd heard those names . . .

It came to her quickly. Emelda Higgens was the woman from the past with the dandelion-puff hair whose solar panels they'd stolen that morning. And Pumpkin . . . that was the name of her little dog.

Only, Roman was talking about her like he knew her. Had he lived on that street they'd looted? It made sense, Dorothy supposed. After all, he was the one who'd chosen the neighborhood, and he'd compiled the names of all the people who were going to die in the earthquake. Dorothy hadn't even bothered asking where he'd gotten them.

But why wouldn't he have just told her?

"Don't worry, Cassia, I wouldn't have *actually* kicked him," Roman continued. "It was weird seeing her again, actually. You know, now that I know what happens."

Cassia? There wasn't anyone named Cassia living in the Fairmont. Dorothy tried to remember if she'd seen Roman with a girl she hadn't recognized at the Dead Rabbit in the last week or so, and couldn't think of anyone.

A horrible thought entered her mind . . . Mac had once offered to let the Black Cirkus partake of his services. Not for free, mind, but for cheap. Dorothy had been disgusted by the idea, but what if Roman had taken him up on his offer? What if he knew one of the girls Mac kept in that horrible motel of his?

The thought twisted her stomach, and she quickly pushed it out of her mind. Roman wouldn't do that, she felt certain. But, then, who was he talking to?

She moved closer, and the floorboard beneath her foot gave a long, low creak.

Roman fell abruptly silent.

Blast.

Dorothy glanced over her shoulder, wondering how quickly she could duck back down the hall and around the corner. Before she could decide one way or another, Roman was pulling the door open and she was caught.

"Dorothy." Roman sounded surprised. "What are you doing here?"

"I—I wanted to make sure you were all right," Dorothy said. She'd never minded lying before, but it felt strange to lie to Roman, just as it had felt strange to spy on him. She struggled to remember why she'd actually come here in the first place. "You seemed upset back at the Dead Rabbit."

Roman studied her for another moment and then offered up a quizzical smile. "Right."

Did he know she'd been listening in on his conversation? Dorothy couldn't tell. She rose to tiptoes, hoping the long cloak would mask the movement, and tried to subtly peer past his shoulder.

His eyebrows went up. "Looking for something?"

Her eyes snapped back to his face, cheeks flushing. "Of

course not. It's just . . . I thought I heard voices."

Roman's expression sharpened, giving Dorothy the impression of someone caught in a lie. Before she could call him on it, he stepped aside, flinging the door open so that Dorothy could see the room behind him:

Unmade bed. Dresser scattered with old photos. Armchair covered in dirty clothes. But no sign of who Roman had been speaking to.

"There's no one here," he said. But the light caught his dark eyes, making it seem as though something within them was flickering.

Staring back at him, Dorothy was reminded of a one-man band she and her mother had walked past while they were living in Chicago. The musician wore a mask, which he removed as Dorothy glanced back at him. Beneath, he wore another mask. Dorothy hadn't looked back again after that, but whenever she thought of that moment she imagined that he wore another mask beneath the second, and another beneath that, and another, going on forever.

Roman was like that. Masks on masks on masks. She wondered if she'd ever see his true face.

She rocked back on her heels, disappointed. "I must've imagined it," she said.

But, of course, she knew she hadn't.

26

ASH

Ash took the long way home. Waves rippled around his boat, and the angry growl of the motor cut the night in half. The only things that broke up the darkness around him were the white-barked trees that grew up from the waters, standing like skeletal sentries in the dark. He barely saw them. His head was still too full of Dorothy and the Professor's missing journal entries and the possibility of traveling through time without a vessel.

He didn't even notice the schoolhouse until he was pulling up next to the dock that ran alongside it, one hand automatically reaching back to cut the motor. He tied his boat up and then hauled the window open, grunting again as he climbed inside and landed, hard, on the floor. There was a light on down the hall.

Ash followed it to the kitchen and found Zora at the table, her father's notes and textbooks spread out before her, one foot propped against the lowest rung of her chair, knee hopping up and down.

"Zor," he said.

"You're back," she breathed, standing so quickly she knocked her chair back a foot. "I've been waiting for hours."

Had it been hours? "Yeah, I'm sorry about that." He pushed the damp hair off his forehead, trying to think how he could explain his strange interaction with Dorothy. "Listen—"

"Sit down," she said, yanking a second chair out from under the table. The wood scraped against the floorboards, the sound making Ash cringe.

"You trying to wake the whole place?"

"I don't know." Zora rubbed the spot of skin between her eyes and then released a strange half laugh. "God, maybe we should? Will you please just sit down?"

Ash sat, his frown deepening. "Zor," he said carefully. "What is it?"

"I think I had a breakthrough." She shook her head, as though she couldn't quite believe it herself, and then leaned over the kitchen table, pulling a loose sheet of paper out from under a stack of smudged notebooks and old napkins covered in the Professor's scribbles. "I haven't asked Chandra to look through it yet because I don't know if she'll . . . I just need a second set of eyes on it first. Can you look at it? Please?"

Ash squinted down at the squiggles and scribbles. They could've been written in ancient Greek for how well he understood them, but he frowned, thoughtfully, and scratched his chin. He could feel Zora at his shoulder, practically vibrating as she waited for him to say something.

Finally, he said, "Can you just tell me what I'm supposed to be seeing here?"

"Oh, right. Okay, so you see this number here?" She pointed to a scribbled line of digits that looked like a phone number.

Ash nodded.

"This was recorded after my father's first trips back in time. And these, see how these figures keep going up? They're moving in relation to the frequency and length of the trips my father has taken. It never occurred to me to try to match them all up before, but look here." There was a pause, while Zora waited for Ash to see what she saw. "They fit, perfectly. See?"

Ash frowned. "Zora, I'm going to need you to just tell me what you're trying to say."

"Seattle's on the Cascadia Fault, right?" Zora layered her hands one on top of the other, so that her knuckles were aligned. "It looks like this. Every time we go back in time, there's a tremor."

She moved her hands so that her knuckles bunched together. "The tremors do this to the fault line, right? So the more it happens, the more the energy builds up and the fault line gets all cranky and then—"

She snapped her hands into a fist. "Earthquake."

Ash felt a sinking in his gut.

Zora said, in a rush, "I started thinking about it when we watched the *Black Crow* go through the anil. Remember how the earth trembled? Like there was going to be a quake?"

"There are tremors all the time now," Ash said.

"Exactly," said Zora. "Because the Black Cirkus has been using the anil more frequently. And if you look back at the earthquakes that were largest, historically, they all match up with the patterns of my father's travels. I never put it together, before, because it's not like we go back in time and then suddenly—bam—there's an earthquake. But each trip through time brings us closer to the next earthquake. *See?*"

She pointed and, this time, the lines of notes and numbers made a little more sense. Ash recognized the dates when they'd gone back in time, the magnitude numbers used to quantify the scale of an earthquake. His head started pounding, a deep, steady throb that made his eyesight go bloody.

"That can't be right," he said. "The Professor would've noticed."

"Dad was always inside the time machine when we went back, so he wouldn't have noticed the tremors. And it's like I said, this sort of energy takes time to build up. By the time the earthquakes finally occurred, they seemed random, but . . . but they're not." A breath, and then, "The earthquakes are caused by *time travel*. They're caused by us."

27

DOROTHY

Dorothy let herself into her room, feeling twitchy and cold. Her head was so full of Roman's lies, and Mac's bribes, and the dead, bleak future she'd just seen that she doubted she'd ever be able to drift to sleep. She found herself wishing that she'd taken a few more swigs of the bourbon Mac had brought them, if only to quiet the worries running through her head.

She hesitated at the door, wondering if there was any left at the bar, half considering going back to fetch it.

In the end, she only closed the hotel room door behind her, deciding against it. It would be dawn soon, and then she and Roman would need to climb back into the time machine for their second mission. There was barely time for sleep.

She removed her cloak and wet boots and pulled her white hair away from her face.

And then she touched the small, silver locket hanging from her mirror, like she always did when she got to her room, sending it swaying.

28

ASH

NOVEMBER 8, 2077, NEW SEATTLE

It was near morning, and Ash's eyes glazed as he read through the Professor's notes again.

If x is equal to y at the time of a storm, then the formula for calculating the stabilization of the anil (or S) would become:

$S = P0 + \rho xy$

He swore under his breath, rubbing the skin between his eyes. He could pick out words and phrases that felt familiar, but the second he tried to make sense of them, everything crumbled.

Zora was a lot smarter than he was, though. A hell of a lot smarter. If she thought these notes meant time travel was causing the earthquakes . . .

His head started pounding, a deep, steady throb that made his eyesight go bloody. It would mean they were responsible for the deaths of tens of thousands of people—that they could be responsible for the deaths of *millions* more if they didn't figure out a way to stop the Black Cirkus before they traveled through time again.

There was a creak on the floorboards behind him. Ash whirled around, fingers twitching at his waist, itching to reach for the gun he'd tucked into the back of his jeans.

But it was just Zora. She leaned against the doorframe, eyes going soft as she considered him.

"What do you think?" she asked.

Ash faltered. "You know more than me about all this."

"Yeah, but I'm looking for a second opinion." She took a step closer to the desk. "So?"

Ash was quiet. The numbers swam before him, but even he could see that they added up to something, telling a story he didn't want to believe.

He lifted his eyes to Zora. "You sure about this equation?"

"As sure as I've been about anything." Zora sighed and dropped into the chair next to him, swiping a hand over her forehead. "You know, if my dad were here, he'd do a whole line of experiments to prove exactly this. Come up with a question, form a hypothesis, test the hypothesis, et cetera."

"There isn't time for that," Ash broke in, eyes moving to the window on the other side of the room. The sky outside had grown light around the edges, a ghost haze hovering on the surface of the still, black water. "Just . . . dumb it down for me, will you? What, exactly, are you saying will happen if the Black Cirkus travels through time again?"

Zora thought for a few seconds and then she swept some cogs and gears into a pile on the center of the kitchen table.

"Think of it like this. Every time you go back in time, it's like you're stacking one cog on top of another, right?" She demonstrated. "And the more you do it, the more unsteady the tower gets."

She added a few more cogs. The tower started to wobble. "See that there? How the tower wobbles? That's like the tremors we experience. But you never know which cog is going to cause the tower to fall. It depends on the shape of the cog, whether you gave the tower enough time to stabilize before you placed it on top—"

"Whether someone knocks into the table?" Ash asked.

"It's not a perfect metaphor," Zora said. "All I'm saying is that every single trip we take through time brings us closer to the earthquake that could destroy the world. The next time the Black Cirkus goes into the anil . . ."

She placed another cog on the tower, and the entire thing toppled.

Ash released a ragged sigh. "You think the Black Cirkus's next trip back in time could cause a massive earthquake?"

"Not just a massive earthquake—*the* massive earthquake." Zora squeezed the bridge of her nose. "And I don't actually know. My father's calculations for when the earthquake would hit the city were based on a far less frequent use of the Puget Sound anil. But he was also using metrics from the *Dark Star*, and the *Black Crow* is a smaller ship, so it's possible that it hasn't been doing quite as much damage."

"The size of the ship matters?" Ash asked.

Zora nodded. "Think of a smaller ship like a smaller cog

on the tower. The smaller the cog, the less likely it'll cause the tower to fall over, right? But every cog, no matter the size, makes the tower less stable. It's the same with the anil. It's still dangerous, but there's no way of knowing how dangerous. . . ."

"They leave at dawn," Ash said.

Zora fumbled with the watch at her wrist. "That's not for— Oh, shit."

Ash was already pulling his jacket off the back of his chair. "If we go now, we might still be able to stop them."

29

DOROTHY

NOVEMBER 8, 2077, NEW SEATTLE

It was early, and the Fairmont garage was cool and dark, only the thinnest glimmer of silver light making its way through the dirty glass. Dorothy stood beside a window, fingers twisting in the folds of her coat.

She closed her eyes, breathing as nausea rolled through her. She imagined she could hear the sounds of the crowd past the roar of wind and waves crashing into the concrete walls. She could picture them clapping and stomping their feet as they waited for her and Roman to fly over their heads, and the image was so clear that she could almost feel the vibration spreading through the concrete floor of the garage and trembling up her legs.

It left her on edge. She and Roman were supposed to be going back in time for medical equipment to help the city's sick and downtrodden. But what was the point of saving this city if it was only going to be destroyed again?

"You look like death," Roman said, coming up behind her. "Didn't you sleep?"

Dorothy looked at him, taking in the green cast to his skin, the firm press of his lips. "Did you?"

"Well enough," Roman said, voice falsely cheerful.

Lie, Dorothy thought, bitter. When had they started lying to each other?

She fixed a stiff smile on her face. "Well then, so did I."

Another lie. She hadn't slept at all. She'd sat at the edge of her bed, watching the window and waiting for morning. And, all the while, a cold dread built inside of her.

Butterfly effect, Roman had said. One single moment had the power to change the course of humanity. Why weren't they trying to figure out what it was? Even if it was a fool's mission, it seemed to her that they should at least try.

She felt numb as she followed Roman into the *Black Crow* and settled into the passenger seat beside him, fingers moving woodenly over her seat belt.

She thought of the Fairmont's black walls and broken windows.

"The *Black Crow* is moving into position for departure," Roman said. Dorothy curled her hands into fists.

A moment later, the time machine rumbled to life below them.

30

ASH

Ash crouched at the front of the rickety motorboat, his heart beating in his throat. He leaned forward, as though he could make the boat travel faster through sheer force of will. Sheets of water crashed over him, soaking his shirt, slapping into his face.

He had eyes only for the swirling tunnel in the distance. The anil.

The *Black Crow* was already there, a blight on the landscape; a dark, black smudge in the early-morning light. Ash gritted his teeth.

He turned and shouted over his shoulder, "Can't this thing go any faster?"

"It's a boat, not a plane," Zora called back. "Now will you sit?"

Ash turned his back to her, ignoring this. His throat felt raw, and nerves thrummed through him, seeming to make his whole body vibrate. He pressed the heels of his hands into the side of the boat.

"Come on," he murmured. He hadn't prayed in years, but he felt like doing it now, like offering up this fierce hope to anyone who might be listening.

They were still yards away from the anil when the *Black Crow* began to hover.

"No," said Ash, his voice hushed. Everything inside of him seemed to tense.

The time machine moved forward, into position.

Ash felt his blood boil beneath his skin.

No.

He saw Dorothy's face the way it'd looked during their last meeting, behind the Dead Rabbit. Hair wet and plastered to her skin, fingers anxiously fumbling with her locket.

It isn't possible to travel through time without a vessel. . . .

Yes, but the Professor went on experimenting with it, to see whether he could find a way.

Ash stood, the motorboat rocking beneath him.

"Ash!" Zora shouted. "Sit down!"

He barely registered her voice. He heard a kind of roaring in his ears, something louder than the motorboat's tinny engine and the crashing water and all the other sounds that made up the night around them. His hands had started to tremble, and something, some pressure, was building inside of his chest, making him ache.

He couldn't let this happen. He had to do something. Zora said that a smaller ship wouldn't cause as much damage to the anil. If that were true, then *no* ship shouldn't cause any damage, right?

If there was a way to travel through time without a time machine, without EM . . .

The *Black Crow* was halfway into the anil when Ash dove out of the rowboat. The second he hit the water, he could feel the pull of the time tunnel sucking him toward it, like water into a drain. He couldn't swim, couldn't fight against it.

All he could do was be still and let it take him.

No man had ever survived moving through an anil without a vessel before. Those who'd tried had their skin ripped from their bones, their internal organs liquefied. But Ash wasn't afraid. He'd seen his own death, and so he knew he didn't die here.

The last thing he heard before he disappeared in time was the sound of Zora screaming.

31

DOROTHY

JULY 10, 2074, NEW SEATTLE

Dorothy felt her breath catch as she stared up at the hospital looming above them. It was dark here, past midnight, and every light in the building above them was blazing. The parking lot was filled with cars, and people crowded the sidewalk, unloading stretchers from ambulances and barking orders at one another.

She swallowed. She'd been to the hospital with Avery a few times, back in 1913. The tiny, two-story Providence Medical Center had seemed massive to her then, the doctors who'd filled the halls impossibly impressive in their stark white jackets and scrub caps.

Those old doctors were nothing like the people before her now. It was like comparing a fighter jet to a rickety bicycle. Where the doctors from her time were neat and orderly, mostly older men with gray hair and spectacles, these were young and fast and . . . *sleek*. Their scrubs had a metallic sheen, and their equipment was more advanced than anything Dorothy had seen before.

And wouldn't it be? This was 2074, the most advanced the world would get before the mega-quake took it all away. It was right that Dorothy felt intimidated.

She looked over at Roman and saw that he had one hand pressed to his front shirt pocket, fingers anxiously tapping his chest.

She frowned. "Everything all right?"

Roman dropped his hand, like he was worried about giving something away. "Yes, of course," he said, but there was a rough edge to his voice that betrayed much darker emotions.

Dorothy swallowed, uneasy. She didn't know whether she should push Roman or let him keep his secrets. Every question she could think to ask was a version of one she'd already tried.

"All right, then," she said instead. "Let's get this over with."

Roman had planned this con on his own.

"I wouldn't even call it a con," he'd told her. "The hospitals were a mess in the years after that first earthquake; there were too many patients, too many injured, not enough doctors. A child could've snuck inside."

"I hope your plan is a bit more advanced," she'd said.

A roll of his eyes. "We'll go in through the morgue. No one's going to look twice at two emergency responders returning with bodies. It'll get us through the door, at least, and that's the hardest part. After that, we just need to work quickly."

"B-bodies?" Dorothy had asked, her voice thick.

Roman had only grinned at her. "Body bags," he'd corrected. "And don't worry, they'll be empty."

Empty though the body bags may be, they were still *heavy*. They weren't actually bags but hard, plastic cases attached to stretchers. Dorothy gritted her teeth as she pushed hers before her, careful to hold it steady as the wheels crunched over gravel and concrete.

They crossed the parking lot in silence, carefully avoiding eye contact with the other medical professionals swarming around them. Roman had procured the body bags, and uniforms, which were the same odd metallic scrubs that the other hospital workers were wearing. They didn't have an ambulance, and Dorothy had been concerned that this would look suspicious. Now she could see that it had been foolish of her to worry. There was chaos in the parking lot, so many people rushing into the hospital that it was impossible to see where they were all coming from. She and Roman blended in easily.

They reached the sidewalk that wrapped around the hospital's main entrance, and the uneven ground beneath the wheels of her stretcher became smooth pavement. Her heart thrummed anxiously. She glanced at Roman, but he kept his eyes trained ahead, jaw tensed in concentration.

The front doors whooshed open, releasing a blast of

cool air. Dorothy smelled the sharp, antiseptic smell of the hospital; she heard phones ringing in the distance and the mechanical sound of someone speaking over an intercom. She had to remind herself not to look shocked.

A young man with a clipboard stood just inside the doors. He appeared to be checking people's credentials.

His eyes passed over them, disinterested, and landed back on his clipboard. "Where are you headed?"

Dorothy's palms grew clammy. "We—"

"We have two DOAs," Roman said, nodding at the body bags. "This is just a drop."

The man flicked a hand, already moving to the people who'd come in behind them. "Morgue's in the basement."

And that was it. They were in.

Dorothy sped up a little so that she was walking beside Roman now. She tried, again, to catch his eye and, again, he wouldn't look at her. She noticed that there was sweat glistening on his forehead and a crease wrinkling the skin between his eyes: nerves. But why was he so nervous? They were in. The hard part was over.

They entered an elevator, Dorothy giving a little start as it began to drop. She'd been inside an elevator before, but she was never fully prepared for the surreal sensation of the floor moving beneath her. She braced a hand against the wall, her stomach turning over. She much preferred stairs.

They descended deep into the building, stopping at the basement. The doors opened onto an empty hall. Lights flickered—somewhat ominously, Dorothy thought—and the walls were painted a sickly green. It gave her the feeling of being underwater.

Roman nodded at a sign: MEDICAL STORAGE, MORGUE.

"Here we are," he murmured, moving ahead.

Dorothy swallowed, tasting something bitter at the back of her throat. Glancing at the storage rooms, she saw shelves stuffed with bandages and gauze and glinting glass bottles. Their plan was to sneak inside those rooms and load up the empty body bags with as many supplies as they could manage, and then bring them back to New Seattle.

Roman pushed his stretcher past the storage room with a soft grunt.

Dorothy hesitated. He was supposed to go *into* the storage room and start loading up medication, but he kept moving, pushing his stretcher farther down the hall.

"Where are you going?" she asked.

"I have to find something first," he said. "Don't worry, we'll go back."

Something clenched in Dorothy's chest. He sounded anxious. She'd never heard Roman sound like that before.

The wheels of his stretcher squeaked over the hospital's linoleum floors. Roman was halfway down the hall now, but he didn't slow down, and he didn't turn.

Swallowing, Dorothy followed him.

32

ASH

Something coarse and sharp pressed into Ash's cheek. Rain pelted the back of his neck.

Ash's back arched as he coughed up a lungful of seawater. Everything in his body ached, and the ground seemed to shift and move beneath him.

He forced his eyes open, but the rain obscured his eyesight so that, for a moment, all he saw was gray and black. He could feel water lapping at his feet, the cold seeping into his boots.

The last thing he remembered was leaping out of the motorboat and Zora's screaming. He'd thought that the anil was pulling him in, that he might somehow follow the *Black Crow* into the time tunnel, but he must've been mistaken. The tide must've dragged him back to shore.

Well that was a failed experiment, he thought, pushing himself off the ground. He blinked through the rain, hoping that

Zora wasn't too far, that she might be able to take him home. He lifted his head—

And froze.

The Seattle cityscape spread out before him, dark and glittering. It wasn't the hulking black outline of New Seattle's remaining skyscrapers that Ash was familiar with but the dazzling, lit-up skyline of the city before the flood. The roads were dry, and buildings rose high into the air, every window golden and glowing. The old highway curved through it all and, on it, Ash could just make out the twinkling of headlights as cars and trucks and motorcycles roared past.

And then there was the ground itself. He was on a beach, a real beach. Ash laughed and dug his fingers into the sand, amazed that he hadn't realized it before. There were no beaches left in New Seattle. Everything was underwater.

He'd gone to the past. Somehow, unbelievably, he'd traveled through time without a vessel. Without any exotic matter.

It . . . shouldn't have been possible. Ash gave his head a hard shake and pushed himself to his hands and knees, trying to make sense of what had just happened. People had tried before. The Professor had performed experiment after experiment. This thing that he'd just done should've killed him, but it didn't. *Why?*

Ash found himself wishing that Zora had come back with him, that she were here to offer him some sort of explanation for what he'd just done. But she wasn't, which meant that he'd have to figure out what to do next all on his own. It was a more daunting prospect than it should've been.

Standing, he peered up at the city, shielding his eyes against the fierce glow of light. In her broadcast, Dorothy said that she and Roman were headed back to the old hospital to pick up medical supplies. Ash thought it might be too much to hope that he'd not only traveled back in time but also somehow managed to wind up at the exact moment that Dorothy and Roman had gone back to. But, hell, stranger things had happened today.

He could see the top floors of the hospital from his spot on the beach. It was downtown, one of the largest buildings in the city. Couldn't be more than a mile away.

Pulling his wet leather jacket more firmly around his shoulders, Ash set out for the hospital.

33

DOROTHY

Down dark and twisted hallways. Past more rooms filled with medical equipment and drugs they were supposed to be stealing.

Roman didn't stop, but said only, "This way."

And now, the skin on the back of Dorothy's neck crept. His voice sounded . . .

Feverish. Desperate.

He stopped at a room that looked just like all the others, abandoning his empty body bag at the door. "Come on," he murmured, seeming to speak to himself.

Dorothy stayed in the hall, wary and watchful.

Roman knocked a bottle over with his elbow. It toppled and then rolled off the shelf, exploding on impact with the hard tile floor, spraying the toes of Roman's heavy boots. He appeared not to notice.

Dorothy's palms had started to sweat. Something was very wrong.

"Come on," Roman murmured, digging a hand through his hair. Dorothy came up behind him, reading the medicine labels over his shoulder.

"Insulin?" she read.

Roman's hand jerked forward, snatching a few small bottles off the shelves, knocking even more to the ground. He shoved them into his pockets, his movements erratic.

And then he was in the hall again, running for the exit.

Dorothy followed him up a staircase, through a set of heavy metal doors. She felt the prick of water on her cheeks and, blinking, realized that they were outside and it had started to rain. The streets were dark and glittering, and even the shadows seemed edged in light.

"Roman, wait!" she called, but Roman didn't turn around. He was racing across an expanse of black asphalt, boots slapping wetly against the pavement. They must've exited at the back of the hospital because she saw no sign of the crowd and chaos that had been gathered out front. Swearing, she darted into the street after him—

A sound like a bullhorn blared through the night, shocking her. She stopped short as a car skidded to a stop inches away.

"S-sorry," she said, though she couldn't see the driver beyond the rain-soaked windshield.

Roman had ducked between two buildings. She was going to lose him. Heart pounding, she hurried the rest of the way across the street.

Tall buildings. Thinly gathered trees. Dorothy didn't have time to stop and marvel at the world she was running through. She could only just manage to keep Roman in her sights. He was faster than she'd expected him to be, and he showed no signs of stopping to wait for her. Wind screamed in her ears. The rain came down harder, plastering her uniform to her shoulders.

She caught sight of red brick. Pink cherry blossoms. Black concrete gave way to grass, skyscrapers became tall trees and quaint, brick buildings.

Still, Dorothy didn't know where they were until she saw the first tent.

She slowed to a walk, her chest aching. First it was just one tent, nestled below the trees, door flap fluttering in the wind. And then there were half a dozen, each seeming to appear from the shadows as though by magic, and then the tents were all Dorothy could see.

Her heart seemed to go still inside of her chest. This was Tent City, she realized. Roman had told her about this place a long time ago.

The emergency pop-up shelters had been erected on the grounds of the university in the days right after the first earthquake. The Black Cirkus had started here, as a small gang roaming these tents, looking for food. They'd gotten their name because of how the tents sort of resembled old circus tents. Though the fabric looked near black in the darkness, Dorothy knew they were actually purple. Or they had been when the tents had first gone up. Now they were old and torn, covered in mold and dirt and grime. There were a few old signs propped out front.

The past is our right! Join the Black Cirkus!

It was fascinating to see this place firsthand after hearing about it for so long, but Dorothy was confused. Why had they come here now?

She picked her way through the tents, looking for Roman. There weren't a lot of people out and about in the rain, and every movement made her start, nerves creeping up her neck. Mostly it was just squirrels and raccoons darting between the tents, their glassy eyes reflected back at her in the darkness.

"Roman?" she called softly, eyes straining. She stepped into a clearing surrounded on all sides by tents. "Where—"

She broke off, walking directly into Roman's back. His dark hair and clothes had blended easily with the night so that she hadn't seen him until she was nearly upon him. He stared straight ahead, not seeming to notice that she'd joined him.

Dorothy followed his gaze and saw that they were not alone in the clearing. There, straight ahead, were the two children from their trip to collect the solar panels, the ones who'd been playing in the house next door. They were two years older, but Dorothy immediately recognized the girl's dark braids, the boy's skinny frame. And yet something was wrong.

The boy was on his knees in the clearing between the tents, and he was gasping, his eyes dark pits of grief. The girl lay in his arms. Her eyes were open and staring, her limbs already rigid.

She was . . . dead.

A moan came from Roman. He dropped to his knees. The

bottle of insulin fell from his fingers, landing in the mud.

Yards away, the boy crouching in the grass echoed the sound. "Hold on, Cassia," he whispered, patting the little girl's face. "You have to hold on, okay? Help will be here soon."

Dorothy went cold. She knew that voice. It sounded younger than she'd ever heard it, but it was still, undoubtedly, Roman. The boy crouching in the mud was Roman himself, two years ago. And the dead girl could only be . . .

"Is that . . . your sister?" Dorothy asked, numb.

She couldn't think of anything else to say. Roman knew all her secrets, and yet he'd never trusted her with this.

Had he trusted anyone? Or had he held this grief inside for years, suffering alone?

"I thought . . . if I got to her in time." His voice sounded strangled. "But I was too late."

His eyes shifted up to Dorothy's, his face a silent plea. His skin was nearly as pale as the little girl lying in the mud.

Dorothy opened her mouth, and then closed it again, finding that she couldn't speak. The picture she'd spent the last year forming broke apart inside of her head. All those times Roman had seemed to bite his tongue, all the dark looks and secrets. It had been this. He'd been trying to come up with a plan to save his sister's life.

She lowered herself beside him, placing a hesitant hand on his shoulder. She expected him to swat her away, but he didn't. He reached for her hand and gripped it.

"You—you never told me," she said, her voice thick. "Why—"

But then Roman's eyes shifted to something behind her, and his expression darkened. He dropped her hand and stood.

"What's he doing here?" he spat, bitter.

Dorothy followed his gaze to the rain-drenched figure standing on the other side of the clearing, watching them. She saw soaked leather and dirty-blond hair against sun-burned skin, and, though she recognized those things, she couldn't make sense of them here, not until Ash took a step closer, his eyes moving to hers.

A feeling somewhere between excitement and terror flared through her.

Oh no, oh no, not here.

Ash seemed to understand that it would be a mistake to address her here, and so he turned back to Roman, hands held out before him, as though in surrender.

"Roman," he said, taking another step into the clearing. "I didn't—"

Dorothy would never know what he was about to say. Before he could finish, Roman had leaped forward, his expression twisted into a look of deepest loathing. He crashed into Ash with a grunt and the two of them went tumbling to the ground.

34

ASH

Ash flew backward, his head smacking into the ground with a wet thud. He'd been so surprised by the attack that he hadn't been able to prepare himself for the fall. His arms and legs cartwheeled, cartoonishly, doing nothing to brace his body for the sudden impact with the ground.

He blinked, stunned. For a moment, all he could see was mud and gray sky.

And then, Roman was leaning over him. "Old friend," he murmured. He fisted his hands around the front of Ash's jacket, pushing him deeper into the mud. "How the hell did you get here?"

Ash didn't answer but grabbed Roman by the shoulders and shoved him off. Roman tumbled back into the dirt, a grim smile on his lips. Ash was vaguely aware of a slight, white shape standing in the shadows just behind him. Dorothy.

He waited a beat, hoping she'd jump in and explain about their meeting behind the Dead Rabbit, and how she'd tipped him off on the possibility of traveling through time without any EM. But she only looked at him with a puzzled expression on her face, and said nothing.

"I followed you," Ash said, not sure how else to put it. He'd reached the hospital quickly—it was closer to the shore where he'd washed up than he'd remembered—but he'd been too intimidated by the swarm of medical personnel gathered outside to try going through the front. Instead, he crept around back, reasoning that, in most cases, a back entrance was far easier to break into.

He hadn't been able to put the theory to the test, though. The back door flew open before he got there, and Dorothy and Roman had come stumbling out, running. Ash hadn't known what to do. So he'd gone after them.

Darting past cars and ducking through the rain until, finally, they'd reached Tent City and found a younger Roman kneeling in the clearing, holding his dying sister in his arms.

Ash had felt numb, watching them. The Roman kneeling in the clearing had been younger than he'd been when Ash had known him, but not so much younger. A year, perhaps. And yet Roman had never mentioned a sister. Not once.

"Why didn't you tell me about her?" Ash asked Roman now.

A snort of a laugh and Roman said, "And what, exactly, would you have done about it, *Asher*?" He spat the name, as though it'd left a foul taste in his mouth. "Would you have tried to help? Or would you have been like the Professor, telling me we don't use time travel to change the past with one

243

breath, and then going back to save the people he loved with the next?"

Something heavy settled over Ash's shoulders. He knew exactly what Roman was talking about. After his wife died, the Professor went back in time over and over again, trying to save her. The Professor had always maintained that time travel shouldn't be used to change the past, that they didn't yet know the effects that might have on the world around them. But, when it came to the woman he loved, he hadn't cared.

Ash had always wondered why Roman had betrayed them. Of course he'd wondered. Roman had been one of them, after all. He'd been Ash's best friend. The Professor had thought of him as a son. But, beneath the wonder, there'd been anger, and the anger had a way of rising up to obscure it. It was so much easier to believe that Roman had left because he was selfish, because something about him was wrong. Never had Ash considered that he'd wanted to save someone, too.

Ash found his eyes drawn back to the clearing where Roman's dead sister had lain. She was gone now, and so was the younger Roman, probably frightened by the fighting, but Ash could still see the flattened bit of ground where they'd been.

He could understand why his presence here had set off Roman. Roman was a fiercely private person, and Ash had seen a glimpse of him at his most vulnerable. This was a secret he'd been guarding for years, and now it was out.

"Roman," Ash said, his voice thick. "I didn't know, I swear—"

Apologizing seemed to be the wrong move. A grunt, and Roman was lunging for Ash again, fist swinging. His first punch missed, barely catching Ash on the arm, but his second connected with Ash's jaw, spinning him back a step. Ash blinked, seeing stars. *Damn.*

"Hit me," Roman spat at him, furious. "Come on, Asher. Aren't you going to defend yourself?"

"Wasn't my plan," Ash said, stretching out his injured jaw. He could feel his bones shifting in place where Roman had hit him. The pain wasn't bad, yet, though he knew he'd feel it later. "But I've got to admit, that last punch didn't help."

Roman gave him a withering look. From this distance, his eyes were just dark pools of reflected light. "I barely touched you."

"Still hurts."

"Sorry about that."

Ash looked up at him, hoping for remorse, but the look in Roman's eyes was cold. He sprang, but Ash was ready for him this time. He feinted to the left, and Roman slammed into one of the tents, the fabric billowing around him as he went down.

A second later, Roman was up again, head lowered, charging at him. Ash thought he heard the sound of Dorothy's voice, shouting at them to stop, but it was hard to make out with the blood pumping in his ears. Roman hit him square in the chest, but Ash manage to crack off a single blow to Roman's gut before Roman's fist got him in the eye—bright white burst of pain—and then he was jerking back, swearing.

"You're a better fighter than you used to be," Roman said. "You finally let Zora teach you to throw a punch?"

Ash tasted blood in his mouth. With a jerk of his chin, he spit it into the mud.

It was a joke, sort of. Back when he'd first come to the future, he'd been truly awful in a fight, worse than both Roman and Zora, despite being the only one of them who'd been in a war.

Throat dry, he said, "Well, you know how bossy she can be."

"She didn't do a very good job. You still drop your shoulder." Roman was inching toward him, again, his hands balling into fists.

The muscles in Ash's leg tensed. His heart beat hard and fast in his chest.

"Old habits die hard," he muttered.

Dorothy's voice came from the darkness, "Ash, just *go*."

"Yes, Ash," echoed Roman, mocking. There was a smear of blood on his cheek, but Ash didn't know whose it was. "Just go."

Ash suppressed a grimace. The awful thing was, he didn't think he *could* go. He wasn't sure how he'd gotten here, and he had no idea how he was going to get back.

If they didn't offer him a ride, he might end up stuck.

35

DOROTHY

If these idiot boys didn't kill each other, Dorothy might do it for them.

"What are you thinking?" she snapped. Roman had been inching toward Ash, taunting him. "Are you trying to get us all caught?"

Roman's lip curled in a sneer, and he didn't answer her. It made Dorothy want to slap him. She'd been too shocked by the first few blows to do more than scream. It embarrassed her now, that this had been her reaction, but she couldn't help it. She'd always hated fighting.

She reached out to cup Roman's shoulder, and he finally turned, giving her a long look. He had one eyebrow arched, cool and furious, but, otherwise, she couldn't make sense of the expression on his face.

"You're taking his side?" he asked, in a voice that was more hurt than angry.

Side? "Are you serious? The two of you are acting like

children, and I want to know how he got here."

She was pretty sure Ash hadn't managed to stow away on the *Black Crow*. The ship had been in the Fairmont parking garage since their last trip, guarded by a team of their best Freaks. She'd have heard if he'd managed to sneak in.

A moment passed, and then Roman's shoulders slumped, reminding Dorothy of a chastised child.

"He started it," he muttered. But he let his arm drop.

Children, Dorothy thought.

That should have been the end of it. Dorothy thought it *would* be the end of it—

But then Ash lunged, slamming into Roman and knocking him to the ground. Dorothy turned and found the two of them rolling around in the mud again.

She let her eyes close for a fraction of a second, annoyance thrumming inside of her.

Oh, for heaven's sake.

The last time all three of them had been together, things had gone just as poorly. She still remembered that moment on the docks outside the Fairmont. Roman and Ash would've fought to the death if she hadn't intervened.

Since showing up in New Seattle a year ago, she'd had this fantasy that she might just shove the two of them in a room together and force them to work out their differences but, now, she could see that it wouldn't be that simple. She hated the both of them in that moment.

But she couldn't just let them *kill* each other. She couldn't bear to lose either of them.

She waited until the boys had separated, and then she grabbed Roman from behind, using a hold he'd taught her months ago: she merely grabbed his arm and pinned it behind his back, wrist cranked upward to send pain shooting through his forearm. It was a move designed to use an attacker's own strength against him.

Roman gasped in pain and shot her a furious, betrayed look.

"*Ash*," Dorothy said, and she was surprised by the sound of her own voice, low and pleading. "Please. Just go home."

And now Ash turned his gaze on her, hurt. Dorothy felt something inside of her clench. He looked back at Roman.

"Fine," he spat. His lip was bleeding. He glanced at Dorothy, opened his mouth like he was about to say something else, and then shook his head, apparently deciding against it. Shoulders bunched up around his ears, he turned to go.

36

ASH

Ash should've just asked Dorothy and Roman to give him a ride, but he couldn't bring himself to do it. He opened his mouth wide, stretching his jaw again. His face throbbed where Roman had punched him.

"Asshole," he muttered, even though no one was there to hear him. He was standing on the beach, staring at the anil out on the water, waves lapping against his ankles. The only thing he could think to do was swim out to the anil and see if whatever had allowed him to travel through time the first time would work again. He was . . . more than a little nervous.

He bounced on his toes and clenched and unclenched his hands, working up his adrenaline. And then he dove into the water.

The swim out to the anil was rough. Waves crashed over his head, and the undertow pulled at his feet, wanting to drag him under. He used all his adrenaline from the fight, all his anger and frustration to propel himself forward.

He couldn't make out the anil through the water in his eyes. It was a glimmer of silver light, and then it was yellow liquid pouring through the waves. Blue lighting. Holding his breath, Ash dipped below the surface of the water. He felt that pull, again, but this time he didn't think it was the ocean. It was the anil tugging him toward it, calling to something deep inside him. Acid rose in his throat. There was a strange, static electricity prickle inside of his gut, starting where the piece of the *Second Star* had lodged itself into his body four weeks ago.

The air around him grew thicker, and the water seemed to dissolve so that he wasn't floating through the waves any longer but hanging, suspended, in the thick and heavy air. It felt like he was falling and flying all at once. He opened his eyes and saw that everything had gone black. Distantly, he thought he could make out the pinprick glimmer of stars.

The piece of ship inside of his body stung, painfully. His lungs began to burn. He pulled upward with his arms, thrashed with his legs.

He was underwater again. His brain spun, trying to figure out what was happening. Did it work?

Or . . . was he drowning?

You don't die like this, said a voice in the back of his head.

The water was cold and unforgiving. It pounded at Ash's temples and stung his eyes. He could make out a distant flicker of light above him.

Gathering his strength, he swam. Up and up until he surfaced, gasping. He was conscious of water rising and falling all around him, carrying his body aloft on crashing waves.

Ash could see the bubble of the anil in the distance: swirling light and mist and smoke. It cast a glow over the black water, illuminating . . .

Was that a boat?

He squinted into the darkness, treading water to keep his head above the waves. It *was* a boat—it was his boat. And the figure crouched inside was—

"Zora," he croaked, swimming hard. His muscles burned in protest, but he ignored them. Spitting up water, he called again, louder this time, "Zora!"

Zora whirled, sending the boat rocking beneath her. In the light of the anil, Ash could see that her skin was gray and tears had carved lines down her cheeks.

"Ash?" she said, incredulous. "But you were just . . . How did . . . Holy shit, are you bleeding?"

Ash clawed for the side of the boat. He tried to pull himself over, but his arms screamed with pain, and Zora had to help haul him in.

It wasn't until he was crouched on the bottom of the boat, Zora leaning over him, that he noticed a dark spot of blood just below his ribs, soaking through his T-shirt. His old wound had opened up.

Coughing up a bit of water, he said, "You won't believe what just happened."

LOG ENTRY—JULY 31, 2074
12:16 HOURS
THE WORKSHOP

I've now traveled into that terrible future an additional three times, on three separate occasions.

The horrors I've witnessed have not altered.

I keep thinking about what's going to happen to WCAAT. My whole life was at that school. I first saw Natasha walking across the grass between the physics building and the library, arms filled with books. And then, just two years later, we were married—in WCAAT's courtyard, in April, when all the cherry blossoms were blooming. She waited for me outside of a graduate lecture on space time and quantum mechanics to tell me she was expecting our daughter.

And it's not just personal stuff. WCAAT gave me my first job. The professors there helped me develop the initial concepts that eventually became the seeds to get me interested in time travel.

In just a few short years, it will all be gone.

I think I'm focusing on the school because my brain can't process what else this will mean: the destruction of the city I've lived in my entire life, the death of everyone I've ever known and loved. It's all too much to take.

It seems to me that what I'm witnessing is the result of a butterfly effect.

If that's the case, then it means that in my own timeline, between the last time I traveled into the future and July 12, 2074, something changed, probably something that seemed small, at the time.

But what?

I wish Roman were here. I've taken it for granted, over the years, how easy it is to talk to the boy, to run my ideas past him and get feedback on where I'm making leaps in my thinking. But he's been spending so much time elsewhere recently. I suppose I'll just have to work it out myself.

37

DOROTHY

JULY 10, 2074, NEW SEATTLE

Dorothy took Roman to a twenty-four-hour diner a few blocks from where they'd stowed the *Black Crow*. The Mini Star, the diner was called, and it had likely seen better days. The vinyl booths were cracked, the fluorescent lights flickering. Dorothy ordered heaps of pancakes and eggs and bacon, even though she doubted either of them would be able to eat. But the act of ordering itself brought some comfort. For a moment, at least, she allowed herself to think that her biggest problem was whether to order her eggs scrambled or fried.

She studied Roman after the waitress brought their coffee. He looked most of the way dead himself, with his gray skin and darkly shadowed eyes. He sipped his coffee without seeming to realize that he was doing it, his vacant eyes staring ahead at nothing.

"Do you care to explain what that was all about?" Dorothy asked, after a long moment of silence.

Roman shifted his eyes to her face. "If it's all the same to you, I'd prefer not to."

"Roman," she said, sharp.

Roman rubbed his eyes with two fingers, sighing deeply. "Very well." He placed his coffee back on the table, folding his hands in front of him. "As you guessed, the little girl in the clearing was my sister." He hesitated, and then added, "Cassia."

"Pretty name," Dorothy murmured.

"I . . . talk to her, sometimes. To her picture, I mean. That's what you heard last night." A flush of red spread through Roman's cheeks, and he took another sip of coffee, suddenly awkward.

"What happened to her?"

"She was born with type 1 diabetes. What you just saw . . . her blood sugar plummeted unexpectedly, sending her into shock. We'd run out of insulin the week before and, with the hospitals overrun from the earthquake, there was no one we could go to for help. She went into a diabetic coma, and . . ." Roman looked at Dorothy and away. "Well. You saw what happened."

"She died," Dorothy said, and Roman closed his eyes.

"She did," he added, voice quiet. "It's why I can't leave this city. It's the last place she was ever alive. It'd feel like I'd left her."

"And you thought you could still save her. That's why we came back to this day, isn't it? It wasn't really about bringing medical equipment to the city at all?"

"It's not the only reason." Roman leaned back. The fluorescent lights caught his eyes, turning them a deep, stormy blue. "Back at Fort Hunter, you asked me why I betrayed them. Ash and the others."

"You said we hadn't been acquainted long enough for that story."

"You remember." A ghost of a smile flitted across his lips. "I know what Ash thinks of me, what he probably told you, but I only left the team because of what happened to Cassia. I wanted to go back in time and try to save her life, but the Professor said it wasn't possible. He wouldn't even try. I thought he was being selfish. But the old fool was right." Roman laughed, humorlessly, and shook his head. "But that's not the only reason I wanted to come back here."

Dorothy was confused. "What other reason could there be?"

"You asked me about the butterfly effect before, when you saw what our future was going to become. You asked me why I didn't want to figure out which moment changed the course of human history. Remember?"

"I remember."

Roman looked up at her, miserable. "The moment Cassia died was the moment I first started thinking about defecting to the Black Cirkus. I didn't actually leave until years later, but . . . if she hadn't died, I'd have stayed with the Chronology Protection Agency, and everything would've been different. The Professor never would've gotten lost in the past, we would've found a way to stop the earthquakes. Everything that happened, everything that's going to happen, all of it's my fault."

The silence between them stretched. It felt charged. Dorothy knew that, no matter what she said, she was making a choice.

She thought of black skies and burned cities and no sun.

"It's not too late," she said finally. "Let's try again."

They returned at twilight, three hours before Cassia was going to die. They snuck through the hospital's gold-tinted halls while the sun dipped low in the horizon. They gathered the insulin in silence and then crept out the back door and through the shadow-darkened streets. They hid the medication in Roman's tent while he and his sister were out. They couldn't stay near the tent because that put them at risk of being seen, and so they hid in the trees and watched the clearing.

Dorothy felt her heartbeat thrum in her palms, her breath shallow and quick. She was sure it had worked. It had to have worked.

Three hours passed, and then the scene played out exactly as it had before: A younger Roman stumbled out of the tent, holding his sister. She looked like a broken bird in his arms, her head lolling back, her neck long and pale.

He collapsed in the clearing. Her eyes stared, unblinking, at the sky.

"Thieves," the older Roman whispered, still crouching beside Dorothy. "I'd forgotten."

"Forgotten what?"

"That day, thieves snuck into our tent and stole some of our food. I thought they'd only taken the canned goods I'd been planning for dinner. They must've taken the medicine, too."

His face was stony as he stared ahead, watching his sister die. Dorothy touched his shoulder, her heart heavy.

"Come on," she said softly.

They returned a half hour before his sister's death. Any earlier, and they risked the thieves stealing the medication again. They crept through the halls. Stole the insulin. Made their way to the back staircase.

A burly security guard heading out for a cigarette break intercepted them mere feet from the heavy, double doors that led to the back parking lot. He detained them in a back room, and they only managed to escape when Dorothy found a stray bobby pin on the floor and used it to pick the lock. By the time they made it to the clearing in Tent City, they were too late.

Roman stumbled out of the tent. His sister's head fell back against his arm. Her eyes stared.

"Let's go," Dorothy said again. But her throat felt thick.

She couldn't admit it yet—she didn't even want to *think* it—but, in some deep place, she felt that she was starting to understand.

They returned fifteen minutes before his sister's death. This time, Roman remembered to bring a bottle of insulin from their last theft, so they were able to skip the hospital and fly straight to Tent City. They parked the *Black Crow* as close to the university grounds as they could manage, cutting the engine with nine minutes to spare.

At seven minutes, they were weaving through the black tents, rain beating on their shoulders.

At three minutes, they could see the clearing in the distance. Dorothy watched the younger Roman stumble out of his tent, carrying his sister in his arms.

At two minutes, he dropped to his knees. The Roman beside her started running faster, pulling ahead—

And then he tripped. The root seemed to come from nowhere, tangling around his ankle and bringing him down, hard, in the mud. He gasped and struggled to push himself back to his hands and knees, but it was no use. The mud was thick, and it was everywhere.

"No," he said finally, standing.

Dorothy followed his gaze and saw his younger self kneeling in the clearing, his sister dying again.

Dorothy thought she understood.

"Do you remember holding her in your arms?" she asked.

Roman closed his eyes. "I can't."

She tried to keep her voice gentle. "You *felt* her die. Remember?"

Shaking his head. "I don't know."

"If it were possible to change this, you wouldn't be able to remember her dying because we already would've gone back and prevented it from happening." She gripped his arm.

"Time is a circle, remember?"

She thought he was going to push her away. But he lifted his own hand and dropped it over hers.

For a long while, they stood in the rain.

38

ASH

NOVEMBER 8, 2077, NEW SEATTLE

Zora was staring at him, her mouth agape.

After a moment she said flatly, "That's impossible."

"I know," said Ash. They'd pulled their motorboat up to the dock just outside of Dante's, but Zora had refused to go inside and let Ash order a much-needed drink until she'd bandaged up his open wound using a torn-off bit of her shirt and he'd told her everything.

She didn't believe him.

"You've read my father's research," she said. "You can't enter an anil without any exotic matter. Only two people have ever even tried, and one of them died while the other—"

"—was flayed by the intense winds inside of the time tunnel," Ash finished for her. "I *know*. I'm not arguing with you. All I'm saying is that *I* just went through an anil without any exotic matter."

"And even if you had any exotic matter, you would have

needed to incorporate it into a protective vessel, like a time machine," Zora continued, seeming not to have heard him. "Long before my father came up with the plans for the *Second Star*, he thought that exotic matter might have stabilizing effects inside of an anil, but he found that when the material wasn't properly incorporated into the design of his ship, it failed."

Ash dropped his face into his hands, groaning loudly. "Zora," he said. "You're lecturing."

Zora blinked at him. "Sorry. It's just that . . . well, this doesn't make any sense. Why are you different from my father, and all the other scientists who've tried and failed? It shouldn't—"

"Be possible?" Ash untied the bandage around his ribs and then retied it tighter. There was already blood leaking through the fabric, a deep, dark red. "Yeah, you might have mentioned that."

Zora looked chastened. "Sorry," she said again.

"And you're wrong, anyway. Dorothy went through the anil without a time machine, and she survived."

"True. But she was holding the container of exotic matter," Zora said thoughtfully. "And her hair turned white. All of us got white streaks in our hair after we fell through the anil without a vessel." Absently, she fingered the white braid beneath her ear. "But your hair isn't white."

Ash lifted his eyebrows. "It's not?"

"Nope, dirt blond, as usual."

"Hey," said Ash, but he couldn't even muster up false indignation and the word fell flat. He ran a hand back through his hair.

"Okay, say you *did* travel back in time. Somehow. How did you end up in the *exact* time that Dorothy and Roman went back to?"

Ash, frustrated, said, "I don't know."

"We're missing something," Zora murmured. "I suppose it's possible that Roman and Dorothy left behind a sort of . . . trail."

Ash raised his eyebrows, and Zora, groaning, elaborated. "Okay, think of it like a boat cutting through the water, leaving a wake behind in the waves, right? It's possible that you were dragged along in their wake and that's how you ended up in the same time that they did." Her eyes traveled from his hair to a spot on his abdomen, just below his ribs. She frowned at his bandage. "And, maybe . . ."

Ash lifted a hand, suddenly, stopping her. He'd just caught a scent in the air—engine grease and smoke—and the skin on the back of his neck pricked. He turned, but the morning was sunless and blurred at the edges, and he couldn't see where fog became clouds and water became sky. The world seemed still.

"We shouldn't be talking about this out here," he said, feeling suddenly exposed. He took a step toward Dante's. And then . . .

There. A creak of wood. A soft footfall. Ash reached for

the gun he'd tucked into his waistband. Zora's eyes were suddenly alert.

"Who's there?" Ash called, struggling to breathe against the tightness in his chest. He closed his fingers around the gun's hilt but didn't pull it out. Unnerved, he searched through the soupy, gray light, looking for movement, listening for breathing.

Silence.

Zora nodded at something in the water out past the docks. "What's that?"

Ash followed her gaze and saw a pinprick of light glimmering through the distant trees. He could hear a motor, low and rumbling, churning up black water in its wake. A moment later, a motorboat separated from the shadows and fog.

Ash caught Zora's eye as the boat drew up alongside the dock and pulled to a stop. Something was wrong.

He took a step closer to the edge of the dock, pulling out his gun—

A hand shot out of the fog, and then Ash's arm was being wrenched behind his back, the gun slipping from his fingers.

"Easy now," said a cool voice. The hand was small, but strong, and Ash's first thought was that Dorothy had betrayed him, that she was going to kill him now, prememory be damned.

But, when he turned, he saw pale skin and dark hair. Not Dorothy, but a girl he'd never seen before. Normally he'd be able to overpower her, but she'd caught him by surprise and had his arm twisted in a complicated hold behind his back. Pain shot through his shoulder whenever he moved.

She pointed his own gun at his temple, smiling wickedly. "We haven't been introduced," she said. "My name is Eliza. And that over there is Donovan."

Ash glanced across the dock and saw that a boy had Zora in a similar hold, arms twisted behind her back, a beefy bicep curled around her neck.

"Can't say it's nice to meet you," Zora breathed through clenched teeth.

The boat's engine cut, but the sound of a rumbling motor still ghosted through the air, not quite willing to die. Ash's gaze slid back to the edge of the dock as Mac stepped out of the fog. His crutches made hollow, clomping noises on the dock. As he approached, a few more Cirkus Freaks separated from the fog, their faces grim. Ash counted four, and then six, surrounding him, Zora, Eliza, and Donovan in a tight circle. He felt his first twist of fear. So this was going to be an ambush.

"Impressive," Mac said, his eyes swinging from Eliza to Donovan. "I should have started recruiting Cirkus Freaks years ago."

"Happy to help, sir," Eliza said, holding Ash a little tighter. Ash grimaced.

"Good to see you again, Mac," he said, hoping his light tone would cover his nerves. "Although your friends have been a little rude."

"I figured it was about time to address that little stunt you

266

pulled at my club." Mac glanced lazily over at Zora. "She's prettier than your last girl."

Zora's lips pulled up over clamped teeth, curling into a vicious smile. "Come a little closer and say that."

"Bad tempered, though." Mac stroked his jaw and shook his head. "You didn't think I could let you get away without punishment for what that bitch did to my leg, did you? I've killed men for less than that."

Ash felt a chill work its way down his spine. He clenched his shoulders to keep himself from shuddering.

"You're not going to kill me," Ash said. "I know how I die, and this isn't it."

"You sure about that?" Mac asked. He nodded to Eliza.

Ash saw the blow coming and tried to brace himself, but the butt of his gun caught him hard on the side of his face. He heard something crack, and then his eyesight turned bloody.

"Boom," Eliza whispered into his ear, laughing. She smashed the gun into his face again. And again.

The dock tilted toward him.

And then there was only darkness.

LOG ENTRY—OCTOBER 7, 1899
22:24 HOURS
JUST OUTSIDE COLORADO SPRINGS

This is a little embarrassing, but let me explain.

I was feeling pretty low after everything that happened. Not only the terrible future that will almost certainly come to pass, but my own experiments and failures as well.

And so I had a drink. And then I had a couple of drinks. And then I thought about how nice it would be to talk to another scientist, someone who knows exactly how it feels to fail so horribly at something you believed without a doubt to be true.

And so I got into the *Second Star* and flew into the past to see Nikola. We've been hanging out in his experimental station, and we've had a few more drinks and just . . . talked.

Nikola still thinks I'm a martian, but he understands my frustration, nonetheless.

I wasn't going to write about this little trip at all, but Nikola said something that's stuck with me. I wrote it down as best as I could remember it here.

He said, "Maybe there is something like destiny, or God, working on each of us, determining our paths forward, on and on through the future. Though you might be able to change your own path, you cannot change someone else's."

That seemed really profound to me. Or maybe it's the bourbon.

Before I left, Nikola asked if I would come visit him one last time, before his death. I asked him why, but he only smiled and wouldn't tell me.

"There's something I'd like to give you" was all he said.

PART THREE

How did it get so late so soon? It's night before it's after-noon. December is here before it's June. My goodness how the time has flewn. How did it get so late so soon?

—Dr. Seuss

39

DOROTHY

NOVEMBER 9, 2077, NEW SEATTLE

Wind beat into the sides of the *Black Crow*. Rain lashed at the windshield. And, somewhere far in the distance, stars winked in and out of existence.

Dorothy peered at the sides of the anil, searching first for the exact crest of purple that meant 2077, and then for the subtler changes and shifts in color that meant they were nearing the eighth of November. It was her first time flying the *Black Crow* through the anil on her own, and this was the part she'd been dreading. She was terrible at looking for signs in the swirling black and gray of the time tunnel's walls. It all looked the same to her.

"Does this seem right to you?" She glanced at Roman, but he only stared out the passenger-side window, forehead creased in concentration, eyes glazed.

"I'm sure it's fine," he said distantly.

"All right." Dorothy exhaled and, cringing slightly, she

pulled the *Black Crow* through the misty, swirling sides of the anil.

The rain became thick and black, turning to waves, and then the *Black Crow* was shooting up and up, through dark water, to surface in the familiar dusky twilight of New Seattle, circa 2077.

Dorothy loosened her grip on the time machine's yoke and leaned back in her seat, releasing an anxious sigh. She thought she'd done well. The trip hadn't been quite as smooth as when Roman flew, but she'd held the time machine steady against the battering wind, so she considered it a success. At least she hadn't crashed.

She checked the clock on the time machine's dashboard. Then, blinking, she checked it again.

"Roman," she said, leaning forward suddenly. "Is this right? It says that we landed a full day later than when we left."

Roman turned to her. He seemed not to have noticed that they'd arrived back home at all. The last trip back had taken a toll on him. He looked aged.

"What was that?" he asked.

"Look." Dorothy pointed to the time machine's clock. "We landed twenty-four hours too late." She looked over her shoulder, at the anil still swirling behind her. "Should— should I go back and try again?"

Roman went back to staring out the window. "If you like."

Dorothy tried to think of something to say, but everything that came to mind sounded stupid. He'd spent the day watching his sister die over and over again. She couldn't think of anything more painful than that, and it angered her that she couldn't find the words to comfort him. She, too, had lost her entire family, but she didn't think it was quite the same.

She glanced back at the anil one last time. How much difference would one day really make?

She set the time machine to hover and flew over the dark waves, toward home.

The Fairmont rose in the distance like a golden mountain, lit up and glowing against the otherwise darkening sky. Seeing it, Dorothy felt the anxiety inside of her still. *Home.*

Then, she marked the dark figures standing guard at its main entrance and frowned. That was strange. She didn't recognize half the Freaks on duty.

She swiveled around in her seat as she flew past, trying to catch a final glimpse before rounding the corner.

"Wasn't Donovan's team supposed to be on guard?" she said, half to herself.

It seemed to take Roman a long time to hear the question. He blinked, as though coming out of a trance. "What?"

"Donovan," Dorothy said again, more firmly this time. She deftly flew the *Black Crow* through the dark windows of the parking garage, waiting until she'd landed before explaining. "His team was on guard when we left this morning, wasn't it? I thought you'd told him to hold until we returned?"

Roman nodded slowly. They always left the Fairmont in the hands of one of their more trusted teams when they traveled back in time, just in case something should happen to delay their return.

"I didn't see him out front just now," Dorothy said.

"He must've switched," Roman murmured, but Dorothy could see his brows draw together. That didn't sound like Donovan's team. "I suppose it was a rather long shift; we've been gone for more than a day."

Dorothy cringed, once again feeling guilty for missing their intended time.

They exited the time machine and found the door to the Fairmont's basement ajar, a thin yellow light dribbling into the stairwell. Dorothy could hear the grunting sounds of work being done. It seemed like there was an entire team of people gathered on the other side.

This was . . . also strange. It was nearly evening, the hotel was usually quiet at this time of day. Most of the Cirkus Freaks took to the boats as soon as the sun set to patrol the waters around the Fairmont, while those who were lucky enough to be off duty headed to the Dead Rabbit for a drink.

"Did you assign a job you didn't tell me about?" Dorothy asked. Roman shook his head. His eyes had lost their glaze and now he looked just as anxious as she felt. Frowning, Dorothy eased the door open.

No one saw them, at first. The boys assembled were new recruits, and Dorothy didn't recognize most of them. They were dressed in work clothes rather than standard Cirkus black, and they were moving the solar panels from the corner where they'd been stacked yesterday morning and onto a cart to go . . .

Where? Dorothy wondered, eyes narrowing beneath her hood. She hadn't ordered anything to be done with the panels just yet. She glanced at Roman, and he shook his head. He hadn't ordered this, either.

An older boy looked up then, wiping the sweat from his forehead. She saw his eyes go wide as he spotted her and Roman at the door.

"Quinn," he said, and a lump rose and fell beneath the skin at his throat. "And Roman. You're back."

Dorothy lifted her chin. "Where are these being shipped?"

"H-he didn't tell us," the boy rushed to answer, clearly worried he was in some sort of trouble. "We're only supposed to prepare them for delivery."

"Delivery." Dorothy pressed her lips together, allowing her eyes to travel over the stacks, looking for any sign of where they might be going.

There was a propped-open door at the far corner of the basement, and, though the hall beyond the door was dark, Dorothy knew that it led to an old service elevator. The workers were likely taking the panels up the elevator shaft and through the parking garage. If they had a boat waiting there, they could take the merchandise anywhere in the city.

"Who asked you to prepare them for delivery?" Roman asked.

"Mac Murphy," the boy told them. And then quickly,

"But he said the order came from you."

"Did he?" said Roman, cool.

Mac, Dorothy thought, and anger beat at her chest like a second heart. What right did Mac have to give orders to *her* gang, inside *her* hotel?

And now the strange men standing guard at the entrance to her hotel took on a sinister new meaning. It felt less like a mistake, more like a message.

Was this still her hotel?

The anger in her chest hardened, becoming fear. Mac was giving orders to her Freaks; Mac was having her solar panels delivered God knew where. What else was Mac doing?

"Do you know where Mac is now?" she asked the boy, doing her best to keep her voice controlled.

"In his room, I think."

His room? Who did Mac think he was, taking over one of their rooms? Another sideways glance at Roman told Dorothy that he was equally taken aback by this new sequence of events.

"More happened in the last twenty-four hours than I'd expected," Roman murmured.

"Mac works fast," Dorothy said, bitter. "Perhaps we should go back now and try to return a day earlier, as planned?"

But, even as she said the words, Dorothy knew that this wasn't possible. If their last trip back in time had taught her anything, it was that she could not change the past once it had already been set. They were stuck with this present, for better or worse.

It chilled her, how easily things could change.

"Thank you," she said, turning back to the boy. She cast one last glance around the room, letting her eyes linger on each of the workers in turn. "Those panels aren't to be taken out of this hotel without either Roman's or my express permission. Is that understood?"

A pause. And then each of the Freaks nodded.

40

The sky outside of Ash's hotel room cell looked bruised: purple, with black clouds strewn across the horizon, their edges already turning yellow. He groaned and sat up. He wasn't sure how much time had passed since he'd been brought here. A few hours, at least. Maybe a full day.

His wrists had been tied behind his back, but his feet and legs were still free. He pushed himself off the hotel bed and walked over to the window, letting his head knock gently against the glass.

The windows were barred. No way out. But even if they hadn't been, even if Ash's hands had been free and he'd been able to pry the glass open and climb outside, he doubted he'd have the guts to jump. The water seemed so far below. Eight stories, possibly more.

He exhaled, heavily, his breath ghosting the glass. Dorothy had made this jump. She'd been in the same predicament as he was now, and yet, somehow, she'd managed to pry a window open and find her way outside. She'd stared down at the violent black water and leaped.

Without warning, Zora's voice snaked into his mind: *You have to stop thinking that she's the same girl you knew.*

He swallowed, hard. *Zora.* He was alone in here, but he wondered if Zora was being held in some other room in the Fairmont.

Behind him: the scrape of metal in a lock. A door creaked open, bringing the smell of cigarette smoke into the small room.

Ash stiffened.

Footsteps, and then hands were grasping his shoulders, spinning him around. Mac had brought four Cirkus Freaks with him. Despite his misery, Ash felt his lip twitch.

"Two men for each of my arms," he said, flexing beneath his jacket. "I'm flattered."

"I aim to please," Mac said from the doorway.

"Where's Zora?" Ash asked.

"We left her on the docks. I have no use for mouthy women." He ran a tongue over his chapped lips and then nodded at the men holding Ash's arms.

Ash swallowed.

Well, shit.

As expected, the Cirkus Freaks knocked him around the hotel room a little bit. Ash had a hard time following exactly what they were doing. There were simply too many fists and feet swinging in his direction. He stayed standing for the first few blows to his face and gut, and then one of the Freaks kicked his feet out from beneath him, and he dropped to the ground like a stone.

His hands were still tied behind his back, and so he hit the floor face-first. A spray of blood painted the wood before his eyes.

He remembered, clearly, the first crack of a boot in his ribs, how he curled, bracing to absorb the blow. Pain exploded through his chest, driving the breath from his lungs.

The third, fourth, and fifth kicks blurred together, but the sixth kick was memorable, seeing as it was aimed at his face. He heard the crack of his nose breaking a split second before he felt the burn of pain. The room dissolved into white light and blood.

Finally, Mac said, "Enough."

Ash struggled to stay conscious. He couldn't see past the blood in his eyes. His breath was uneven, his heartbeat sputtering.

Crouching, Mac pulled a wad of paper napkins from his pocket and began cleaning the blood from Ash's face.

"Hey, look, I'm sorry I had to do that," he said conversationally. "But you see where I'm coming from, right? You came into my club, waved a gun around, demanded things. I'm respected around these parts, son. I can't let you get away with that."

Ash closed his eyes. Well, he closed one of them. The right one was already swollen shut.

"You should consider yourself lucky." A grunt, and Mac

wiped the blood from Ash's eye with his thumb. "If you were anyone else, I'd have shot you back at the docks and been done with it."

"Do you expect me to thank you?" Ash laughed, spitting up blood.

Mac frowned, and Ash got the feeling he didn't have a lot of experience with sarcasm.

"Why keep me alive at all?" Ash choked out. "You're already working with the Black Cirkus, and they're the ones with the time machine. You don't need me."

Mac studied him, the tip of his tongue peeking out from between his lips.

"Let me tell you a story," he said after a moment. "About a month ago, my contact with the Center offered me a boat-load of money if I could get them a time machine." A shrug. "I guess their fancy scientists still haven't been able to figure it out. Between you and me, I'd never given much thought to time travel. But, well, this amount of money could've had me sitting pretty for years. I would've been able to expand my little operation, take over Aurora, live like a king."

Mac grinned, revealing nicotine-stained teeth. "It was enough to start me wondering whether this place was even worth it. Twice in recent memory, an earthquake has come damn close to wiping New Seattle off the map. I had to ask myself: Did I really want to build my empire without some sort of guarantee that it wouldn't happen again?"

Ash blinked at him, his eyelashes still thick with blood.

"That's why you're suddenly so interested in time travel? You want to know whether an earthquake's going to destroy your whorehouses?"

Mac held out his palms: *What do you expect?* "What can I say? I like to think ahead. And, when I got to the future, I saw that I had a pretty good reason to be worried. This next earthquake isn't just wiping out the city, it's wiping out *everything*, the whole coast. Anyone still living out here is gonna die."

For a moment Ash couldn't hear anything over the blood pounding in his ears.

Anyone still living out here is gonna die.

It was just as they'd feared. The next earthquake was going to kill them all.

"I'm not keeping you alive out of the goodness of my heart," Mac said. "I have a feeling that Roman and Quinn aren't going to play nice once they find out I took over their precious Black Cirkus. I have a plan to take care of them, don't you worry about that. But once they're gone, I'll need someone else to fly my new time machine." Mac sniffed. "I'm thinking I'll go back in time. Use my money to set up a tech company in Seattle in 2015 or play the stock market in 1980. You know, something fun. I just need someone to fly the time machine for me." He took Ash's chin in one hand, grinning gleefully. "That's where you come in."

Ash swallowed, tasting blood. "I'd rather die than help you," he said.

Mac shrugged. "That can also be arranged."

41

DOROTHY

"Mac is busy right now. What do you need?"

Dorothy had been standing in the hallway with her back to the hotel room door, studying a water spot on the wallpaper—and she turned around at the voice. Eliza was leaning head and shoulders into the hallway, the door held close behind her.

Dorothy glanced from the girl's face to the new cloak hanging from her shoulders to the shiny boots on her feet. "Those are new," she said, shocked.

Eliza grinned. "Mac asked me to do him a favor."

"You're working for Mac now?" Roman asked.

"Don't look so surprised. You were the one who gave me the idea," Eliza said innocently. "Or don't you remember our conversation back at the Dead Rabbit?"

A choked scream issued from inside the hotel room. Roman stiffened, and Dorothy saw his eyes travel past Eliza's head, narrowing in curiosity.

"Who's in there?" Dorothy asked.

"No one you need concern yourself with," said Eliza. Was it Dorothy's imagination, or did she seem to hold the door ever so slightly tighter? "Mac can find you after he's done."

Roman made a noise in his throat. Mac didn't give orders in their hotel, no matter what treasures he brought their Freaks. It'd been too long since they'd reminded the Black Cirkus who they were.

Dorothy removed a long, thin dagger from her sleeve. The blade was smaller in diameter than a pencil, and so sharp that Eliza would have to squint to see where its point ended.

"Do you know how much pressure it takes to rupture an eardrum?" Dorothy held the blade up to the light and a line of silver appeared along its edge. "I don't know, myself, but I hear people used to do it by accident, with hairpins and cotton swabs. Imagine the damage *this* could do."

Eliza stared at the blade and licked her lips. Dorothy imagined she was thinking of how the metal might scrape against the inner membrane of her ear, how it might *pop*, feeling hollow at first, and then wet as pus and blood trickled down her neck.

Dorothy smiled in a slow, practiced way that showed off all her small white teeth.

"Tell Mac I need to speak with him now," she said.

Something flickered through Eliza's eyes. Fear? Disgust? Dorothy couldn't say for sure, but Eliza murmured, "Yes, ma'am," and then pushed the door closed again, leaving Dorothy and Roman alone in the hall once more.

"Mac has become a problem," Roman said under his breath.

"Do you have your gun?" Dorothy asked, slipping her dagger back up her sleeve.

A pause, and then Roman said, "Naturally."

Dorothy pressed her lips together, her mind spinning. She'd never killed a man before, no matter what her reputation was, and she wasn't sure she was capable of taking a life, even one as loathsome as Mac's.

Surely there was still another way?

Another scream issued from the other side of the door. Dorothy felt as though the air had been sucked out of the hallway. She heard the muffled sound of voices and then footsteps.

She rolled her wrists, feeling the cold steel of her daggers beneath her sleeves.

The door opened, and Mac's voice entered the hallway before he did. He was singing.

"Close your windows tight, little children, the Fox and Crow are scratching at the glass . . ."

Dorothy stiffened. It was the nursery rhyme the residents of New Seattle had made up about Quinn and Roman, and she'd always been morbidly proud of it. It had felt like proof that she'd made herself into a person to be reckoned with, even if it was in reputation only. Now, though, it felt like Mac was mocking her with it.

"I'm glad the two of you stopped by," Mac said cheerfully, as though Dorothy hadn't just threatened a member of her own gang to force him to speak with them. His leg was still bandaged and, though he limped a bit, he seemed to no longer need his crutches to walk. "I've been thinking it's time we took another little trip."

He held a cloth in his hands, and he was using it to wipe the blood from his skin. It wasn't doing much good. There was simply too much blood, too little cloth.

Dorothy stared at him, momentarily taken aback.

Was he joking?

Roman was the one who spoke. "And why would we do that?"

"I'm afraid you aren't in the position to be making such demands," Dorothy said.

Mac blinked at her and said, as though baffled, "Aren't I? I was under the impression that we were working together here. You scratch my back, I scratch yours."

The idea of touching Mac's back caused Dorothy to shudder involuntarily.

"Don't worry, you'll like my new plan," Mac told her. "I've seen enough of the future. If that's what this world is going to look like in just a few short years, then I want no part of it. I'd rather go back in time and live like a king."

He lifted his fist, studying a yellowed fingernail. "All you have to do is take me back in time. I want to vet a few time periods before deciding on one. And then you can leave me there, and we're all happy." He looked back up at her, grinning. "What do you say?

Dorothy hesitated. His desire to go back in time seemed

true enough, but she doubted very much that he would just let them leave him there. Mac liked power too much to let their time machine fall through his fingers. This was a trick.

She was about to tell him what she thought of his little plan when another choked cry from inside the hotel room stopped her. The hairs on the back of her neck stood up.

"Who do you have in there?" she asked instead.

Mac grinned, and Dorothy felt duped. Clearly, he'd wanted her to ask.

"See for yourself," he said, throwing the door wide.

Dorothy didn't want to look, but her eyes seemed to move on their own, zeroing in on the figure lying utterly still on the floor.

Ash had been beaten, that much was clear, but it wasn't the beating itself that caused horror to rise in her throat. It was *how* he'd been beaten, how he'd been kicked and carved and sliced. His skin was white except for where it was red and clotted with blood. *God*, there was so much blood. Where had it all come from? It pooled around him and stained his clothes and hands and feet. A roaring sound filled Dorothy's ears.

Whatever had been done to him had been done *gleefully*.

Dorothy's first thought was that he was dead. This monster had killed him. But then she noticed that he was shaking, whether from the shock or the blood loss she couldn't tell.

Not dead yet. But close.

Mac was studying her now, his eyes narrowing like lenses. Dorothy had to work hard to keep the emotion from her face. He knew. Somehow, impossibly, he knew about her history with Ash. He knew what he meant to her. *How?*

It didn't matter. Mac was going to kill Ash if she didn't stop him. Her stomach roiled and her fingers curled around her hidden daggers. She wanted to pull them free and slice the smile off Mac's face. She wanted to add his own blood to the blood that already painted his clothes. The want was so strong inside of her that it felt like heat.

He's near, she thought. Near enough that she if she struck now she could drive a dagger through his chest.

But could she do it? Could she end a man's life?

She eased her daggers out of their harnesses.

Yes, she thought.

As though reading her mind, Mac hobbled out of easy reach. Her Cirkus Freaks closed around him, making it so that Dorothy couldn't reach him, not unless she was willing to go through them.

And were they hers any longer? Eliza, it seemed, had already defected. What about the others? Were they working for Mac now, too?

Dorothy felt her heartbeat pulsing in her palm, vibrating through her daggers. She couldn't risk it.

Mac held out his hand and, as though on cue, one of the Cirkus Freaks handed him a knife.

Smiling at her, he said, "Let me just finish this guy off and then we'll discuss this further."

Finish him off?

The thought made her feel like screaming.

"If you really want to go back in time, we should leave

now," Dorothy said, her mind working quickly. From the corner of her eye, she thought she saw Roman's gaze flicker and settle on her. Dorothy didn't look at him. In this moment, all she could think about was getting Mac away from Ash. Not just five years this time. Decades, centuries. "Before—"

But her mind froze, and she could think of no reason that they should leave now, before Mac had a chance to kill Ash.

Roman cleared his throat. "As I'm sure you know, the person you're torturing is Jonathan Asher," he explained. "He should have a public death, don't you think?"

Roman said all of this as though it were obvious, his expression blank.

Mac's eyes flicked between the two of them, suspicious, but he lowered his knife. "That's not a bad idea." Over his shoulder, he added, "Keep him alive until I get back."

Skin humming, Dorothy turned and started down the hallway, trusting the others to follow her. She slid her daggers back into their holsters.

She may have let one moment pass, but there would be another. She'd make sure of it. For now, Mac wanted to go back in time, and so they would take him.

He just couldn't be allowed to return.

42

ASH

"Ash . . . come on now, time to wake up."

The voice drifted out of the black, tugging him from unconsciousness. It was familiar.

He struggled to raise his heavy lids. "Dorothy?" he murmured.

And that's how he knew he was dreaming. Because Dorothy couldn't be here.

A cool hand touched his cheek. The voice spoke again. "Hurry. You don't have a lot of time."

Ash still didn't open his eyes. There was blood crusted in his eyelashes, holding them shut.

"You aren't here," he said. It was a struggle to speak. His tongue felt too big for his mouth.

"You have to get out," Dorothy was saying. "Mac won't be long, and if you're still here when he returns, he'll kill you."

"I don't die today," Ash muttered. His thoughts were still soupy. "I know when I die."

"Lucky you. Now *go.*"

Either a moment or an hour later, Ash opened his eyes and found that he was alone in the small hotel room. Dorothy wasn't there. She'd never been there.

He was about to let his eyes drop closed, to let himself fall unconscious again, when he noticed that the Cirkus Freaks weren't there, either.

And the door to his room was open, the darkened hallway twisting before him.

And . . . his gun was lying on the floor in front of him. He blinked to make sure he wasn't seeing things.

The gun stayed where it was.

Now go.

Was that possible? Could he even stand?

I have a plan to take care of them, he thought, and the words worked like a salve, easing the pain in his body somewhat. He slid his hands under his shoulders and, cringing, began to peel his body off the floor.

He rose to his forearms first. Then, arms trembling, pushed himself to hands and knees.

It was a mistake. Pain crashed over him, leaving him dizzy. He tilted to the side, and he thought he was going to fall back to the ground again but he steadied himself against the side of the bed.

He breathed. Sitting upright became a little easier. He grabbed his gun, hands thick and clumsy. It took a few more tries but, eventually, he made his way to his feet and stumbled for the door, his heartbeat hammering in a small, panicky way.

I have a plan to take care of them, he remembered again.

Whatever Mac's plan was, he had to stop it.

Ash followed the twisting docks through New Seattle without stopping to think about where he was going. His feet seemed to lead the way, carrying him through the dusty, damp buildings and out into open water. Downtown, the docks all converged and overlapped in a strange labyrinth. But once he got to the edge of the city, the docks stopped, leaving only empty, black water dotted with white trees.

Ash stood at the edge of the final dock, breathing hard. There was a little over a mile of water from where he stood to the anil. He was reasonably sure he could make it.

And then . . .

What?

What was his plan, here? He had no idea how long it had been since he heard Dorothy, Roman, and Mac planning to go back in time, but he was sure he was too late to catch up to the *Black Crow*. Which meant that he was going to have to try to go through the anil on his own, again, and hope that he'd be pulled through time by the *Black Crow*'s wake.

Would it work?

Shouting cut through the streets behind him. Ash looked

over his shoulder and saw lights flicker in and out between the buildings, figures moving. He swallowed, tasting blood. The Black Cirkus wasn't far behind. It's not like he had another choice.

He shrugged off his jacket, an ache moving through him as it dropped to the dock. It was a good jacket, and he was sad to see it go, but the leather would just get waterlogged and drag him down.

Gunshots blasted through the air behind him.

Ash jumped.

He sank into the black water, cold pressing against his skin and seeping into his ears, blocking out all other sound and leaving him with a deep ache in his skull. He surfaced, gasping, and started to swim, hoping the exercise would pump some warmth back into his blood.

His arms and legs began to stiffen after a few minutes, and his skin burned with cold. His trousers quickly filled with water, slowing him down. Another ten minutes of this and everything below his neck had gone numb. He was vaguely aware that he'd slowed down, that it was harder to move his limbs through the water.

It can't be much farther, he told himself. His chest ached and he could barely catch his breath. He heard the sound of a motor growling in the distance. The cackle of laughter. It wouldn't be long before the Cirkus found him.

Pain prickled just below his ribs, where the piece of the *Second Star* had lodged itself into his gut. Cringing, Ash pressed a hand to his belly. He could feel the hard edge of his ship just below his navel, shifting inside of him, and he realized that the wound must've opened up, again.

He lifted his hand. It was damp . . . but not with blood. The substance that clung to his fingers was thicker than water, and silvery.

Ash blinked, and the substance changed, hardening into a solid, black mass that coated his hand like a glove.

And then it changed again, this time becoming gaseous and green. Ash watched, amazed, as it drifted into the inky-blue sky around him and was gone.

Exotic matter acted like that, he knew. It shifted and changed in that canister the Professor had built for it, so that he never really got a handle on what he was looking at. But Ash didn't have any exotic matter in his body.

Did he?

It was true that, when they crashed the *Second Star*, he got a piece of something lodged inside his belly, just below his ribs. He'd thought it was part of his ship, but what if he'd guessed wrong? What if there was exotic matter inside of him, lodged deep into his belly along with the old piece of the *Second Star*? Would that explain why he'd been able to travel through the anil without a time machine?

Was it possible that *he* was the time machine?

Ash closed his eyes now, swimming hard toward the anil. The sound of shouting bounced over the waves, so near. He felt the spray of a boat on his cheeks.

The anil was just a few yards ahead. As Ash swam closer, he felt something, some faint pressure slip beneath his ribs, tugging him forward. It was so slight that he could've been imagining it. Just a needle's prick of pain. A sharp tug. It took his breath away.

Ash had thought he'd understood time travel, but in all the years he'd flown through the anil, first in the *Dark Star*, and then in the *Second Star*, he had never felt anything like that sensation.

It was like fate, like magic.

He dove down into the water, and through time itself.

43

DOROTHY

Dorothy lifted a hand, fingers trembling as she pressed them to the bulge of fabric at her neck. She'd tucked her old locket beneath her shirt and now she relished the chill of cool silver on her skin. It was familiar. The closest feeling to home she could conjure.

The locket had come with her on her first trip into the future. It felt fitting that it come with her for this trip, too.

They were in the *Black Crow*, flying low over the water on their way to the anil. Dorothy and Roman sat up front while Mac lounged in the passenger cabin, his bad leg propped up on the seat opposite him, as he carefully polished one of his guns. The rhythm was almost hypnotic. He'd hold the gun up so that the barrel caught the green light coming off the control panel and then shake his head and lower it again, spit, and rub the metal with the edge of his bloodstained shirt.

Roman, sitting in the captain's seat, glanced at Dorothy

and away. His hands were tight on the yoke, his shoulders stiff.

There hadn't been another chance to kill Mac. The Freaks he'd wooed over to his side had surrounded him as they'd made their way through the twisting hotel hallways, and down the stairs to the parking garage where the *Black Crow* waited. The Freaks had stood outside the time machine's doors while the three of them crawled inside and, once he was seated, Mac had pulled out his gun and busied himself polishing the barrel.

It had all felt carefully, perfectly planned, and now Dorothy stared straight ahead, worrying that she would only ever have that one chance, back at the hotel. She'd let it pass, and now there wouldn't be another.

No, she told herself, focusing on the daggers beneath her sleeves. Once the three of them landed in the past, she would find another moment, or she would make one.

The Puget Sound anil yawned ahead of them. It was light dancing on the waves. A great, reflective bubble. A swirl of smoke and shifting color.

Roman aimed the nose of the ship toward the tunnel. Dorothy swallowed.

"The *Black Crow* is moving into position for departure," he said, plunging them through the crack in time. The ship shuddered, and they were through.

Lightning flickered from the curved edges of the tunnel, and vicious winds howled outside the ship's thin walls, but their full supply of EM kept the ship itself steady.

Mac picked at his teeth with his thumb. "I want to see the golden age of piracy first. That was, what? The 1700s? 1600s? I always thought I'd make a great privateer."

"Very well," Roman said, unreadable. He pulled back on the ship's yoke, shooting them forward. Dorothy noticed, with some interest, that he didn't turn left to take them back in time. He turned right, toward the future.

Mac, still picking at his teeth, noticed nothing.

44

ASH

MAY 2, 2082, NEW SEATTLE

When Ash came to, he was crouching in the dirt. He had one leg curled beneath him, the other propped in a low lunge, hands braced against the earth to either side of his foot.

Earth, he thought, distantly. Actual, solid, earth. He curled his hands into the ground below, his fingers digging past the dirt to brush against something hard and flat.

Not earth. Wood.

Where was he?

He noticed the cold, next. It seeped into his skin, curling around his bones until his teeth were chattering and he was breathing, hard. He didn't even realize he'd opened his eyes until he felt the cold press against them, drying them instantly so that he had to blink, rapidly, to keep them from freezing.

He saw nothing. The dark around him was perfect.

Nerves trembled over his skin. He stood, fingers numb with cold as he fumbled in his pocket for the pack of waterproof matches he'd taken from the Dead Rabbit. He pulled a single match loose and struck it against the box—once, twice, three times—clenching and unclenching his hands to keep his blood flowing. Light leaped between his fingers.

It didn't illuminate much. He appeared to be standing on a small dirt pathway. A single, craggy mountain rose before him, black and decaying and covered in rubble.

Ash made his way to the edge of the pathway, shivering. He was only wearing a wet T-shirt and jeans, and he wouldn't last long out here if he didn't find some sort of shelter. The wind was fierce, and it blew him back a step, threatening to knock him over. It carried the smell of fire and dirt and rot. He tried to keep a hand cupped around the match to stop it from blowing out, but the flame flickered, and then died completely. Darkness swallowed him once more.

"Hell," Ash said out loud. His voice sounded strange. Closer. Like he was speaking directly into his own ear.

He lit another match and, when that one died, he lit another. Slowly, the scene around him began to come into clearer focus. The mountain wasn't a mountain at all but a building. Weeds had grown up over the walls and threaded through the openings. From the glow of his match, Ash could see that it had been reduced to rock and rubble. He squinted through the flickering light . . .

Oh God. That building was the Fairmont hotel. He recognized the old columns out front, and the architectural details above the windows. Which meant that this was New Seattle and this . . . this *rot* was all that was left of his home.

A nasty shiver went down his spine.

How?

Ash remembered, vividly, the first time he'd stepped out of the *Dark Star* and into the New Seattle of 2075. It was one of his favorite memories, how the blazing light had nearly burned his eyes, how he'd strained his neck trying to lean back far enough to see the tops of the skyscrapers. Everywhere he'd turned, he'd seen some new, fantastical thing: cars that looked sleek and fast as airplanes; people dressed in the strangest, most extraordinary clothing; buildings clustered so closely together they were practically on top of one another. The Fairmont hotel had been at the center of all that, the old building an elegant contrast to all that was sleek and new.

He'd had to throw his hands over his ears because everything was so *loud* and still he'd been grinning. Because the future was overwhelming and messy and wonderful. It had been scary, yes, but also exhilarating. Life had seemed to get bigger than he'd ever thought possible.

He had the opposite feeling now, staring out over this dark, dead city. Life hadn't gotten bigger.

Life had rotted and died.

Eventually, Ash found a door. It rose up from the darkness so suddenly that he actually slammed into it and then stumbled backward a few steps, forehead smarting from the impact. He fumbled for it again and, this time, his fingers wrapped around the cool metal of a doorknob.

He pulled, and the entire door snapped off at the hinges,

creaking forward and slamming into the ground before him with a thud that vibrated through the dirt.

Ash hesitated, staring into the black. He tried to calculate where he was standing based on where he was relative to the old Fairmont hotel and realized, with a start, that he must be standing on the docks outside of the Dead Rabbit.

It felt like he'd only just been sitting at the bar inside, watching the bartender build a tower out of matchboxes. The thought sent a chill through him. Should he even go inside? Would it be safe?

He looked over his shoulder, into the eerie darkness of this dead, futuristic world. At least, inside, he might find something to burn.

Swallowing hard, Ash ducked through the door. The smell of something old and musty rose up around him. He tried his best to breathe through his mouth but, still, the smell persisted.

And something was dripping. The sound came at even intervals, like it had been timed. It bounced off the walls and echoed over itself until Ash didn't know if it was coming from right beside him or deeper inside.

And then, from outside, a light.

Ash stood, frozen, as the light came closer.

45

DOROTHY

MAY 2, 2082, NEW SEATTLE

Roman landed the *Black Crow* on the docks outside of the skeletal remains of the Fairmont. Dorothy found herself morbidly curious, her gaze drawn to the old hotel's rotting walls and broken windows. And so it was a relief when the ship kicked up a plume of black ash that blackened their headlight, sending them plunging into darkness again. Anything to block her view of the Fairmont.

Her eyes flicked, instead, to the rearview mirror. Mac's face was bathed in shadow, but the silver gun on his lap reflected the green light of the control panel. It glowed, menacingly, in the dark.

Dorothy was staring at the gun when his voice reached out for her from the darkness. "Well. This doesn't look like the 1700s."

There was a beat of silence, and then Roman said easily, "There must be a problem with the ship's navigational controls. Let me go take a look."

And then, with a heavy sigh, he pushed the door open and stepped outside.

Dorothy threw her door open, too, and followed him. She didn't want to spend a single moment alone with Mac.

Roman was waiting for her in the circle of the time machine's headlights. Cold wind bit into her cheeks and blew through her coat as she came to stand beside him. She gritted her teeth, pulling her collar tighter around her neck.

Roman looked terrified. He dragged a hand over his sweaty forehead and whispered, "I don't know what I was thinking. I guess I thought it would be easier to take him out here, where no one could interrupt us."

"Stay calm," Dorothy hissed back. Her daggers rustled inside her sleeves, restless.

Mac's shadow reached the circle of the headlights a second before the man himself, and this was how Dorothy knew he had his gun out and aimed at them. The shape of it stretched across the ground, larger than it was in real life.

In an instant, Dorothy's hands were on the daggers hidden up her sleeves. She spun around, her heart crashing wildly inside her chest.

"Hands where I can see them, Miss Fox," Mac said, and she froze, fingers twitching. He had his gun aimed at her face. She was fast with her daggers, but she doubted she was faster than a bullet.

"I don't think you've thought this through," Roman said. "It's two on one, old man."

"I've done the math, thanks," Mac said. "According to my

calculations I'm the only one holding a gun."

There seemed to be a smile playing at Roman's lips, as though the thought that they could be so easily disposed amused him. "You have to know we won't go down without a fight."

"Fight?" Mac laughed, swinging the gun around so that it pointed at Roman now. "Who said anything about a fight? I could just leave the two of you here to rot. I was planning on doing that once we all got to the past, but this works, too."

And, with that, he took a step toward the time machine's cockpit. He was closer than they were, Dorothy saw. He'd get there first.

"You don't know how to fly it," Roman pointed out, but he didn't sound nearly as confident as he had a moment ago. His eyes darted, nervously, to the gun pointed at his chest.

Mac looked between the two of them, his smile hardening into a sneer. "Yeah, well I only need one of you for that, don't I?"

And Dorothy heard the click of his thumb against his gun's hammer. The air around her seemed to shiver.

This is it, her blades whispered.

It would be the only moment she ever got.

She flicked her wrists and her daggers leaped into her hands, blades glinting in the steady beam of the time machine's headlights.

Mac kept his gun aimed at Roman. He clearly didn't consider her a threat. "You really think you're going to kill me, sweetheart?"

Sweetheart. Dorothy smiled at him, grateful that he was making this easy.

"Yes," she said.

And she would've, too. She would've pierced Mac's neck with her dagger and laughed as she watched the life drain from his eyes.

But, at that moment, a bullet whizzed past her cheek, close enough that she felt the burn of gunpowder flare across her skin. She stumbled backward, gasping, and she had just enough time to lift one hand to her face, her dagger falling to the ground in a cloud of ash.

46

ASH

Mac stood between Roman and Dorothy, backlit by the *Black Crow*'s headlights. Ash had a clear shot. He pulled his gun free and dropped to one knee, eye squinting shut to take aim.

He exhaled, releasing the tension in his shoulders at the same time that he eased his finger over the trigger.

Here goes nothing.

And then Dorothy shifted to the side, moving half in front of Mac as she whipped something loose of her cloak. The two moments happened back-to-back, practically overlapping. Ash pulled the trigger, and then Dorothy moved. He didn't have time to stop the shot, but he pulled his arm up at the last second, and his bullet missed her by a breath.

It missed Mac, too, and bounced off the time machine, harmless.

Ash whipped back around the wall, his heartbeat cannon fire. *Damn.*

He could picture the three of them on the other side of

the wall, their weapons out, scanning the darkness for the intruder. He closed his eyes and exhaled, silently, through his mouth.

Then, from the other side of the wall: the soft shuffle of a boot.

Roman's voice. "Ash?"

Ash's breath frosted the air in front of him. He didn't want to fight Roman, but things were different now, weren't they? They both wanted to take down Mac. And, anyway, he wouldn't be found hiding here like a child, either.

He had just stepped out from behind the wall when Roman tackled him.

47

DOROTHY

Mac was gone.

Dorothy turned in place, her mind racing. She didn't know when it had happened. A fraction of a second had passed since Ash had fired at them but, sometime between the moment he'd stepped out from behind the wall and the moment Roman had gone to find him, Mac had just . . .

Vanished.

She tightened her grip on her daggers.

Where did that bastard go?

There weren't many places on the docks where he could've hidden. The time machine was still here, its doors yawning open, and Dorothy could see that the cockpit was empty. Its headlight illuminated a wide swath of floor, but left the rest of the docks dark as pitch.

Dorothy squinted into the shadows. Her palms were sweating, and her breath had become a low rasp. She inched forward, peering around the side of the time machine.

And then a hand flashed out of the darkness and clamped around her chest, drawing her back.

"I've found the best place to watch the show," Mac murmured, his hot breath tickling her ear. He brought the barrel of his gun to her cheek, the cold metal soft as a kiss.

"Let go of me." Dorothy got her arm free and twisted, but Mac's hold on her wasn't as strong as she'd thought it would be. It broke the moment she pulled away, sending her stumbling back into the time machine.

Mac snickered, and Dorothy spun toward the sound, daggers raised. They were just outside the glow of the headlight, and the contrast of light to dark was so strong that it hid Mac entirely. Even standing a foot away, staring at the place where his face should be, Dorothy couldn't separate the lines of his jaw and nose from the shadows.

She dragged her dagger blades over one another, the sound echoing through the air around them. "Afraid to step into the light?"

"Are you in such a rush to kill me, little Fox? I thought we might talk a while first."

"I'm done talking to you."

"Fine, then. You can listen. You've chosen the losing team." Mac clucked his tongue. "But, hey, I'm not such a bad guy. There's still time to change your mind."

Dorothy fixed him with a cool stare. "Is that so?"

"Do you really think you can win this game?" His nose separated from the darkness first, and then his big, thick lips. "I've already bribed the rest of your gang. They were cheap, too. Eliza turned her back on you for a new pair of boots. Donovan was more expensive; he wanted a knife."

Dorothy felt a sharp twist in her gut. "You're lying."

"Bennett was the cheapest," Mac continued, grinning. "All he'd wanted was a peach. One lousy peach." Mac laughed, shaking his head. "They must've *hated* you. And, once those two idiots take each other out, you'll be all alone, again. And what am I supposed to do with you then?"

Dorothy tilted her dagger, letting her blade catch the light. "Come closer and tell me."

She could see his eyes now. They were flat and black, like a shark's, and they slid past her, coming to rest on the scene unfolding on the other side of the room.

A smile twitched at the corner of his lips. "I mean it. They're going to kill each other. And then you and me will have a very different conversation."

Kill each other?

Dorothy hesitated, and a rushing sound filled her ears.

Hands still tight on her daggers, she turned—

48

ASH

Ash slammed into the ground, his fingers twitching, his mouth filling with dust and dirt. Jagged, black rocks scraped into his cheeks, and remnants of shattered glass bit into his skin.

He coughed, hard, and tried to push himself back up, but Roman was on his back, one arm braced against his neck and the base of his skull.

There was a click that could've been a thumb sliding over the hammer of a gun—that was *probably* a thumb sliding over the hammer of a gun—and cold metal pressed up against the back of Ash's neck.

Ash closed his eyes. Everything inside of him went still.

A second passed, and then another. Roman swore under his breath. But he didn't fire.

Ash was sweating, shaking, trying to think. There was a rushing sound in his ears, and blood in his eyes.

Why wasn't he firing?

The answer came to him in a flash of image: *a boy on his knees in a muddy clearing, surrounded on all sides by black tents. A little girl lying in his arms, limbs rigid, eyes vacant and staring . . .*

Ash felt like he was still standing at the edge of that clearing, mud beneath his boots and rain pounding at his shoulders as he watched Roman's little sister die on the ground before him.

"Why didn't you tell me about her?" he asked, his voice thick. It was the same question he'd asked Roman back at the clearing in 2074, and he found that he couldn't let it go. "Did you really think I wouldn't have understood?"

Roman was breathing hard. Through clenched teeth, he said, "Don't you dare talk to me about Cassia."

"You were my best friend," Ash continued. And now another memory was invading his mind, crowding out the images of Cassia's death:

It was the morning after Roman's betrayal. Ash had woken to find his gun stolen, and a crumpled piece of notebook paper in its place. Scrawled across it were the words *So long, old friend,* written in Roman's familiar, slanted hand.

Ash had kept the note with him that entire day, clenched in one hand as he watched the still, black waters, waiting for Roman to return. He would've forgiven him. He would've forgiven Roman almost anything, back then. But Roman had never come back.

Now, Roman clenched his eyes shut. His hand, still holding the gun, was trembling. "Don't."

How long had he been holding on to this pain? Ash

wondered. It had been two years since Cassia died, a year since Roman had defected to the Black Cirkus. And all that time he'd spent plotting and planning, trying to find a way back to her.

"I would've helped you," Ash said, and meant it. He would've done whatever Roman had asked of him and needed no explanation, just as he would've for Chandra or Willis or Zora. "If you had told me what you wanted to do, I would've helped you. We could have tried to save her together."

"You're lying." Roman's voice sounded strangled. "You wouldn't have."

"Let me help you now," Ash said, and, after a moment's hesitation, he leaned forward and—slowly, slowly, his eyes holding Roman's—he placed his own gun on the ground between them. "We shouldn't be fighting each other. We should be fighting him."

There was no trace of anger left on Roman's face. His expression was anguish; it was pain.

Too much has happened, Ash thought, hopeless. They could never go back to what they were. But, still, he wanted to show Roman that he was no longer his enemy. That he didn't blame him for what he'd had to do.

"I saw this moment," Roman said. "I've always known this was going to happen like this."

He lowered his gun and held out his hand.

As Ash reached for it, a gunshot cracked through the air.

49

DOROTHY

The shot echoed through Dorothy's head, seeming to ring in her ears long after it should've gone silent.

Time hitched. She almost thought it was a time-travel thing, how the world around her seemed to slow down so that she saw every moment of what happened next in vivid, excruciating slow motion.

The bullet hit Roman on the right side of his chest, jerking him backward. He swayed forward, landing on the ground cheek-first, plumes of dust and ashes billowing up around him. His gun skidded away from his body, fingers twitching.

The ashes obscuring his face cleared, and then he was staring at her, his eyes not quite focusing. He swallowed, with difficulty. Dorothy watched the slow rise and fall of his Adam's apple beneath the skin at his throat. A single drop of blood oozed past his lips and down his chin to stain the ground below his face.

Mac raised his gun to his lips and blew the smoke from the barrel.

He aimed at Ash and fired again.

50

ASH

Two years ago, Ash had arrived in New Seattle an outsider. He'd been a farm boy and a soldier, fresh off flying fighter jets across the German sky during World War II. Time travel was a concept he didn't think he'd ever fully grasp. He didn't even have a high school diploma. Who was he to talk about theoretical physics?

It was a world he never should've been a part of, and he'd felt like an impostor from the moment he'd stepped off the time machine and seen the bright new city before him.

In those days, the Professor and his family had been living in university housing, an entire floor of rooms in an old redbrick building with creaky floorboards and drafty windows. Ash had hauled his army-green duffel onto a twin bed in one of those rooms, but he hadn't been able to unpack. All his energy had been focused on trying to breathe like a normal person. Inhale first, then exhale.

And then he'd heard a creak of floorboards, followed by a voice. "Do you golf?"

Ash didn't know what he'd expected to see standing in his doorway—if time travel were real, did that mean ghosts were, too? What about bigfoot?—but it had been Roman, his head cocked, that infuriating smile playing at the corner of his lips. He'd been holding a dirty golf ball in one hand, rolling it between his fingers.

"Golf?" Ash remembered saying, frowning. He'd never golfed before, and it struck him as a strange, sort of fussy sport. His old man had liked football and boxing. Golf was for rich people and snobs.

He'd snorted, but Roman either didn't notice or didn't care. He'd tossed him the ball and jerked his head down the hallway. "C'mon," he'd said. "You'll like it, I promise."

He'd taken Ash to a door at the end of the hall, and up several flights of stairs to the roof. Ash hadn't realized how high the university building towered over the city until they'd walked out onto that roof. The whole of Seattle lay before them, gleaming with white light as ferries moved across Elliott Bay, office lights blazed from skyscrapers, and bars and restaurants stayed lit for the evening. He could make out the distant, blue-tinted light of the Space Needle, and the dizzying glow of the waterfront. It looked strange and futuristic and alien, and the only thing that felt familiar was the moon hanging above them, close enough that Ash almost thought he could reach up and pluck it out of the sky.

Roman had handed him a rusted golf club and nodded at

a bucket of balls sitting beside the edge of the roof. "Aim for the Needle," he'd said.

They'd spent the next few hours smacking golf balls off the roof, aiming at the tiny, blue prick of light in the distance that Ash knew was the Space Needle. They hadn't spoken more than that, but Ash still remembered how grateful he'd been to Roman, that night, for giving him some sense of ease in this strange, new world.

They'd been friends before they were enemies. It was so easy to forget that, after everything that had happened.

Ash clenched his eyes shut a moment before the bullet hit him and threw himself backward off the building. He fell past the broken docks and crashed into the ice, hitting the hard, frozen surface of the water with a crack that moved through his whole body.

He blinked up at the sky and, for a moment, he saw nothing but swirling black darkness.

Then, he heard footsteps. Mac's voice called to him from the darkness, "Go ahead and run, boy. I don't think you're going to find anything to help you out there."

And then, cackling, he walked away.

Ash tried to stand, and collapsed, gasping. He was injured, and his first thought was of Mac's gun, the bullet that had been speeding toward him a moment before he disappeared and wound up here. He clutched his side, gasping, but when he looked down he didn't see blood oozing out from below his ribs but something else.

It was a milky, iridescent liquid. And then Ash blinked and it wasn't liquid at all but a solid, steel spike protruding from his ribs. And then it was purple electricity prickling over his skin. And then something goopy and thick and a deep, bloody red.

Ash grimaced as he pressed his hand to his wound. He needed to get back to his time, to Zora.

There was a noise above him, and he looked up in time to see the *Black Crow* zoom overhead and disappear into the distance. Staring after it, Ash thought of Dorothy and felt a pang deep within his chest. He knew he should be worried for himself just now. He was badly injured and alone here in this strange time. But, still, he couldn't help thinking about her. Was she okay? Would she be safe with Mac?

He sighed and gave his head a hard shake. He supposed none of that mattered right now. He had to find a way home.

He thought he could make out the anil in the distance. It was a pinprick of light, like a distant star. It wasn't far, and the water beneath him was frozen solid. He was pretty sure he could walk there.

He stood and, limping a bit, started toward the tunnel that would take him home.

Nikola asked me to visit him one last time before his death. And so here I am.

He was still alive when I entered his hotel room, but only just. I think he was happy to see me. He opened his eyes when I walked in and said, his voice weak, "I was hoping it would be you, my friend."

I felt pretty terrible just then. Perhaps I should have visited more often over the years. But when I attempted to apologize, Nikola only shook his head and gestured to a stack of trunks in the corner of his hotel room and told me that they were for me.

"I only meant that I wanted you to have them before the leeches at the FBI came sniffing around," he told me. "Hopefully they will help you with your research into time travel."

I was quite blown away by this. Of course I've heard rumors that several of Nikola's trunks went missing after his death, but it never occurred to me that I'd been the one to take them. I immediately went over to the stacks of trunks and opened the first one, anxious to see what Nikola thought I might find useful.

The trunk was filled to the brim with notes written in Nikola's small, cramped handwriting. And when I read the first few pages, I couldn't believe what they contained.

Time travel. Nikola was looking into *time travel*.

"Won't someone notice these missing?" I asked Nikola, as

I eagerly looked through the pages of notes.

He only shrugged and told me, "I don't think so. They all think I'm working on a death ray."

I think that was supposed to be a joke. Apparently Nikola doesn't realize that, for centuries, the world believed he really did have some supersecret plans for a death ray. He'd explained how that was all a lie, intended to throw the press and Edison off his trail. For the last twenty years, his primary focus has been time travel.

There are twenty trunks filled with time-travel research, in total. It'll take me years to read through them all.

I can't wait to see what he's discovered.

51

DOROTHY

Dorothy didn't remember making her way back to the *Black Crow* or climbing into the pilot's seat. But, suddenly, there she was. The leather was cool beneath her legs. The dashboard gleamed before her.

Mac climbed into the seat beside her, gun aimed at her face. "You can fly this thing, right?"

Dorothy swallowed, her eyes moving over the dashboard.

She had to check that the wing flaps were . . . yes, they were up. And now the carburetor needed to be put in position. She pushed the throttle to 3,000 RPMs, her eyes flicking to the EM gauge. Full capacity. Good.

Her heartbeat felt like gunfire inside of her chest. She could do this.

And then she looked up, and saw Roman's body lying in the ashes, illuminated by the time machine's headlights. Something caught in her throat. She fumbled with her seat belt.

"We can't just leave him there," she said, grasping for the door.

Mac grabbed her shoulder, pinning her back in place. He lifted his gun, almost lazily, so that it pointed between her eyes. "The only reason you're not lying on the ground next to him is that I need someone to fly this piece of shit." He pressed the cold barrel of his gun into her skin. "You got that?"

Dorothy had a hard time drawing in breath. What were her options? She supposed she could refuse. She could stay here, in this ruined city. Only that wasn't really a choice, was it? There was nothing here. There was *no one* here.

She found herself reaching for the yoke, fingers numbly switching dials and flipping buttons. Mac lowered his gun.

"That's a good girl," he said, voice dripping with condescension. Dorothy's eyes closed for a moment, bile rising in her throat.

"The *Black Crow* is moving into position for departure," she said. Somehow, she managed to bring the time machine to hover, and flew them across the barren landscape, and back into the anil. She piloted the *Black Crow* through the tunnel of stars and purple clouds and black sky. She blinked hard, refusing to cry as the air around her thickened, growing heavy and wet. Water pounded against the windshield, making the glass creak.

And then they were surfacing, and New Seattle's ominous, dark skyline lay before them.

Home sweet home, Dorothy thought, numb.

52

ASH

NOVEMBER 10, 2077, NEW SEATTLE

"Oh my God, you're alive."

That was Chandra. Willis stood beside her, aggressively washing a teapot in the kitchen sink, but he looked up at the sound of Chandra's voice. It was very late, and Ash had only just made it back to the schoolhouse, somehow managing to pull himself through the window and down the hallway to the kitchen. He groaned as Zora launched herself across the room and into his arms.

"Damn you," she said, hugging him hard. "I thought we'd lost you this time."

"I'm okay," Ash said.

"*Okay* is maybe not the word that I would have used," Chandra said, nose wrinkling. "You look like death warmed over."

Ash lifted a hand to his cheek, cringing at the feel of dry blood and raw flesh. He'd forgotten about the mess that Mac and his cohorts had made of his face. So much had happened since then.

"It'll heal," he said, and pulled away from Zora. He tugged his shirt straight, motioning to the wound below his ribs. "This is what I'm really worried about."

It was sparking again, blue electricity leaping over his skin. And then it was seeping something thick and black. Ash looked away before it could change, again. It was giving him a headache. "Anyone want to tell me what the hell is going on here?"

Chandra was sitting on a barstool in the corner of the kitchen, anxiously braiding and unbraiding her hair, and now she leaned forward to get a better look.

"Gross," she said, but she sounded excited. "What *is* that?"

"Exotic matter," said Zora, frowning. She looked up at Ash, and he could see that she was making the same calculation he'd made back on the dock. "Do you think this is why you can travel through time without a vessel or any EM?"

"I was hoping you'd be able to tell me."

Zora shook her head. "I've never heard of anything like this before."

"There's nothing in your father's notes?" Ash asked, urgent. "Nothing at all?"

"You've read all the same books I have. He never mentioned experimenting with this."

"You said there were pages missing from his journal, didn't you?" Willis said. "They have to be somewhere."

"We could look through the notes in his office again,"

added Chandra, hopping off her stool. "I could help."

"Wait," Ash said, before they could disperse. "There's more."

They all turned and looked at him, waiting. Now was the time to tell them, Ash knew. Their friend and former comrade, Roman Estrada, was dead. Ash saw the bullet hit him. He saw him fall to the ground.

But something rose in Ash's throat, and he found he couldn't say the words out loud. Not yet. He gave his head a hard shake and said, instead, "But, uh, it can wait."

Leaving them, Ash made his way back to the small schoolhouse room that had been his home for the last two years. It wasn't much more than what he'd had back in the army: a thin cot and a few blankets, a trunk to hold his possessions, a window that looked out on the water. Right now, the world beyond that window was black, either because it was late at night or very early in the morning. Ash couldn't tell which.

There was a small slip of paper on the bed beside him, sitting on top of a tangle of sheets and blankets. Frowning, he picked it up.

Outside the anil. Midnight, it read.

53

DOROTHY

NOVEMBER 10, 2077, NEW SEATTLE

Dorothy landed the *Black Crow* in the Fairmont garage and cut the engine. Her eyes moved restlessly over the clouded windows and rusted pipes. It seemed strange, she thought, that this place should look so normal and familiar when everything had gone so horribly wrong.

Woodenly, she began to fumble with her seat belt. She wanted to be back in her room, alone, so she could finally break down, but she couldn't seem to make her fingers work fast enough. The buckle felt large and foreign in her hands, and she was all too aware of Mac's gun, still pointed at her.

And then they weren't alone, anymore. Cirkus Freaks had begun to gather around the time machine, seeming to crawl out of the woodwork like cockroaches. Her fingers went still.

Had Mac been telling the truth, before? Had they all turned their backs on her?

Was she alone, again?

"It's good that they're here," Mac said, pushing his door open. "They'll want to know what happened to their comrade, won't they?"

He holstered his gun, and Dorothy inhaled, her nose filling with the city's familiar smell of salt and mold. Steeling herself, she exited the time machine.

"Where's Roman?" The question came before the door had even slammed shut behind her. Eliza was pushing her way to the front of the crowd of Freaks, eyeing Dorothy's blood-soaked cloak with great suspicion. "Didn't he come back with you?"

"He . . ." Dorothy opened her mouth to explain, and found that she couldn't speak. She heard the crack of a gunshot, saw Roman's body spinning in place, and then falling to the ground.

She closed her mouth and pressed a hand to her chest, breathing hard. She couldn't say it.

She was vaguely aware of Mac lifting his hands to quiet the crowd. She looked up at him, wondering how he planned to explain Roman's death. Did he honestly think he could tell them the truth, hoping their allegiance would protect him?

They'll tear you apart, she thought, savage. And she found that she was anticipating this. Roman had been well liked. The Freaks would be furious once they'd learned what had happened to him.

"Friends," Mac said in a grave voice, "I am sorry to report that there has been a great tragedy in our midst today. Our

Crow, Roman Estrada, has been murdered."

Whispers erupted like wildfire. Dorothy's face suddenly felt very hot.

"We cannot let this stand," continued Mac, his gaze tracking over the crowd. "And so I am offering a reward to anyone who brings me Roman's murderer."

Murderer? Dorothy felt the hair on the back of her neck stand straight up. Did he really plan to pretend he hadn't been the one who pulled the trigger?

She felt a sudden chill and realized what he was going to say a second before the words left his mouth.

"Jonathan Asher killed Roman Estrada."

It sickened Dorothy, the hugeness of this lie, but she saw immediately how easily it would be accepted. The gathered crowd was already nodding, their mouths pressed into hard lines, their eyes glittering with malice. It made sense to them, that the man they'd held captive would've escaped to kill one of their own. Already, they were shouting for vengeance.

"Liar," Dorothy breathed, but her voice was drowned out by the jeers and shouts of the Freaks. Even so, Mac looked right at her, as though he alone had heard. He smiled, viciously. A dare.

Dorothy swallowed. Her throat felt thick as she looked around, at the faces surrounding her. If she spoke up now it would be her word against his. Would anyone believe her?

Perhaps some would. But the others would want Ash's blood. They'd be out tonight, looking for him. *Hunting* him.

Someone had to warn him.

Dorothy backed up a few steps, and then she turned and began pushing her way through the crowd of Freaks. She'd almost made it to the back of the room and the door that led—*blessedly*—out onto the docks when Eliza slid in front of her, blocking her way.

"Going somewhere, little Fox?" she said.

Dorothy froze, her skin creeping. She couldn't tell whether she was being mocked.

"Yes," she snapped, allowing a sharpness to creep into her voice. "I'm going back to my room. It's been a long day. Or haven't you been listening?"

Eliza tilted her head, considering her through narrowed eyes. "I saw you, you know," she said. "*Both* of you."

"Both of us?"

"You and Asher. Two nights ago, you met him on the docks behind the Dead Rabbit." Eliza fixed her with a cool stare. "You looked . . . intimate."

Dorothy's mouth felt dry.

But . . . but she *hadn't* met Ash on the docks that night at the Dead Rabbit. She'd left him there and gone after Roman. *What was this?*

Whether Eliza had intended to or not, she'd caused a stir. The other Freaks were turning to face them now, frowning, *listening*.

Dorothy flushed, and tried to come up with something to say in response. But the truth—*no you didn't*—seemed so thin . . .

"And I saw you again, this morning," Eliza spit, fury

lighting her face. "You snuck into the room where Ash was being held prisoner and set him free. If it weren't for you, Roman would still be alive."

What? No, she hadn't. Dorothy had gone right to the *Black Crow*, with Mac and Roman. There hadn't been time to set Ash free first.

Dorothy was still frowning, trying to decide whether to untangle the threads of the argument when Eliza moved closer, invading her space. She took an unconscious step backward, slamming into the wall.

A vicious smile flitted across Eliza's face.

"*Traitor*," she hissed. She reached for Dorothy, hand closing around her arm.

"Don't touch me," Dorothy said, yanking her arm free. She saw some confusion in the crowd around her, nervous glances flitting back and forth, whispers, and said, full-voiced, "You're lying."

"Enough," came Mac's voice. The crowd parted, and suddenly he was moving toward her. With Eliza at her back and Freaks pressed in around her, there was nowhere for Dorothy to go. A brief stunned silence hung over them all.

"I imagine our Quinn must feel remorse." Mac's voice was a low threat. "After all, what did Asher do after you set him free? He came after you. Killed your only ally."

"That's not what happened." Dorothy pushed the words through clenched teeth. They could lie about her if they wanted, but she wasn't going to go down without a fight. "You *know* it's not what happened."

Mac leaned closer to her and spoke directly into her ear, low enough that no one else would hear his words.

"Look at the position you're in, sweetheart. You've been . . . what's the phrase? Fraternizing with the enemy. Do you really want to go telling tales on me now? You think they'll believe a word you say?" Mac paused and, when Dorothy didn't immediately respond, he seemed to take it as acceptance and continued. "I could probably convince them that it's in their best interests to keep you around if you were to do something to prove your loyalty."

Sickened, Dorothy asked, "And how would I do that?"

He said, like it was obvious, "All you have to do is find Asher for me. And kill him yourself."

54

ASH

OUTSIDE THE ANIL. MIDNIGHT.

Ash read the note again, a chill moving through him. He grabbed his father's pocket watch off the wooden crate beside his bed and checked the time. Not quite midnight, but close. He'd lost all sense of day and night over the last week but, now, he did the math in his head, counting back.

"Damn," he murmured. He had about ten minutes left until November 11, 2077. A year ago, today, his prememories had started.

He let the paper float back onto his bed, his skin crawling.

There was a knock at the door, and then Chandra stepped into the room. "Hey, Zora wanted me to ask if—"

Ash cut her off. "You're supposed to wait until someone says 'Come in' to open the door." He tried to fold the note and tuck it into his pocket, but Chandra had already seen it.

Her eyes shifted from the note to Ash's face. "What's that?"

Did it make sense to hide it? Ash supposed it was too late

for that. He could feel Chandra staring at it, wondering, and so, with a sigh, he handed it over.

Chandra read it quickly. The skin around her eyes tightened a tiny bit.

"So that's it, then? Today's the day you're supposed to die?" Chandra was hoarse. She dropped onto the bed next to him.

"You're not going to try to stop me from going?"

"Would that work? Okay, then *I* think you should hide under your cot and hope Quinn Fox or Dorothy or whoever she really is never finds you. Ooh, or we could all run away. How's that sound?"

Despite everything, Ash felt himself grin. "Not so bad right now, actually."

"Then let's do it. Grab a bag, we can leave tonight."

A minute passed, and then another. Neither of them moved. Chandra let her head fall onto his shoulder. "Yeah, that's what I thought."

Ash rubbed his eyelids with two fingers. "You don't have any sage wisdom for me?"

Chandra scoffed. "Sage wisdom?"

"You know, advice. How to face your death like a man and all that."

"You need Willis for that. Want me to get him?"

Ash shook his head. "What about movie advice, then? If this were a movie, what would the hero do now? Would he go, knowing he was about to die?"

"Well." Chandra was quiet for a moment, considering.

"In a love story, there's always a moment near the end of the movie when the protagonist has to make a choice. Either she does the easy thing and life continues as usual, or she does the hard thing and everything changes. She faces her fears and winds up with everything she ever wanted."

"This isn't a love story, Chandra."

Chandra looked up at him. "Isn't it? Could've fooled me."

She kissed him on the cheek, and then stood and crossed the room, walking in a quick, jerky way that told Ash she was trying to make it to the hallway before she started to cry.

She paused at the door and said, without turning to look at him again, "Maybe I do have some sage wisdom after all. Have you ever heard the parable of the blind men and the elephant?" Her voice was thick and choked, but she continued anyway. "So the story goes that these three blind men stumbled upon an elephant, right? Only they'd never met an elephant before, so they didn't know what it was, so they groped around, trying to figure it out. And one blind man touched its trunk and said, hey this thing sort of feels like a big snake. And the other touched its leg and said, hey it's kind of like a big column, right? And the third one touched its ear and thought it was, like, this big fan. But none of them really knew what it was because they were only seeing one part."

Ash thought about this story for a moment, and then he said, "I don't get it."

"That prememory you keep having is, what? Five minutes long?" Chandra lifted a hand and moved it across her cheek, still facing the door. "How do you know you're seeing the whole thing?"

Ash felt his eyebrows draw together. "You think there's more to it?"

A shrug. "There always is."

55

DOROTHY

Dorothy sat in Roman's room, darkness gathering around her like an old friend. She didn't know what time it was, only that the sky outside was black and starless. A candle and matches sat on Roman's bedside table, but she couldn't bring herself to light them. She didn't think she could bear to look at Roman's things; just sitting here was painful enough. If she closed her eyes she could even pretend that Roman was beside her. The sheets on his bed still smelled like him, and the walls still seemed to hold the echo of his voice.

Have you seen the future? she remembered asking him, back when they first met.

Perhaps, he'd answered. *Perhaps I've even seen yours.*

A lump formed in her throat, making it difficult to breathe. She could feel the sobs rising in her chest and, for a moment, she considered letting herself break down. It would be such a relief, to cry. But she only blinked, hard, and focused on her hands clenched, tightly, in her lap.

There were guards outside her door, at least three of them, she thought, from the sound of their voices. She'd told them she needed something from Roman's room, and so they were giving her a few moments to gather whatever it was before they dragged her off to find Ash.

But she'd lied to them. There wasn't anything here that she needed. She only wanted to say goodbye, and now she had, so it was time to go.

She looked around the room for something she could pretend she'd come here for and found her eyes drawn to Roman's bedside table. The top drawer was cracked, and something glinted from within.

Leaning over, Dorothy inched the drawer open further and found a dagger.

Her breath caught. She'd left her own daggers in the future, with Roman's body, but they'd been long, thin blades, designed to cause sharp pain and leave little trace.

This was different. It was heavier, for one thing. The blade was nearly as thick around as her wrist. Dorothy picked it up, focusing on its weight in her hand. It was meant to do damage, to cut through bone and flesh like it was butter.

Below the dagger, she saw a small, folded note, Roman's handwriting staring up at her.

Breathless, she pulled it out.

Dearest Dorothy,

It's funny, I was never quite sure when to tell you this. Or, perhaps I didn't want to admit that it was finally time. That's the problem with knowing when and how you are going to die, I suppose. You have months and months to set all your grand plans into motion, but when the time comes, it's too hard to go through with any of it. Strange, how the knowing doesn't make death any easier to face.

I should explain. Ever since you and I first traveled back in time, I've been haunted by memories of my own death. I know exactly how and approximately when it is going to happen.

We will go to the future. Ash and I will fight, and I will be shot. I will bleed to death in the ashes of our ruined world. My last memory will be of that black, sunless sky.

We planned to save the world together, you and I, and my one regret is that I will not be alive to see it happen. But you, Dorothy. You still have so much life ahead of you.

Use it well.

Roman

Dorothy closed her eyes and now the tears finally fell. It wasn't the breakdown she'd been picturing, though. This felt more like she was gathering her strength.

She knew what she had to do.

She wiped her cheeks with the back of her hand and pushed herself to her feet, curling her fingers around Roman's dagger.

She didn't think he'd meant to leave the dagger for her, but she decided to take it all the same. She had an idea of how she might use it to save the world, like they'd planned.

It was time.

56

ASH

Ash stood in the small boat, easing his weight from leg to leg to keep his balance. Black water lapped at the sides, sending the boat rocking, but Ash moved, easily, with the motion. He'd grown used to the water over the years.

Trees seemed to glow in the darkness around him. Ghost trees. Dead trees. Water pressed against their hollow, white trunks, moving with the wind.

Ash counted ripples to pass the time while he waited. Seven. Twelve. Twenty-three. He lost track and was about to start again when her light appeared in the distant black. It was small, like the single headlight of a motorcycle, followed by the rumbling sound of an engine. He stood straighter. Part of him hadn't expected her to come. But of course she would. She always did.

Leave now, he told himself. There was still time. He felt sure that she wouldn't come after him if he left before she got here. He knew how this night would end if he stayed.

He'd seen this exact moment a dozen times. A hundred, if he counted dreams. But he stayed still, his hand clenching and unclenching at his side.

He wanted to see her, even knowing what it meant. He had to see her one last time.

The boat drew closer. She was hidden beneath that hood, but her hair had blown loose. Long, white strands dancing in the darkness.

She pulled up next to him and cut the engine.

"I didn't think you'd come." Her voice was lower than he'd expected, practically a purr. She reached up, pushed those white strands of hair back under her hood with a flick of her hand.

Ash swallowed. He didn't see the knife, but he knew she had it. "It doesn't have to end like this."

Her hand disappeared inside her coat. "Of course it does."

57

DOROTHY

NOVEMBER 11, 2077, NEW SEATTLE

Dorothy was about to open the door when it flew open on its own, slamming into the wall with a crack.

Zora stood before her, gun in hand.

"You *bitch*." She shoved Dorothy against the wall and pressed the barrel of her gun to her forehead.

"What—" Dorothy tried to squirm away, but Zora had an arm angled across her collarbone, and she leaned into it, increasing the pressure on Dorothy's chest.

Dimly, Dorothy registered the bodies of three men lying in the hallway behind her, unconscious.

The guards, she realized, with growing horror. Zora had taken them all out.

"What did you do to him?" Zora said, and Dorothy heard the hammer of her gun click into place. "Tell me or I swear to God I'll shoot off the rest of your face!"

"I don't know what you're talking about," Dorothy said through the tightness in her throat.

Zora cocked her head, and now Dorothy could see that, beneath all that anger, she was barely holding herself together. She was breathing fast, and her eyes were wet and wide and desperately unhappy. Something was very badly wrong.

A chill went through Dorothy, and it had nothing to do with the gun still pressed to her forehead. "Zora," she asked, more firmly now. "What happened?"

Doubt flickered across Zora's face. She lowered the gun. "You really don't know."

She didn't say it like it was a question and, before Dorothy could respond, she'd dug something out of her pocket and thrust it into Dorothy's hands.

It was a note.

Outside the anil. Midnight.

Whatever Dorothy had braced herself for, it wasn't this. Her eyes traveled over the words scrawled across the ripped sheet of paper, the way they looped and curved, angling slightly to the left.

This note—it was written in her handwriting.

Dorothy breathed and read the note again, trying to understand. It was her handwriting and yet she hadn't written it.

And that wasn't all. *There*—that splotch of ink over the word *anil*, it reminded her of the fountain pens in Avery's study, so unlike the cheap plastic things people used now. As far as she knew, there was only one such pen left in the entire world, and it was down in the basement of this hotel, along with the rest of the things she and Roman had taken from the past.

She looked up at Zora, her mind spinning. "Where did you get this?"

A flash of fury lit Zora's face. "You left it in Ash's room an hour ago, *Fox*. I found it on his bed."

But . . . but she didn't. She hadn't. She was about to say so when—

Oh God. Dorothy brought a trembling hand to her mouth, remembering. Back in the parking garage, hadn't Eliza claimed to see her meeting with Ash on the docks outside the Dead Rabbit?

And then, again, she said she'd *seen* Dorothy helping Ash escape from Mac. Dorothy had done neither of those things, and so she'd assumed that Eliza was lying. It hadn't even occurred to her to consider the alternative, and now she felt stupid for not seeing it.

She lived in a world where time travel was real.

It was possible she just hadn't done those things *yet*.

Dorothy took a step closer to Zora, feeling as though her breath and her heartbeat were lodged in her throat together. "You asked me what I did to him? What do you think I did to him?"

Zora's voice was steel as she said, "Let me show you."

The anil looked iridescent in the distance, a soap bubble sitting atop the waves. And then it looked like a jagged crack through ice, its sharp edges spiderwebbing into the sky. It was a tunnel made of mist and smoke. A distant star. The beginning of a tornado.

Dorothy blinked and looked away, her heart speeding up. She tightened her grip around Zora's waist. She felt her breath coming faster.

Zora cut the engine on the Jet Ski and came to a stop, sending a spray of water between them and the anil. When the water settled and the growl of her motor died down, she jerked her chin. "See for yourself."

An object sat in the water just before the time tunnel, rocking gently on the waves. Dimly, Dorothy registered that it was a boat. *Ash's* boat. Something deep and red stained the water around it. Dorothy wouldn't have seen it if they weren't so close to the anil, the light of the time tunnel illuminating the blood.

There's so much of it, she thought, horror rising inside of her. Everywhere she looked, there was red. It coated the water like a veil.

"He knew he was going to die like this," Zora said, her voice strangely distant. "He'd seen it happen."

Dorothy thought of Roman's note.

I've been haunted by memories of my own death.

A chill moved through her.

"I didn't do this," she insisted. Her fingers curled into Zora's shoulders, but Zora didn't flinch. "Zora, I swear to you, I *didn't*."

Zora stared at the anil. Her dark eyes absorbed the otherworldly light and shone like an animal's.

Finally, she spoke.

"But you will."

LOG ENTRY—AUGUST 6, 2074
17:41 HOURS
THE WORKSHOP

I don't know what I was expecting to find in Nikola's notes, but this is beyond my wildest dreams.

Apparently, Nikola never got over his brush with time travel. Remember how I wrote that he was once shocked by a jolt of electricity coming off one of his coils? He's always claimed that, at that moment, he "saw the Past, Present, and Future at the same time."

After we talked about this, I was certain that what he saw was just a product of his brain short-circuiting. A near-death experience that he's interpreted as time travel. Real time travel, as you know, requires three things:

The presence of an anil

Exotic matter

A vessel

Nikola had none of these things on him at the time that the jolt of electricity went through him so, despite my initial hopes, I had to eventually admit that he didn't actually travel through time.

Now, though, I wonder.

Nikola's greatest dream was to be able to prove that you could harness the electrical power of the earth and use it to create a kind of "free energy." Now, over the years, that theory has been proven false. His theories about how the earth transmitted energy just weren't true.

But the strange thing is that those very theories are true inside of an anil.

So what if he really was on to something? What if there's a way to travel through time without an anil or exotic matter, or a vessel?

Tesla's notes include very detailed information on how to do just that. All I'll have to do is inject a tiny bit of the exotic matter directly into my person.

This sounds crazy ... but someone has to test it.

Here goes nothing.

PART FOUR

The present is theirs; the future, for which I really worked, is mine.

—Nikola Tesla

58

DOROTHY

JUNE 12, 1913, JUST OUTSIDE SEATTLE

Dorothy hesitated outside the closed office door, unsure of how to proceed. This was her house—or, well, it would've been her house, if she'd gone through with the wedding. Now she supposed it was only Avery's house.

Should she just . . . knock? She didn't want to interrupt anything. She didn't know how genius worked, but it seemed entirely possible that the man inside this room was on the verge of some grand discovery and she was about to break his concentration. One knock could alter the entire future of the human race and, frankly, she'd done enough of that already.

Holding her breath, she lowered her hand to the doorknob and let herself in.

The man was hunched over Avery's ornate, wooden writing desk, scribbling furiously. He didn't look up as Dorothy swept across the room, stopping before the narrow table where Roman's dagger sat on a stained and rumpled handkerchief.

Staring down at the dagger, Dorothy felt her stomach turn over. Ash's blood still coated the thick blade and stained the white cloth. It'd been days, and yet she hadn't been able to bring herself to clean it. She could still remember the feel of that dagger against her palm, the sudden give of skin and bone as she thrust it into Ash's chest.

Fingers twitching, she picked it up.

"Dear?"

Dorothy's eyes snapped back to the hunched-over man at the writing desk. He still hadn't turned around, but now he lifted a hand, fingers held a few inches apart. "Do you know whether they've started making those little brownies yet? The fudgy chocolate ones with the nuts?"

Dorothy hurriedly wrapped her mother's handkerchief around Roman's dagger. "Brownies?" she asked, distracted.

"The Little—oh wait." The man pinched his nose between two fingers, and said, almost to himself, "Little Debbie wasn't founded until 1960, and then they only sold those awful oatmeal pies. One does forget these things."

"I could bring you coffee?" Dorothy offered. Avery made good coffee, thick and rich. It was one of the few things he did well. "Or tea?"

"Coffee would be grand." The man swiveled around in his chair. He had his back to the small desk lamp now, and it left his features bathed in shadow. Dorothy could only make out the bottom half of his nose, and his wide, bright smile.

When he saw the dagger clutched in Dorothy's hands,

the smile faded. He scratched his chin. "Aw, yes. I suppose it's time to deal with that."

Dorothy swallowed. "I'm sorry, did you want to—"

"No, no, dear, you've proven yourself quite adept." He smiled, again, but this time it was tinged with sadness.

Dorothy began to turn toward the door.

"Wait," the man said, and Dorothy hesitated, dread creeping up her skin.

The man cleared his throat. It seemed to take him a moment to work out what he wanted to say and, when he finally spoke, his words were hesitant.

"Does my . . . does my daughter know that I'm still alive?"

Dorothy closed her eyes. Her palms had grown clammy, and her heart was beating loud and fast in her ears. It embarrassed her, a little, that she was so nervous. She'd been expecting this question since she first brought the man here and, honestly, it came as something of a relief that he'd finally asked. But that didn't make the answer any easier to give.

"No, Professor Walker," she said, looking up. "Zora thinks that you died at Fort Hunter in 1980."

ACKNOWLEDGMENTS

As always, there are so many people I want to thank! *Twisted Fates* has a fantastic team of people supporting it behind the scenes, so big thanks to everyone at HarperTeen for everything they did to bring this book out into the world. Thank you to my editors, Erica Sussman and Elizabeth Lynch, who have been championing this series from the beginning, and also to Louisa Currigan, and to Shannon Cox and Sabrina Abballe in marketing, Alison Donalty and Jenna Stempel-Lobell in design, Alexandra Rakaczki in copyediting and, finally, to Jean McGinley, Rachel Horowitz, Alpha Wong, Sheala Howley, and Kaitlin Loss in subrights for taking care of the Chronology Protection Agency abroad. Also, thank you to the entire Harper sales team for helping this book find its people!

And, of course, a huge thanks to my husband, Ron Williams, who let me read him chapters while he was cooking, and who asked great questions and pointed out dumb mistakes, and still tells people that this is his favorite series ever.